# Slave Skin

## By Derek E Pearson

First published 2017
Published by GB Publishing.org

Copyright © 2017 Derek E Pearson
All rights reserved
ISBN: 978-0-9935072-8-1 (paperback)
978-0-9935072-9-8 (eBook)
978-1-912031-00-9 (Kindle)

GBP

GB Publishing.org
www.gbpublishing.co.uk

To Sue, for whom I am the portrait in her attic. And for Christopher and Dana Durban who understand why friendship matters, even from across the pond, and in memory of Denise Elisabeth Windebank who was taken too soon.

## Acknowledgement
*As always, my thanks go out to the team at GB Publishing.org. George, Bee and Christopher help me tend my curious garden and watch strange flowers grow.*

# CONTENT

# [1]

The day had a dense, still quality to it. It seemed to be holding its breath as if waiting for something terrible to happen. Even insects had ceased their interminable stridulation, exhausted by the treacly air.

Philippe wiped sweat from his upper lip and glanced across at Melba, something he liked to do as often as possible. She had tied her shirt up under her breasts to fend off the humidity. He admired the way the healthy curve of her firm belly arced down into the waistband of her belted shorts. She was strong; she carried her rucksack as easily as any man, but there was nothing masculine about her. Nothing at all.

Melba stopped and pulled her thick mop of sun-bleached hair back into a plain, black scrunchie. The back of her neck was moist. Her movements opened her shirt slightly and Philippe got a brief yet tantalising view of the upper swell of her breasts. What he saw glowed with the same evenly gold tan as her legs, and there was no hint of a brassiere.

'You want to climb a bit higher, you have to be careful.' The young woman spoke without looking at him. She was studying the slope above them.

He replied, 'Yeah. Don't stress it. I'll be okay.'

'Yeah, well, look there. See? There's been a rock fall recently. Watch out for loose scree. You slide on that stuff, you'll scrape the hide off your ass, and I don't want to be stuck with carrying you back to the spa. Just watch where you put your feet. Okay?'

'Thanks for caring.'

She continued her sure-footed ascent and he scrambled after her. Unlike his guide, he often had to resort to using his hands. He gazed up at her well-proportioned behind and drank in the sight of her long, tanned legs.

He panted, 'I think it's worth the effort for the view.'

She looked back briefly, with hooded eyes. Philippe wondered if he had just stepped too far beyond the pale. He lifted both hands and offered a typically Parisian shrug, putting all his Gallic charm into the gesture. He smiled. She shook her head and returned a twisted grimace.

At that exact moment, the ground crumbled under his feet and he found himself sliding backwards into dust-filled darkness. He heard Melba call his name in alarm. Then the sound of her voice was lost. He became deaf to everything except the harsh rattle of loose stones and gravel. He had no time to cry out or be afraid.

In the cave below him, something squatted in the shadows. It heard the scrabbling sound of Philippe's descent and reacted with sluggish interest. It was a ship not of Earth, unthinkably ancient, and its systems had almost ceased to function. Over long years it had managed to survive by sipping the merest trickle of background radiation, sucking in just enough juice to keep it minimally alert. It had been waiting for something to happen. Something like this.

When it had been flung into the ocean and careered miles down into the murk of the smooth seabed, the most advanced creature on the planet had been a horseshoe-shaped crab the size of a big man's shoe. The ship had been designed to travel along sophisticated pathways from a far distant star, but within minutes had found itself hopelessly mired in glue-like silt and clinging ooze. Its thrusters quickly became too clogged to be of use.

The ship's mind instantly dispatched thousands of DNA-based parasite slave matrices into the ocean, and then – without waiting for the resultant army of newly-infected slave workers to turn up and dig it free from the mud – it got on with a systems survey of its damaged Finder, the most important unit in its crew.

Within minutes the area immediately around the ship was swarming with thousands of crabs, jellyfish and tiny, worm-like creatures – hemichordata. Its hull disappeared under a roiling blanket of marine life, which began to churn up the silt in a doomed attempt to loosen the great disc from the clinging muck. Their mindless efforts served only to further churn up and loosen the seabed until, slowly but surely, the craft began to sink under its own weight. It was sucked deeper and ever deeper into the sediment. Eventually even light from the great, forward-facing viewports disappeared completely under the surface and the focus for the frantically working marine creatures' futile labours became lost in a floating bloom of thick silt.

The little creatures soldiered on until the giant craft had completely vanished, its passage marked only by great belching domes of escaping gas and air. Then, like puppets freed from their strings, the swarm of creatures stopped working. They crowded around for hours waiting for more instructions. When none came they finally dispersed and everything around the crash site became still once more.

The ship's situation was going from bad to worse. It had discovered the Finder to be damaged beyond repair; the creature's brainstem had been snapped like a twig during the jolting violence of the crash. Its long, ovoid head now angled awkwardly backwards from the slender, broken pillar of its neck, and its multi-jointed limbs dangled bonelessly from its complex nest of shoulders. The mind reclaimed the Finder's body, leaving only its core pod behind. When a suitable host presented itself, a new Finder could be transformed.

The ship's mind began to take stock of its situation and discovered the horrifying extent of its problems. It sent its sensors roaming around its tool bays and crew berths, and with mounting despair discovered that nearly every element had ceased to function. All crew and tool units had been terminally damaged, all except three repair techs quietly reweaving the damaged fabric of its hull.

The ship had been crippled and sent spinning out of control by a crunching strike of white-hot, high-speed volcanic ejectile. The damage had been compounded during the resultant crash into the sea. Everything it suffered could have been fixed if it had access to the right facilities – or even suitable hosts to regrow its crew. None of which was going to happen while it was mired in the cloying mud of the deep-sea floor.

The future looked bleak. Although they had reacted well to slave matrix seeding, the planet's indigenous life forms were obviously too small and primitive to host its tool units. The ship mind decided to ignore them as irrelevant. And none of its library of programmed protocols could provide useful solutions to its problems. It was on virgin ground.

What to do? The ship knew it was sinking deeper into the mire. It had to accept that fact and consider the best way to survive. It was time to make tough decisions. First it reclaimed the physical bodies of the ship's company, absorbing everything useful while leaving core pods where they fell. It then powered down everything except the three repair techs. They were performing essential duties worthy of their drain on its precious energy reserves. If they weren't allowed to complete their work, the pressure caused by miles of sea water pressing down on the clay-like mud in which it was trapped would eventually crush its hull like an egg and, the ship thought, that mustn't be allowed to happen.

The mind then selected its ultimate fall-back position: endurance mode. This meant dispersing its intelligence throughout the fabric of the ship; very much a last-ditch survival tactic. Once it entered endurance mode, only the craft's complete destruction could kill its mind and thus eliminate even the smallest hope of escape. Then it waited to see what would happen next.

The repair techs worked tirelessly for hours until their job was complete and full structural integrity had been restored. Each tech was an incredibly

3

complex organism over six feet long and four feet wide. They were squat, flat and extremely strong – strong enough to survive the collision. Compartments in their undersides bristled with a formidable array of precision instruments. They had been designed to be the ultimate engineering tools, and looked as if an insane manufacturer had been given free rein and an unlimited budget to build the universal gadget of their dreams – or to create the monstrous creatures that haunted their worst nightmares.

Job done, the last living tool units in the ship were given their final instructions. They moved together in the pitch darkness until their forward corners touched. Tender instrumentation reached out and locked together. They had worked as a close team since launch so the ship mind allowed them their final farewells; it gave them time to relax and accept their lot. And then it killed and reclaimed them.

The last three core pods formed the points of a perfect equilateral triangle, and the ship mind was alone in the achingly still blackness. Thick mud pressed in on all sides. What happened next would be entirely in the hands of fate. Its only hope was that time would somehow present it with an opportunity to escape. The ship mind was patient. It knew how to wait.

More than two million years later and just over seven thousand light years from Earth, two super-dense neutron stars began to coalesce. Their combined mass rapidly condensed into one hyper-dense ball which rotated at a fantastic rate. Gravity squeezed it like a fist, and as it shrank energetic gamma rays poured from its poles. This phenomenon, known in scientific communities as a gamma ray burst or GRB, was considered by some researchers to be quite common and, in fact, usually harmless. Throughout the visible universe, GRBs had been seen to occur as often as three hundred thousand times a year with no appreciable adverse effects, much as a random bullet fired into the air would almost invariably fall harmlessly to the ground. The universe was very large and there was a vast amount of empty space in it, but this time the GRB did not dissipate harmlessly into the ether. It was pointed directly at Earth.

A column of gamma radiation sliced into the atmosphere with devastating effect, scorching the planet's surface with the equivalent destructive energy of three thousand megatons of nuclear warheads exploding simultaneously. Creatures inhabiting shallow seas were slaughtered in their millions by an intense burst of hard radiation. In the alchemical crucible thus created, nitrogen and oxygen atoms in the atmosphere were ripped apart – and then recombined to form a thick fog of dense nitrous oxide compounds. These blocked the sun for several months, resulting in a punishing nuclear winter that made it hard for the toughest plants to survive and even the hardiest insects to flourish.

The GRB caused the second greatest extinction event ever recorded on Earth. Named the Ordovician-Silurian extinction, it was almost twice as severe as the K-T event at the end of the Cretaceous Period, which was believed to have ended the reign of the dinosaurs.

Barely conscious and buried deep in its sedimentary bed, the ship was untroubled by the slaughter around it. The relatively few global life forms that survived that terrible GRB phenomenon were nearly all shielded in the deepest oceans. Most were the distant progeny of creatures that had once been infected by the ship's slave parasite and had received the alien matrix with their DNA.

One hundred and forty-three million years after the great Ordovician-Silurian extinction, life on Earth thrived and had developed along many extraordinary pathways, but the slave matrices remained buried in their cells, like genetic triggers waiting to be squeezed.

One of those primordial sea creatures' most evolved offspring had now fallen through a weakened shell of limestone and found himself helplessly tumbling into a cave chamber – a chamber which had been hollowed over time from ancient sedimentary rock.

The ship's burial site was no longer deep under the ocean but was now perched high among the peaks of Manitoba's Duck Mountain Provincial Park. The ship heard Philippe's fall and sensed Melba's presence. It stirred. After countless years of waiting, opportunity had finally knocked. It was time to wake up and answer the call.

# [2]

Philippe landed hard. He thumped to the ground like a sack of grain, his breath knocked painfully from his body. He wondered what he had done to deserve it. Perhaps he was being punished for admiring Melba's ass, but that, he reasoned, would be patently stupid. If every man who admired a woman's ass got dropped down a hole, humanity would have died out long before it climbed down from the trees.

He gingerly peeled off his rucksack and examined himself, paying particular attention to his elbows, shoulders and knees. Nothing seemed broken or dislocated. He was battered and his dignity had taken a real bruising, but he was still physically sound. It looked like Melba wouldn't need to carry him home after all. *Shame.*

There was enough light pouring through the hole he'd made to illuminate most of his landing site. He took a moment to regain his breath while he looked around. And then he stopped and stared.

'*What the...?*'

'You alive down there? Hey, Philippe! Come on, kid! Speak to me!'

He realised Melba had been shouting at him for the last several seconds and turned to gaze up at where she was silhouetted against the afternoon sky. There was a rising touch of panic in her voice.

'What's up? Did you break your tongue or something? Come on, Philippe! Talk to me.'

'Melba, I'm okay, but you have got to come down here and see this.'

He could hear the relief in her voice at his response. She chuckled. 'Oh please! Why does every boy in the dark find something I really need to see? No chance. Get your raggedy ass back up here. There are plenty of handholds, so you don't need my help. Come on, climb back up here.'

'No, I mean it, really. You *have* to see this.'

'Yeah? Well let me tell you something. You waste my time and I don't care how bruised you are! I'll kick your ass all the way back to base, understand?'

There was the sound of controlled scrabbling and moments later she skidded to a halt at his side. He had to jump out of her way or she would have taken his feet from under him. She stood tall by his side. Both were now coated with a fine layer of dust.

'Okay, show me. What?'

He pointed into the darker shadows at the back of the cave. Her gaze followed his finger. Her jaw swung open.

'The fuck? What is that?'

Buried in the stone at one end of the cave they could clearly see the wall of what appeared to be a two-storey building. It was curved and glazed, with big windows mounted into ornate, metallic frames. They found themselves walking towards it, stumbling across the stony floor of the cave and craning forward to see inside.

Philippe began to ramble. 'You going to kick me? Huh? Well, are you?'

Melba waved her hand at him without answering.

He continued, 'Thought not. This is too cool, yeah. I've seen buildings like this back home in France. They were built by the Germans during the Second World War. But I don't get it. How did this one get to Manitoba? Must be like a spy base or something. What d'ya think?'

Philippe was seventeen. Melba wondered how anyone so stupid had managed to live that long. She used her right hand to wipe dust from the nearest window and pressed her nose against it, squinting to make sense of vague shapes in the shadows. Whatever this insane building was, she was dead sure it wasn't German. It didn't look very Canadian either. A trickle like a sharp electric charge bit at her skin, making her jerk her head back in surprise. She rubbed at her nose. Beside her, Philippe was shaking his hand.

'I felt something. Did you feel it too? I bet you did, didn't you! I bet this place has a kind of electric security field around it, but it would have to be over sixty years old now and it's barely working. I bet that's it. I bet that would have burned us alive a few years ago.'

He made a crisp electrocution noise at the back of his throat.

Melba regarded him sideways. 'You've become quite the gambler suddenly.'

She pressed her hand back against the glass. Her flesh crawled as if hundreds of tiny, needle-sharp legs were scuttling across it. The fine hairs on her arm stood on end. Then a cold certainty settled in her gut. Something about the building had suddenly changed, and although she couldn't be sure what had happened, or even how she knew it, she became acutely nervous.

'I think we should go.'

'Not yet. Come on, please! This is so cool.'

'Philippe, I mean it. We should go. We need to report this.'

He was right in one respect – everything about the building felt foreign. Under the dust the metal frames were curved and looked woven, almost organic. Even the windows had a curve to them. She got the distinct impression that the structure was brooding, as if it was waiting for something; waiting for something to come home. She realised she was spooking herself badly.

And how had it become buried like this in the cave wall? The rock seemed to have flowed around it and set hard. *How could that happen?* She stroked the stone. It vibrated. That was too much.

'Philippe, we're going. Now!'

There was no reply. She looked around. The boy had disappeared. *What now?*

'Philippe, this isn't funny. Where are you?'

'Up here. Look, see, this window's open. Man, it's so thick! Look at it! Funny hinges too, they look like big chicken bones or something.'

'Get back down here! We don't know what this place is or what's in there. It could be full of snakes or spiders. Come on, get down.'

'Snakes, really? Like Indiana Jones? That would be so amazing. Cool!'

He leaned forward, trying to see inside. His foot slipped, and with a high-pitched squeal he fell through the narrow opening. Without hesitation Melba flew into action. While she climbed up towards where the teenager had been, she yelled: 'I've just about had enough of this. If you're not dead I'm going to kill you, you fucking idiot. I shit you not!'

She reached the opening and cautiously slid through. She found herself poised some ten feet above the ground. The floor below her was in almost total darkness, and she had left her torch back in her rucksack.

*Not thinking straight, Melba. Come on, calm down girl. Man! This is so stupid.*

She heard a groan.

'Philippe?'

There came a drawn-out retching sound. A weak voice said, 'I fell.'

'I saw. Don't worry. I'll come and get you, okay?'

'I fell down. My arm hurts. I banged my head on something.'

'Okay, honey, I'm coming down. Don't move. Try not to touch anything, okay.'

'I fell down.'

She looked around, wishing she had a rope. *Damn, even Indiana Jones' whip would be better than nothing.* The inside of the thick window frame was impressed with deep ribs and its arc outwards and downwards was relatively slight. It looked like her best option. The boy was retching again. He was likely to be heavily concussed. What if he was brain-damaged? He was in her charge when it happened. She would get the blame. *Shit! This might cost me my job. This was not how I planned to spend my afternoon today.*

Melba swung herself around until she was straddling the inside of the window frame, holding on with fingers, knees and boot tips. She gingerly began to climb down. Her boots were just a little too large for the ribbing and they slipped a few times, leaving her swinging from her fingertips. Ten feet began to feel more like a hundred and she jumped the last few feet, landing heavily. She stood up, breathing heavily and pumped with adrenaline. She tasted acid and bile in her mouth. She wanted to vomit but refused to. She didn't want to scare Philippe.

Her sight was becoming more accustomed to the gloom, but it wasn't helping her make sense of her surroundings. When a person enters a darkened room, she thought, experience normally helps them navigate through it. Even a strange room will contain familiar items that one's fingertips will recognise. Chairs, tables, beds and lamps create a Braille lexicon that informs the blind mind and helps it 'see' in the darkness. Such was not the case here. Hard objects and pieces of strange architecture caught at her and tried to trip her up. Nothing made sense or was where it should be.

Even the floor wasn't flat. Instead it offered a series of obstacles that seemed desperate to catch her out, as though it was made up of holes and ridges. There was no logic to it. She caught herself emitting an involuntary whimper, and firmly reminded herself that she was the adult in this situation. Her charge might only be three years younger than her, but she was the one getting paid to be there. She was *trained.*

*How do you train for shit like this?*

The boy had stopped groaning. Was that a good or a bad thing? Why fool herself? She was certain it wasn't good.

'Philippe, honey, say something, will you? Where are you?' Her voice sounded feeble in her ears. She tried again. 'Philippe, honey, come on! Speak to me.'

There was a skittering sound. Something was scuttling around her very fast. There was a flickering movement in the shadows. She crouched down, her hands out in a defensive posture. Whatever it was, it was moving too fast to register as anything other than a dark blur. For a moment, she was badly rattled, to the point she just wanted to cut and run. When she felt hands pulling apart her blouse and grabbing at her breasts, she was almost relieved. Was that what this was all about? Philippe was trying for a little grope?

'Cut it out, you little freak. Back off.'

9

And then she felt a brief sting in the flesh of her chest, and with a rush of cold clarity she suddenly discovered what the building had been waiting for.

It had been waiting for her.

'The only virgin there, Budail, will be you. And what use will you be if your stupid backside has been blown halfway across the planet?'

The young man in the front row looked shocked. He had come to mock the spiritualist fraud, but now the infidel bitch was taunting *him*! A woman talking to him like that was unforgivable. And she was doing so in his dead father's voice. It was monstrous.

The tiny, dark figure on the stage crouched forward and low on the edge of her big chair. Hands clasped, knees together, head down and eyes shut under the spotlight. She seemed frail and tenderly fragile, as if the merest breath of wind would blow her to rags and tatters. By contrast the impossibly powerful male voice booming from her could rattle windows a city block away.

'Stick your stupid anger back in your pocket, boy. Show some respect to the world and you might get somewhere, like decent Muslims have done for generations. Allahu Akbar means "God is great"! Not God is a grenade with the pin pulled out. I died and left you alone when you were too young. Okay, I'm sorry, but I had no choice. I died from cancer. Why don't you use that educated brain of yours to help find a cure and save lives, instead of wasting it like this? Why are you talking with half-wit tujjar al'iibil and plotting jaban ways to kill women and children? You disgust me, boy! Go on, get out of my sight. Look at him. See him? See him there? He thinks he's a warrior. Moxxu gazma! His mind is low and dirty as a shoe. He is not my son! I will not be father to such a liar!'

With a scream of rage the slender young man launched himself at the stage, his hands outstretched like claws towards the diminutive medium's slender throat. But before he could touch her, she raised her face to the light and opened her huge eyes. Her gaze was like ice-cold steel. It froze his blood. He paused, and with a growing sense of horror realised he could see his father standing over the woman, his hands placed protectively on her shoulders. The dead man stood firm and regarded Budail as if he was less than dirt.

From his own father's lips, he heard, 'Hamagi kaddaab, you *will* not raise your hands against me. Find a shovel and dig a hole deep enough to bury yourself so I won't have to suffer your foul stink a moment longer. Now go! This place is too clean for such as you.'

Budail's legs crumpled. He staggered and almost fell when he turned to run from the little theatre. He sprinted up the aisle with every eye in the place following him. He got as far as the lobby before he was grabbed by two plain-clothed police officers who had been listening to the medium's performance with mounting interest.

'Good evening, sir,' said the young blonde as she took a stronger grip on the whimpering youth's arm. 'I believe you might be able to help us with our enquiries.'

Minutes later the squad car they had called screamed to a halt in front of the theatre, pulling up right in the middle of a zebra crossing. It earned a shouted protest from an elderly woman who was halfway across at the time. The driver leapt out and consoled her.

'Sorry, missus. Terrorist alert.'

'Where?'

'There.'

And then she saw the limp young man being dragged from the theatre by two plain-clothed officers and watched as he was bundled into the back of the car. With its lights flashing and siren wailing, the car tore away.

'Shoot the little fucker!' she yelled at the departing vehicle. 'Save the taxpayers some money.'

The next day was Thursday, and she now had something juicy to share with her cronies at her local church's regular coffee morning. She almost scampered on her way home, a rare lightness to her step. She decided she would microwave herself some 'chip shop' style fish and chips when she got home. She was in the proper mood for a treat. Might even buy some cider on the way for a little touch of mid-week wickedness.

*Terrorists, ha! She'd told them. "Shoot the little fucker," she'd said. Ha!*

Back on stage Medina Bishop was forced to spend a few moments calming her audience after the father-and-son drama had concluded in such an intense fashion.

'I never know where the spirits will take me,' she explained.

A member of the audience shouted, 'Go on! That was all staged!'

Another at the back of the stalls replied, 'It wasn't. That kid was carted off by the police. I saw it happen.'

There was a hubbub of building noise that threatened to get out of hand. People were looking at each other instead of at the stage. Stagehands wondered whether they should surrender to events and bring up the houselights. Then Medina held up her arms and her surprisingly powerful voice rang out across the auditorium.

12

'There are spirits here,' she boomed. 'They are with me now, and they have messages they want me to share with their loved ones. Will you deny them? I ask you, WILL YOU DENY THEM?'

There was a slight squeal of feedback from the sound system, but she had regained their attention. The rest of the evening could easily have been a wash-out. She knew Budail's confrontation with his furious father would be a tough act to follow, but it went very well.

Medina channelled messages from several people including a soldier who had died in Iraq when his daughter was just a baby. The daughter had never met her father, only seen pictures of him and heard stories. That night she was seated in the stalls with her husband. Through Medina the soldier told his daughter how he was looking forward to seeing his grandson in eight months' time. The woman screamed – she didn't even know she was pregnant.

A husband told his wife where his savings book was hidden; a daughter told her parents she was happy and in a good place. A grandmother told her grandson he should trust his fiancée. The girl loved him and he should best ignore those wicked lies from his 'so-called friends' which, she said, 'were just green fruit fallen from a bitter tree'.

A slender, well-presented woman in her middle years was told to take down the awful portrait painting in her dead husband's study and have a professional de-frame it. It hid a rather beautiful Turner watercolour. She protested that she rather liked the portrait and thought it very fine. Her husband laughed, agreed that Frampton had done a passable job, and then asked if she wouldn't rather have both where she could see them? Wouldn't they make a fascinating and lovely conversation piece?

The woman smiled through her tears.

She said, 'Darling, I miss you so much. When will we be together again?'

He replied, 'Steady on, old love. We can't go giving out that sort of information, can we? Classified, you know. Anyway, soon enough as these things go – but don't be shy about borrowing any library books. And anyway, wherever you are, I'll always be there with you.'

A sergeant who had died on the Somme in August 1916 told his stunned granddaughter some facts about his family tree, to help restart her stalled research into her ancestry. She scrambled to make notes while he spoke. A child told his bereft mother about his new friends and the fields where they played.

'We're allowed to paddle in the lake. It's so lovely, mummy. I wish you could see it.'

Each voice was clear and distinctive. Whether the souls she channelled were men, women or children, they all had different accents, individual verbal styles and pacing. If Medina Bishop was acting, she was a genius. Each recipient of her gift was touched by wonder and joy, and although some wept freely, all felt a great weight drop from their hearts.

She concluded with her customary Q&A session, which she loathed, but her sponsors insisted on. There was so little she, a living soul, could say to her audience about the afterlife. And the questions rarely varied. Was there a Heaven? Was there a God? Was there a Hell? Did demons exist? Such questions she would always leave to Sister Honoria – an eighteenth-century Carmelite nun with a wicked sense of humour.

'There could be heaven here on Earth if you sinners tried a little harder. Is there a God? Why do you ask? Have faith! What have they lost, those who believe and live a righteous life? Nothing, and the world is a better place with them in it. What have you lost if you don't believe and then find out He's there after all? Everything, and you'll bring nothing of value to the table. Righteousness is the bread of life, but it don't thicken the belly like too many dinners. Looks like a good few of you here could do with learning that lesson.'

There was some laughter at that and a few rueful smiles.

'Is there a Hell? Read your newspapers, watch the news. There's your answer, and it's the same when it comes to demons. One thing I will say: the first steps towards redemption begin when you take a good honest look at your own faults and start putting them right, rather than judging everyone around you. I was once as guilty of that as the worst of you here. Judge not, that ye be not judged. Are you listening to me, Stella Matthews?'

A large black woman in a tightly-buttoned lavender dress gaped at the stage. The man next to her stifled a grin.

'One last question. Yes? You, sir.'

'Do atheists survive into the afterlife?'

'Not for long. Think about it.'

And with that Medina came out of her trance and stood to take her bows. The curtains swung closed to rousing applause. She took three curtain calls before the house lights came up and the spotlights turned down, and then at last the chattering audience spilled out of the theatre and took their leave under the orange light of streetlamps.

Acknowledging the congratulations of stagehands, Medina retired back to her changing room and removed her make-up. Her hands shook with exhaustion. The fresh vodka and tonic on the little side table went down far too easily, but she needed it and welcomed its cool warmth. A knock at her door heralded flowers from the management and a note to say her usual requirements had all been met.

Experience had taught Medina never to exit a theatre by its stage door. Too many people with too many questions and grieving hearts awaited her there. She didn't have the energy to face it all again after two solid hours on the stage. She changed into black jeans and a black top, pulled on a big hat and an ankle-length black coat, and then she stuffed her dark professional garb into a black rucksack, which she slung over her shoulders.

She took the long walk through the empty stalls to the theatre's lobby and joined some of the staff who had been waiting for her. They all left by one of the main doors and walked out into the cool, fresh-tasting night. Just workers at the end of the day heading for home. One with a bunch of flowers. Two of the women stayed by her side until the theatre was out of sight.

'Okay if we leave you here, Medina?'

'Yes, thanks. Kind of you. Goodnight.'

'Night.'

It seemed an elaborate ruse, but Medina knew it was necessary. Her admirers sometimes waited around the stage door until midnight, hoping vainly for a personal message from, or news about, a lost loved one.

They were there, crowded around the side of the theatre and waiting. They stayed until the doorkeeper walked out for the umpteenth time and growled, 'She ain't comin'. How many times have I got to tell yer? She ain't comin'. Go 'ome will yer? Go on, all of yer. We're grateful for yer custom but we don't like yer hours. Me, I've got a date with a beer and a bed. I suggest you go do the same.'

Then he locked the door behind him and sauntered away with his hands in his pockets and a tuneless whistle on his lips.

By then Medina had safely reached her hotel. She sourced a vase big enough for her flowers, ate her pre-arranged cold dinner and drank a few more vodkas. And then she enjoyed a long, hot shower before finally retiring for the night in the vain hope of dreamless sleep. She had barely tucked herself into bed, and gratefully rested her head on the pillow, before she heard a clear voice say, 'Talker with Spirits, we need your help.'

She sighed and sat up.

# [4]

Melba and Philippe worked until dark collecting all the richly purple and slightly larger than walnut-sized core pods from throughout the ship. They had emptied their rucksacks and carefully filled them again with nearly two hundred of the pods. They toiled silently, both now navigating the interior of the ship with confidence. The ship mind watched them work and communicated with them in its alien tongue. They understood every word.

Once they had collected all the pods, the ship opened one of its lower viewports and they climbed back out into the cave. Since the sun had gone down, the air had cooled rapidly. Melba felt the sweat drying on her skin. Part of her mind was struggling in panic, like a forest creature caught in a snare. That part wanted to know what was happening and why her body was doing its own thing. It wanted to know why her muscles were refusing to respond to her demands. The rest of her knew exactly what it was doing and why. It was the Finder, and it wanted to go home. But first it had to help impress a brand-new crew.

The ship needed to be freed from its stony prison, and at last the indigenous species had evolved enough to be of value. If its surface could be opened to the sun's rays once more it would begin to refuel, and once its crew and tool units were restored to life it would soon be on its way out towards space – and home.

Philippe's awareness fluttered around his stolen mind like a bird in a locked room. He was terrified and confused. His traitor hand had pressed the nearest pod to his breast and his body had instantly started working under its own agenda. He had been horrified by his attack on Melba, too stunned by events to even begin to understand how he had could move so swiftly in the dark and with such fluid grace, despite his injuries. The pod anchored firmly against his ribs had assessed his physical condition as being 'damaged but temporarily acceptable' pending the discovery of a better unit. Fine filaments of super conductive crystal had woven themselves around Philippe's brain stem. If the pod found itself a better host, they would tear free and embed themselves in the new body. The teenager's mind would be free once more – and dead in seconds from total neurological failure.

After a walk of several miles they sat unseen on a hill overlooking the Duck Mountain spa complex and waited until the lights had all gone out.

They were neither hungry nor thirsty. Finally, the only remaining light was in the entrance lobby. It was time. They made their move.

Tony 'the night guy' was sitting at his desk watching his CCTV monitors when he recognised the pair letting themselves in through the main entrance. Melba looked like a foxy poster girl, as usual, but Philippe looked badly knocked about. Tony leapt to his feet and rushed over, his face a picture of real concern. Melba smiled and deftly reached her hand inside his open-collared shirt. Even as he was leaning forward to get a closer look at the blood on Philippe's oddly expressionless face, Tony became the third member of the resurrected crew.

The next morning the alarm was raised when the spa's unwitting survivors realised that almost four-fifths of the people who should be in the refectory for breakfast had not turned up. A search party was formed and the buildings and grounds combed. The realisation that they were not victims of some massive practical joke arrived with tragic force when they discovered the bloody corpse of Philippe Bourdain sprawled across his bed. The injuries to his head and body were grave enough, but what gave people pause was the trauma to his chest. It looked as though something had exploded *out* of his body. The pathologist's report would later add another veil of mystery to the case. It observed that the teenager's nervous system appeared to have disintegrated – although how and why was a mystery.

Days later, researchers were still studying the CCTV recordings and trying to understand events at the spa during that strange night – and at daybreak the following morning. Crystal-clear digital images showed the trio leaving the lobby and heading up towards the dorms. They followed them along corridors and right up to the moment when they reached and then entered the first dormitory's door. There were no cameras in the spa's private quarters. The researchers had no clue what happened in there.

Several minutes later a small crowd of people came back out into the corridor and dispersed, heading for the rest of the building's sleeping quarters. Before long nearly every guest had been visited. A girl who woke up the next day and found herself alone in a room that usually slept five, and a small group in the most distant dorm, plus the management personnel, kitchen staff and groundsmen who slept in a separate building, enjoyed an undisturbed night. After a few hours of intense activity, the nightwalkers, as they were later dubbed, returned to their beds. Including Melba. Tony the night guy abandoned his post. He was filmed heading for his quarters at the back of the complex. And then all was still.

No further movement was recorded until sunrise the next morning, which at that time of year happened just after six o'clock. As soon as sunlight poured through the spa's windows, the most baffling episode of the Duck Mountain mystery took place. All the affected people climbed out of their beds and gathered in the corridors. Recordings showed one hundred and eighty-four souls marching down into the lobby in a column forty-six rows long, each row consisting of four victims. That they were victims would become very clear, but victims of what? Nobody knew.

The last camera viewpoint was outside and showed the bank of steps leading down to the main road from the lobby's entrance, also known as 'smoker's corner' because it held the spa's only ashtray/trash-can. Out of focus at the bottom of a steep two-hundred-yard slope was the spa's full-size outdoor swimming pool and stacks of folded sun-loungers. The CCTV view of the pool was maintained strictly out of focus for the same reason there were no security cameras mounted in private and sleeping quarters: it might prove too tempting to record fit young people in their underwear, bathing costumes or less.

This last camera showed the victims' final moments as little more than a frustrating blur against an idyllic background of blue sky, grass of an almost surreal green and the turquoise waters of the rectangular pool. Some of the world's most sophisticated image analysis software was brought to bear in a futile attempt to clarify details of the next sequence of events. The column of marchers was clearly seen stepping out of the building and then down the steps leading to the road. They crossed the road and continued onto the lawns. They then executed a looping manoeuvre down the hill, at the end of which the first row of four approached the deep end of the pool. Without any hesitation, each row of four dived into the water. Most were in their nightwear. They caused barely a splash.

The next sequence of events had investigators almost foaming at the mouth with frustration. After diving into the deep end the victims swam the length of the pool. Their dark, blurred shapes moved like torpedoes under the water. When they emerged from the shallow end they hustled away too fast to be seen. The figures that had dived into the water were patently the one hundred and eighty-four patrons and staff from the Duck Mountain spa. The blurred recordings of the pool were studied until researchers' eyes ached, but everyone who saw them agreed on one fact: the swimmers' shapes seemed to change while they traversed the length of the pool. Some seemed to lengthen while others became wider, and when they left the pool they did so at a pace that beggared belief.

By the end of the swimming sequence the level of water in the pool was drastically reduced. The last of the 'swimmers' practically slid along the bottom of the deep end and emerged like rockets into the almost dry shallow end. Their progress in the light looked awkward. Some seemed to find it difficult to rise above all-fours, while others looked as if their limbs had become oddly truncated.

One of the scientists leading the team on behalf of D Division of the Royal Canadian Mounted Police (RCMP) watched the swimming pool sequence for the tenth time. He pushed his hands through his thick mop of hair and sighed.

He said, 'I honestly believe when those young folks dived into that pool they were human. I couldn't say what climbed out the other side, but it sure as hell didn't look human to me. And where the hell do we go from here?'

## 5

An explosion of screaming terror rocked through the Realm of Light in a way none had experienced before. Legions of adept mentors were accustomed to greeting and calming newly-arrived souls. They knew how to soothe those stricken by tragedy and disaster, or those blown suddenly and violently into their new state of existence by war and wickedness. They held out a welcoming hand to those brought to the Light by age or sickness.

But this was new.

The Light was a living, cogent force. It recognised the nobility of some souls and the poor quality of others, and it would shape them accordingly. It would weave the spirit form of the noble from finer cloth and the latter, less evolved souls from baser materials. Thus, some souls might have ruled empires on Earth but now they stalked the marshlands of the Realm like half-made mud creatures. Others might have spent their mortal lives in poverty with nothing but love and compassion to offer their fellows, and they walked through the Light in humble glory, exquisitely drawn and beautiful.

Most souls, however, had muddled through life as decent enough people, and they retained a great deal of the shape that had cloaked them in life. Enough that previously lost loved ones might recognise them and, if they chose to, greet them on arrival. Overall the newly dead were given a friendly reception and offered an experienced hand to help them learn the ropes.

Not so these latest arrivals, quickly named the Banshees from Manitoba. They came into the first Realm of the dead tearing at themselves with horror and lashed out at the gentle souls who approached them. The depth of their terror disturbed the very fabric of the Realm, causing widespread psychic distress among its people; while the terrible force of the new arrivals' screams tore at their sanity. Even the brutish, half-formed clay creatures looked up from their clumsy nests and whimpered with fear. More advanced spirits felt the anguish of the Manitoba incursion as physical blows.

With the worlds of the living and the dead connected by tenuous links, echoes of the extraordinary trauma afflicting the Realm manifested on the Earthly plane as a spate of particularly nasty and mischievous poltergeist phenomena.

One family in Glasgow stood mutely around a baffled plumber who could find no reason why their toilet would flush every time the tank refilled. A young student in Reykjavik ran terrified from her study carrel when her chair was forcefully ripped out from under her and her breasts squeezed hard by invisible hands. The librarian, a noted and vocal champion of the feminine cause, was similarly accosted when she investigated.

The library remained locked to students for forty-eight hours before the librarian, who checked on a regular basis, finally announced she was no longer being molested by the mysterious assailant and that she believed the room was now safe. Those who knew her best thought they noted a hint of regret in her voice.

One spectacular event created world-wide headlines. The eyes of the Black Madonna at Montserrat began to weep blood, or at least a blood-like substance. Pilgrims broke the glass that separated them from the ancient wooden figure and noisily fought to dip handkerchiefs, scarves or even strips torn from their clothes into the ruddy streams. It took several of the Basilica's burliest monks to force their way up the narrow steps to the throne room and form a protective wall before their beloved and sacred 'La Moreneta'.

Once the area had been cleared and the door from the atrium securely locked, the question arose of how to preserve the precious fluid. One of the monks had a brainwave. He plunged back into the gathering crowd of worshippers and begged a bowl-like plastic bib from the mother of a toddler, who looked to the monk as if he could suffer to go without food for a few hours. The monk dashed back up the stairs and placed it around the Madonna's neck (it was balanced on the Christ child's head, but that nugget of information never made it into formal reports). For two days, a parade of trusted monks and nuns took it in turns, day and night, to funnel the miraculous 'blood' into bottles, all of which were locked away safely.

By the time the mysterious flow had stopped as suddenly as it started, the Virgin had wept nearly three gallons of liquid. Research later discovered that the miracle had indeed produced human blood, and that it was as ancient as the sculpture itself. How and why such a thing should happen would fuel debate for years afterwards. The Pope made a special pilgrimage and was photographed while kneeling to kiss the Madonna's foot. His lead was followed by many heads of state.

All over the globe petty tricks and irritating nonsense pricked at the living for forty-eight hours. Mysterious burn marks, stigmata, moving furniture and locked doors mysteriously opening were just a few of the things that confused and unnerved the people of Earth, but once it had ended the alarm soon died down. Everyday life beckoned once more.

In the spirit world, however, the Banshees from Manitoba were creating a crisis. Their increasingly panic-stricken wails sounded ever louder throughout the Realm, like an unceasing and particularly aggressive smoke alarm. It became unbearable.

The ancient, adept and wise creatures of the Realm called for an emergency Council meeting at the communication gateway known to its builders as Prydain-Shelba, and by others, much more recently, as Stonehenge.

The hierarchy of the Realm had been long established yet the nature of its 'ruling' class, perforce, had always remained flexible. The Realm was not a democracy, nor did it cling to the ermined folly of aristocracy. By its very nature, it had become that rare thing – an honest meritocracy.

The most ancient ones had largely earned the right to be taken up, or 'Sublimed' to the next state of being, but some had chosen to remain as teachers, advisers and guides. They formed the basis of the Council. Others, more recently arrived, who had been deemed worthy were also welcomed into its ranks. Some of the oldest members were barely recognisable as human. They had been shaped by the Light, time and wisdom into more abstract shapes.

The Council communed in a spiral around the heart of the stone circle and asked the elemental sprites – supernatural creatures who, when not in their home city, lived in permanent transition between spirit, dream and flesh – to help erect a barrier between the Manitoban uproar and the gateway. They sighed in relief when silence fell about them for the first time in too many hours, and they were at last able to speak and think coherently.

The meeting started with a review of the facts. It was quickly ascertained that all they knew for sure was that nearly two hundred souls had departed from a single location in Canada and exploded into the Realm like a tornado, rattling it to its foundations. The sensitive sprites had also been affected by the disturbance and were eager to help in any way they could. Many of them were immensely ancient, but not even the oldest could remember anything similar in the past. Neither legend nor myth spoke of such a thing and the meeting quickly descended into baffled silence.

Some younger heads suggested forcefully transfiguring the problem souls to a higher Realm where their needs might be better served, but they were glared at until they stuttered into silence.

One ancient, who could remember a frozen world of aurochs and woolly rhinos before the sarsens of Prydain-Shelba had been erected, voiced her opinion.

'It is not our way to hand our problems on to others, you know that. These troubled spirits have suffered an unprecedented event, but what that was we don't know. We do know it was extremely localised because we are not suffering an influx of such agitated souls from elsewhere. Something happened in Manitoba, and only in Manitoba, that has driven these poor creatures beyond the point of madness. To treat them we need to find the cause, and once we know the cause we might find a path to its cure.'

The old soul, who looked as if she had been fashioned whole from crystalline stone, looked around at her fellows.

'Our sprite friends are as baffled as we are. We have no recourse but to reach beyond our Realm to the world of the living and seek help. Has anyone here any suggestions as to how that might be done?'

There followed a susurration, a sound like a breeze drifting through dry leaves, and then one clear voice rose above the others.

'There is a remarkable young woman,' it said. 'Her name is Medina Bishop. I have spoken with her before.'

The old soul nodded. 'Then, please, do so again. Ask for her help.'

The meeting adjourned. Council members reluctantly returned to the pitiless agony of sound that had become the Realm.

## 6

'Shimon, really? Can't this wait? I'm sorry, but I'm really exhausted.'

'No. Please. You must listen to this.'

Medina suddenly buckled under an onslaught of sound akin to a million fingernails screeching down a thousand blackboards, all played through a concert-level sound system with added feedback. It was pure aural agony and more. It washed over her for long, paralysing seconds; seconds during which she coiled tightly into a defensive foetal ball, her mouth stretched open in an agonised O. Her breath was shocked and stilled in her throat or she would have screamed. And then it ceased. She could breathe again.

She panted. 'Owww! What was that? Why did you do that to me?'

'That noise has been tearing the spirit Realm apart for days.'

'What is it?'

'That is the sound of many souls in torment, the sound of unspeakable terror. We don't understand why, but that disturbance is the result of one hundred and eighty-five souls coming to the Light in a state of complete and ungovernable shock. Mentors can't reach them; even the Council are at a loss. The Realm has become Hell for all of us. Some Council members are even talking about transfiguring the poor creatures to a higher state.'

'You can't do that. They aren't ready. They obviously aren't ready. They might dissipate and be lost completely. You can't do that to them.'

'Yes, yes, of course you're right. Elemental sprites are even now working to screen the afflicted from the rest of us...' It paused, and then sighed with relief. 'Ah, at last, they seem to have succeeded. Thank God. That has been torture. Hour upon hour...'

'Good. I'm glad for you. I can't imagine what it's been like.'

She shuddered at the thought of such a sound ripping apart her sanity for days on end. It made her eyes water.

'What do you want me to do?'

'Something must have happened to those poor creatures and we need to know what it was. We may have succeeded in locking them away in a soundproof bubble, but we can't forget them. Spirit Talker, Medina Bishop, we beg you to help us find whatever caused this terrible thing. You have been a true friend to the Realm in the past. Will you help us now?'

The soul's voice was becoming distant. Despite her best efforts, sleep was claiming her, its inexorable grip tightening by the second. She could no longer fight its demands. Her eyes had already closed and her breathing deepened when she murmured, 'Where did they come from, those poor souls?'

'Manitoba, Duck Mountain Provincial Park.'

'Good name, Duck...' And she was lost to dreams.

The tormented cries of screaming souls blighted her sleep. She awoke sweating to the sound of someone pounding on her door. She pulled on a robe before answering it. She found herself gazing up at a furious looking man. His thinning grey hair was in disarray and his dressing gown cinched tightly around his thickening waist. He glared at her through smeared spectacles.

'Are you drunk?'

'I'm sorry?'

'I said, are you drunk? I could hear you shouting from down the hall. Everyone could! What's the matter with you? It's barely three in the morning. Are you drunk or are you mad?'

'I'm sorry, I was asleep. I was having a nightmare. Sorry.'

The man's angry expression changed to one of concern.

'Are you alright?'

'Nightmare, as I said. Some friends of mine are in trouble and I was thinking about them when I fell asleep. Silly of me. I'm really sorry.'

'Drugs?'

'Sorry?'

'Your friends. Is it drugs?'

'No, no really, nothing like that.'

His eyes became kind, gentle. 'Okay, goodnight. Let's both try to get some sleep. Hope you can rest more peacefully now.'

'Yeah, sorry about the fuss. By the way, your brother says thanks for the flowers yesterday, it means a lot. He's okay and so are your parents.'

The man frowned, 'Which brother?'

'He says his name is, yes? Goose? Goose? Really? Does that work?'

The man pushed his hand through his hair and took off his glasses to squint more closely at Medina. He breathed out heavily. She could smell something minty and a little chemical on his breath.

'How did you know that?'

'What? Your brother's name? He told me. It's what I do. I'm a medium.'

'Extraordinary. What's your name?'

'Medina Bishop. I was at the theatre down the road last night.'

'Edward, Edward Louis.' He shook her damp hand. 'Strange meetings in the night are what I do. Nice to meet you, Medina. And now, please, go back to bed. Good night. Think peaceful thoughts.'

She watched him saunter down the corridor. Just before he rounded the corner he turned, smiled and waved, and then he was gone.

Her bed was cold and damp with sweat, but sleep stole her clotted wits within minutes. The next morning − once she was showered, dressed and wondering what she should choose from the breakfast menu − she found a simple business card had been pushed under her door. 'Edward Louis BA(Hons). Novelist. Journalist. Photographer.' It listed a website, social media details, an email address and a mobile phone number. On the back was a list of newspapers and journals, under which was written in a tidy hand, 'Please, stay in touch.' She tucked it into her purse and decided she would Google Mr Louis before the day was out. He wasn't in the breakfast room so she ate alone. She had become used to eating lonely meals and always had something to read in her bag. She enjoyed a good mystery story but avoided the gorier, Grand Guignol horror tales. In her line of work, it wasn't wise to clutter her imagination with such things.

On the breakfast room's wall-mounted TV a news story was unfolding about a group of young people who had gone missing two days before from a spa in a Canadian mountain range. Helicopter and drone shots showed an aerial view of a pleasant looking complex of buildings and a startlingly blue yet half-empty swimming pool. Green lawns and white roads completed the picture. The sound, as usual, was off. She forked scrambled eggs and smoked salmon into her mouth. When she saw the legend 'Duck Mountain Spa Resort' and realised the scrolling news stream was telling her about one hundred and eighty-four people – a mixture of teenage guests and staff – who had gone missing from the resort, she nearly choked on her food. Everything she had been told the night before came crashing back into her mind.

*Those kids aren't just missing. They're screaming up a storm in the Realm.*

She finished her breakfast at high speed and hustled down the road to the local library. She was in town alone so often, she had her own library card and was no stranger to the shelves. She followed the building's index to the geography section and scoured the shelves for information about Manitoba and the Duck Mountain range. Nothing. Even general works about Canada were missing. She sighed in frustration.

'Miss Bishop, how nice to see you again.'

She spun and met the merry blue eyes of Edward Louis.

26

'What a coincidence to meet you here by the reference shelves for Canada. To be more specific... Manitoba?'

'But... I'm... you... Why?'

He pointed at his chest. 'Journalist. Those kids disappeared a couple of days ago, and the nationals want information about the area. Where could they have gone? Is there somewhere around there you could hide nearly two hundred people? Is there a history of this kind of thing? You see what I mean? And what about you? What's your interest?'

'Shall we just say that I've been asked to consider the case? Friends of mine are interested.' She fetched a white Moleskine notebook and pen from her big woven bag. 'Going to make a few notes about the place. Same as you I suppose, get an idea about the terrain.'

'Come, join me at my table. I've got all the books over there and I've only just started. I'd be very pleased to share with a colleague.'

Two hours later they were swapping notes over mugs of disappointing coffee.

Duck Mountain Provincial Park had proved to be nearly one-point-five thousand square kilometres of wilderness in western Manitoba, located within the larger Duck Mountain Provincial Forest.

A rise of forested land between the Saskatchewan prairie to the west and the Manitoba lowlands to the east, the Duck Mountains rose some 200 metres higher than the floor of the Assiniboine River valley to the west, and 400 metres higher than the Manitoba lowlands. The tallest, Baldy Mountain, was also the highest point in Manitoba.

The nearest conurbation of any note, Dauphin to the south, was a city of over eight thousand inhabitants. The RCMP, D Division personnel investigating the spa case had helicoptered in from there.

'I believe the population of moose, black bears and wolves outnumbers the humans up there in the north-west,' observed Louis. 'It's a wild place, barely touched since the glaciers retreated, and there's plenty of room for a couple of hundred people to get lost in, that's for sure.' He leaned back in his chair and fiddled with his coffee mug, moving it around the table. Then he tapped his notes.

'I know what I'm doing, Medina, and why. But *your* involvement fascinates me. Nearly two hundred people go missing and I find a world-famous medium – and yes, I Googled you – researching the case. Last night you were having nightmares because, you said, friends of yours are in trouble. Today you tell me that "friends of yours" are interested in Duck

27

Mountain and what happened there.' He leaned forward and gazed at her, his head slightly to one side. She felt herself colouring under his scrutiny.

'Tell me,' he asked quietly. 'Are they going to find them alive?'

'No,' she answered. 'No, I'm afraid they're not.'

## 7

Nearly eight hours later in the CID offices of the striking, south-west London Metropolitan Police building in Sutton, a single table lamp was providing the only illumination for a large, dark office. It was still officially daylight, but heavy cloud had turned the early evening dark as night. The room was filled with an abundance of chairs and a large evidence board. Only two of the chairs were occupied and they had been pulled up to a small side table by a wall.

'Lucky we had a couple of officers in the audience.'

'Don't be daft. We always have bodies on the ground when Bishop's in town. She's a goldmine, an honest-to-God marvel.'

DCI Page Worker and DI Felicity Chike sipped slowly and gratefully at heavy, thick-bottomed glasses filled with good malt whiskey. The squat bottle sat on the table between them. They had become friends a few years before when Worker had discovered his nickname throughout the CID was 'The Bee', and that Chike's was 'The Flea'. At first they shared time together to commiserate and then they did so because they enjoyed each other's company. They were both smart, hard-working people who shared a wry sense of humour. They had quickly found each other's brand of wit a welcome relief from the more prosaic, beer-fuelled banter of their colleagues.

As is so often the case the rare combination of intelligence and wit had begun to prove a very effective aphrodisiac. Their relationship blossomed until they regularly enjoyed illicitly playful nights together, something they believed to be a well-kept secret. It wasn't, but for members of the police force infidelity was the all too common wage for long hours and too many lonely, stressful nights on the job. Those in the know kept mum and turned a blind eye, while The Flea and The Bee carried on with their 'secret' trysts.

'Why didn't I know about this?'

'Page, honestly I thought you did. I thought everybody did. She was the one who found that Imani boy, remember? The thakathi case? Come on, you must remember. His own mother thought the boy was possessed. She and her sister were going to cut him into six pieces and burn him in a ritual fire to save his soul. Remember? Something about releasing the python in his belly. Poor kid's dad reported him missing. The boy was only four and his dad was going frantic, and I mean he was in a real state, but the mother just kept on saying the lad would be fine. Well, Bishop was here downstairs when the dad

29

came in – she'd been brought in for something or other. Oh yes, that's right. Someone made a complaint about something she'd said on stage that, you know, had pissed them off. And then, when uniforms looked into it, it turned out she was right after all. Anyway, she looked straight at that poor man and she said, "Your son is under his auntie's bed." Just like that. And he was, poor little tyke, trussed up like a chicken for the roasting. Luckily, he was still alive.'

'That was her?'

'That was Bishop.'

'Why isn't she on speed dial?'

'Check "special consultant, freelance" next time you're on your laptop. You'll find Ms Bishop. M. comes up quite a few times. She's my sangoma of choice. What? You think I got where I am because I'm Sherlock Holmes in a frock or some sort of lucky copper? Thanks to her I could cut the stepping stones that made my career.'

'Oh, right. I always thought you were a very good, if a bit gobby, plonk with a cute arse. Luck always follows a cute arse. Likes to lend it a bit of a helping hand.'

'I'll take that sort of chat from you, and only from you, mister Worker Bee with the deadly sting. Cheers.'

They touched glasses and sipped, smiling at each other.

Chike was a strikingly attractive woman; chocolate brown, Zulu slim and six feet tall even before she climbed into her trademark high heels. Worker was a little older, but even in his mid-forties he still drew a lot of attention when he walked into a room.

'Imagine someone mated Sean Connery with George Clooney and they had a son. That's The Bee,' swooned one besotted DC to her friend.

Her friend agreed. 'He could pollinate me any time.'

'Don't go there. Don't even think about it, I'm warning you. The Flea would rip you a brand-new backside.'

'No harm in thinking.'

'Yeah? Well, don't think about it when The Flea's around. She can hear what you're thinking through solid walls and eats cocky DCs like you for breakfast.'

The unknowing subjects of such badinage put their glasses down. There was business to be discussed.

'What's the skinny on the suspect?'

'Suspect? Think again. Perp! Budail Al Rashid, born in Croydon. He's twenty-two, will be twenty-three in September, and is currently in a shitload of grief. His mum says she knew nothing about it and we believe her. She's in a terrible state, poor woman. Heartbroken. The father's been dead just over two years, pancreatic cancer. Fit as a fiddle until he was diagnosed and gone less than a month later. Hell of a shock. Son fell in with the wrong crowd and now his room looks like ground zero for an al Qaeda campaign headquarters. You wouldn't believe the shit we found under his bed and on his hard drive. He must have recorded every beheading IS ever broadcast. You know something? He even filmed himself masturbating while he watched the killings.'

'Nothing surprises me anymore.'

'I could think of a few things.'

'Lock the door first.'

'Later. Ms Bishop has put our feet on a very interesting path. Seems Al Rashid and his friends were planning a Paris-style attack in Oxford Street during the run-up to Christmas. They've got guns stashed away, ammo up to *here*, and even a legitimate black cab they were going to ram down the access stairs at Oxford Circus Tube and explode. It would have caused carnage. They were going to give John Lewis their special attention and one of them was planning to give Ann Summers a right pasting.'

'Ann Summers?'

'An obscene affront to decency and Islam.'

'John Lewis?'

'They support Israel.'

'Do they?'

Chike shrugged and rolled her eyes. 'Do they need to? These guys are crazy mad. Listen to this.' She keyed her tablet. 'Here we are, "The John Lewis Partnership is one of the only large retailers to sell Ahava Dead Sea beauty products. Ahava is a settlement company based on the illegal settlement of Mitzpe Shalem. Waitrose also sells dates from settler company Hadiklaim." That was found on some rant on Al Rashid's hard drive. Just another mad excuse. I think his mum buys his underpants at M&S so at least they were off the list.'

'SO15 on it?'

'Like a rash.'

The Bee poured more whiskey and The Flea studied her refreshed glass.

She said, 'We working late tonight? We could walk to the Holiday Inn from here. No need to drive. I've got my overnight bag in my office.'

'Tempting, really tempting, but no. Little Mike has his dental appointment in the morning and I promised Clare I'd take him so she could go for coffee or something with an old school friend.'

'Shame. Martin's away on another course.'

'Another one? You sure *he's* not playing an away game?'

'Who? Martin?'

They both visualised her amiable, orthodontist husband for a moment and grinned at the thought.

Chike's phone vibrated. She looked at the screen and swiped *Accept*.

'Medina, Hello. What can I do for you? Yes. Yes. What, now? Where? Sure. I'll bring DCI Page Worker with me. Have you eaten? No? Then dinner's on us. I insist. Yeah, cool. Okay, see you in about ten minutes.'

She turned off the phone. 'Talk of the devil. You'd better let Clare know you're working late. I'll grab my overnight bag and meet you downstairs.'

'Ms Bishop?'

'Yeah, she says it's important and she needs our help. Real urgent. She sounds worried. We're meeting her at the Thatched House Hotel.'

Page took out his own phone and keyed the menu. The Flea looked at him quizzically. 'Ringing the missus?'

'I'll do that later.' His phone connected. 'Hello, yes, Thatched House Hotel? Great, I wonder, would you have a decent sized double room free for tonight? In ten minutes. Yes, please, table for three in about half an hour. Worker, W.O.R.K... That's right, yes, like Charlie Drake. My word, you're showing your age. Repeats on BBC2? Ah. Yes. Okay. See you soon.'

He grinned at The Flea. 'We got the bridal suite. See you downstairs.'

# [8]

The area immediately around the ship had become a hive of activity. Above ground all appeared serene and the cave was practically invisible, but there were subtle signs that something odd was under way. The ship mind instinctively knew its recovery had to be kept secret, but there were some important projects that had to be completed first and fast. Oddly symmetrical holes had appeared in the rock above the ship. They opened directly over its highly efficient solar energy collection points, and after two clear, sunny days it had already recouped a sizeable percentage of its lost power.

Some of its crew would remain redundant until take off. They slid into their work stations and powered down. Most of the recovery and repair work would be carried out by basic tool units and would take some time to complete. Weeks of hard labour lay before the century of workers, but after millions of years of enforced stasis the ship could afford to be patient for just a little while longer.

Its plan was to clear away the rock around its hull and shave the ceiling of the cave until it was thin enough for final breakthrough. Larger mining tech units ground away at the stone like giant, starving mouths. They chewed and splintered the rock and then spewed it out as a fine powder. Closer to the hull smaller, more delicate creatures smoothed away the clinging, marble-like blanket of stone with exquisite precision. The resultant mounds of white, powdery waste were hurled away after dark in a fine spray of crystalline dust that became lost in the forests surrounding the escarpment.

The ship's mission had been to explore new worlds and assess them for mineral wealth and mining potential. It had departed its home planet with everything it needed to perform such a task, and after more than four hundred and forty million years encased in sedimentary stone it was basking in its slow return to former glory. It felt alive and vital, revelling in its place as the focus of so much slavish activity.

No one examining the creatures the ship thought of as its 'tools' would have recognised the bizarrely altered bodies of the missing spa people. The ship's parasite matrix had become deeply rooted in the DNA of nearly all of Earth's fauna, including humanity. Even long aeons after the devastating Ordovician-Silurian extinction, the parasite trigger in the survivors' highly evolved offspring had worked with precise efficiency. The cell-deep slave matrix responded to the touch of the core pods exactly as it was designed to do. Skeletons, internal organs, the very muscles and flesh of the victims' bodies, stretched and altered to fit an ancient and very alien template.

All the pods needed was access to hosts, water and sunlight to convert slave bodies to their new purpose. The agony of conversion had driven the hosts' shocked and screaming spirits into the afterlife, where they had joined with Philippe's terrified shade. Confusion, pain and horror had stripped them of their wits and by the time they arrived in the Realm of Light they were quite insane. Their dreadful, biting howl began and didn't cease.

Altered beyond recognition, the ship's full muster of tools and crew members had scrabbled, pounded, loped and galloped the miles back to their trapped mistress. They poured into the cave like misshapen demons returning to their underworld home. And they were welcomed with but two terse commands.

'Deep space personnel, you will all power down to conserve energy until I need you. The rest of you, you have work to do. Get on with it.'

Two days later the forward part of the ship had already been cleared of its rocky mantle, but its main hull was still deeply embedded in stone. The great double bank of windows now fully demonstrated their beautiful symmetry, arching out and down towards the freshly smoothed cave floor.

A mass of workers surrounded the elegant structure and crawled around upside down on the cave's ceiling like ravening termites. The ship's hull described a wide, oblate disc stretching back almost one hundred and fifty feet into the fossilised seabed. It was about twenty feet tall.

Its apparent delicacy of design belied the fact that it had not only survived the impact of its crash but had also shrugged off the stresses that forced its surrounding strata to rise from its original home under the seabed to almost two thousand feet above sea level. It had shared its prison with just a few simple fossils, the remains of which were being scoured away by relentless tool units.

The ship was pragmatic rather than cruel. It didn't pursue a deliberate policy of working its tools to death, but it also knew it couldn't afford the luxury of allowing them to take it easy. Workers were expendable and replaceable; they always had been.

The canopies of the tall forests of its home planet clamoured with the whoops and chitterings of the long-armed kvult, a powerful, hairless ape-like creature easily caught in specially designed elastic nets. Once captured they would fight furiously for their freedom, but the nets would tighten around them until they were helplessly pinioned. The core pods could be administered safely and then the beasts were cut loose and led meekly to a conversion pool. The kvult climbed into the pool and a tool unit or crew member climbed out.

To the ship a human was simply a weaker form of kvult. They were an unsatisfactory material to work with – but better than nothing.

Due to the human body's inherent weakness, not all the conversions had been entirely successful, and some few had buckled and burst under the strain of the recovery work. They fell like broken, bloodied toys to the ground. Their core pods were stored until it was dark and a special team of two crew personnel plus a climber and a pair of hunters were sent out into the night to find replacements. These crew were dark and spindly with long, ovoid and featureless heads connected to slender necks by a pair of golden rings. The climber was squat with a long and powerfully prehensile barbed tail, while the hunters were low, fast and spiderlike with sixteen multi-jointed legs. They had senses more sophisticated than their human prey and for them the pitch-dark wild terrain was an easy traverse. The hosts had to be harvested from the local area by necessity. The collection team couldn't operate further away than the distance they could run during the nighttime, and still return with their victims for an early morning dip. There would come a time when the circle of slow but steady attrition might focus official attention on that area. One day soon, perhaps, but not quite yet.

On the first night, they found a healthy young couple asleep in their tent and took them without a struggle. Water was provided by the nearby Lake Manitoba and in the morning light, a pair of fresh workers were soon loping eagerly towards the cave entrance.

The next night the team found three hunters sitting around a carefully constructed camp fire. The men had dined on a haunch of roast moose and were enjoying a bottle of good Canadian whiskey while swapping lies in the comfortable firelight. Two of them had been taken by surprise and succumbed to the sting of the core pods before they even knew what was happening, but the third was a man of a completely different calibre. He was a seasoned special ops veteran, retired, who had survived the worst both Iraq and Afghanistan could throw at him. He had a trained warrior's sixth sense, and when he saw his friends taken by what seemed to be the night made flesh he became instantly alert, rolled out of the circle of light and sprinted for his rifle.

Snatching it up he had thrown himself flat and then clicked off its safety. He took a bead on the area around the fire, squinting into the gloom to find his targets. He had to be careful; his buddies were out there somewhere so he couldn't just blast away in the hope of hitting something. He waited. There was a pattering sound followed by a faint slithering noise, a distant spill of pebbles, and then silence. There was no sign of anything, neither his companions nor the nightmare things that had taken them. He found himself lying alone in the pitch dark of a moonless night, a night made darker by the bright glow of the fire. He waited for several taut and sweaty minutes until he was certain the coast was clear, then quickly collected together everything he could carry, threw the bundle in a pile onto the back seat of his Ford pick-up and hightailed it down the brutally rutted track and back towards the road. He knew he was probably some way over the legal drink-drive limit, but he would rather face a breathalyser test than stay in that campsite and come face-to-face with whatever had swooped out of the night and stolen away his friends.

## 9

For the RCMP in the Dauphin branch of D Division, a recent spate of missing persons in the Duck Mountain Provincial Park area was further exacerbated by a report of an apparent 'alien abduction'. A hunter had roared his pick-up into the car park in Hedderly Street in the early hours and burst into the reception area of the neat, modern, red brick building like a madman. He was patently terrified and almost incoherent while he blurted out his tale about dark creatures in the night.

'They were black and scrawny, but they took my friends like they were puppy dogs. Just picked 'em up and they were gone, slick as shit. I fetched my rifle and would have shot the bastards for sure, but I was worried I might hit my friends. It was too dark to see anything properly and the firelight made the woods look darker, you know? And those things, those things... They had no faces. I'm telling you ma'am, no faces at all!'

Sergeant Maelie Rawkins had dealt with drunks before and she was very aware of the smell of whiskey on the man's breath, but he was convincing for all that. She called a constable to take over at the desk and led the man to a comfortable interview room where she bade him to take a seat. She fetched him a coffee with milk and two sugars and waited until he'd calmed down enough to catch his breath. He sat scrunching his hat between his two big hands as if it was a stress toy. He stared at his hat as if he might find answers there.

Rawkins made no notes while they talked. Everything would be automatically recorded and filmed as soon as she shut the door behind her.

She identified herself to the room and gave the date and time, then asked her witness to state his name and recount the story he had begun at the counter in the lobby.

The hunter told her his name was 'Marshall, Marshall Fellows' and explained he had been out moose-hunting with his 'good buddies, Phil Crane and Tully Carson'. He added that Phil and Tully were both married men. Phil and his wife were childless, but Tully had a beautiful teenage daughter, who gave him sleepless nights on too many occasions. Rawkins knew what that felt like.

'We go out there in the wild to shoot the breeze more than we do any animals,' Marshall explained, 'but we'd brought down a moose and I field-butchered it. I learned that during basic training with Special Ops, you know?'

He lifted his eyes from his strangled hat and rested them on hers. She was very aware that he wanted to establish his credentials as a witness. In mentioning the Special Ops, Fellows was telling her he wasn't some green-belly who panicked over nothing. She nodded at him to continue.

'We left the skin, the head and the guts for whatever might take a shine to them. The rest is still out there in a chill box in the bed of my pick-up. Everything's there bar the haunch we ate last night.'

Once his coffee was cool enough he slurped at it like he'd just crossed a desert and was dying of thirst. His eyes were red and hot in an otherwise ruggedly pleasant, tanned face. He reminded Rawkins of her colleagues: a breed of capable men who saw what was in front of their faces, not fanciful dreamers. Fellows had seen something that shocked him to the core the previous night. She wondered what it could have been.

He continued, and as he spoke his eyes wandered back down to his hat as if he was wondering what it was. He began wringing at it again and she saw his lips twisting and working hard to spit out the words as if they had become foul in his mouth.

'We'd eaten well and Tully dug out a bottle of Crown Royal so we could toast Mikey...'

'Sorry, who?'

'Mikey? Yeah, that's what we called the moose. Mikey the moose. Stupid, I know but, you know? Guys together get stupid.'

'Amen to that.'

'Yeah. Amen to that. Tully offered us glasses and hung on to the bottle, taking sips while he was talking and topping us up when we ran dry. Ma'am, we were drinking, not drunking – I can promise you that. I know my limits. Phil and Tully enjoy a drink in company but they're both professional men, you know? They know not to get pie-eyed out in the woods, and so do I.'

He blinked rapidly. 'Tully was telling us what Cassy – she's his daughter – had been up to and we were laughing. Tully told a great story. He's a natural. They were still laughing when those thin black arms grabbed them and pulled them back out of the firelight and into the night. I got the impression of heads, long and narrow. Heads without faces. No eyes, no nose, no nothing. They were black too. Not like you, ma'am, no offense intended, not human black, you know? Not even that African black like ebony, I've seen that. No, these things were so black they were blue. Like a gun barrel, you know?'

38

'Could they have been wearing crash helmets, do you think?'

'No way, ma'am. Too narrow. Not crash helmets.'

He lifted his coffee cup and was surprised to find it empty. He looked as if he was going to burst into tears. The blinking of his eyes became more rapid.

'Mr Fellows, would you like a break while I get you some more coffee?'

'Please, that would be nice of you. Could I have some water too, please?'

Rawkins declared the session suspended, noted the time, then went into the kitchen where she made a proper mug of coffee and fetched a tumbler of ice water from the cooler. Fellows gave her a grateful smile and downed the water in one. One of his eyes winced shut at the sudden, ice-cream headache in his sinuses.

He shook his head. 'Damn, drank it too fast.'

Rawkins noted the time and date. 'Mr Fellows, you were telling me those things were blue-black, like a gun barrel?'

'Marshall, please. Yeah, they were, just like that. Blued steel. Well, I've been in situations where you need to move fast or... let's just say I've seen stuff that'd turn you white. No offense, ma'am.'

'None taken.'

'I rolled out of the firelight and ran for my rifle, got down on my belly and chambered a round. I stayed still as a log and I swear I heard them moving away. Phil and Tully said nothing; they stayed quiet as the grave. Not a peep out of them, not a murmur. One minute they were laughing and the next they were gone. Just like somebody popped their balloons. They were gone. They were just gone.'

'Mr Fellows, Marshall, do you think you could find your campsite again in daylight?' She had to stay with him, to keep his memory out of the nightmare.

'I could, yes, for sure.'

'Then would you be willing to go back there with a team and show them where this happened?'

'In daylight?'

'As I said.'

He drained his coffee.

'Let's go.'

It took a while for Rawkins to assemble her people and wait for sun-up, which gave Fellows enough time to grab a few hours' sleep, freshen up, change his shirt, and sort out his vehicle. The moose meat was still chilled in its box. He was shocked at how little time had passed since he had first caught the moose in the reticules of his reliable Redfield scope. He looked at

39

his watch. Just before seven in the morning. He dozed some more on his truck's back seat. It was almost ten-thirty before he was woken by a voice at his window.

'Good morning, sir. Sergeant Rawkins sent me to fetch you. Sorry about the wait.'

Fellows sat up and found himself confronted by a powerful looking young man wearing a stab-proof vest with *Police* emblazoned on it.

'You might want to bring your rifle along, sir, just in case.'

The hunter grunted and walked around his pick-up. He pulled his gleaming rifle from its place on the passenger seat.

'Nice gun. She looks well cared for.'

'My BAR. Yeah, she's a nice gun. I bought her second-hand about ten years ago, and I've hunted moose, deer, hogs, coyotes, and the occasional bobcat every season since. After zeroing the BOSS to 150 grain Remington Core-Lokts I can get one-and-a-half-inch groups all day long.'

They chatted about firearms while they walked, which Fellows found to be relaxing, almost comforting after the madness of the previous night. The constable, named Monkton but known to all as 'Monk', drew out his police issue 5946 Smith & Wesson.

'Be nice to get a Glock, but I guess Dauphin is hardly downtown Toronto. These S&Ws are standard issue but loaded with hollow point, nine-millimetres they'll stop most things if you aim right.'

'And do you aim right?'

'Yeah, I do. Here we are.'

Rawkins was standing with three men by a recent model, unmarked, silver-grey Mercedes Sprinter Traveliner TL9. Two of the men wore police outfits but the third cut a very individual figure indeed. The sergeant introduced her officers and then the tall slender man who had a lean, red-tanned face and long, sleek black hair parted in the middle. He was wearing a long jacket, hand-sewn from patches of different coloured leather, over a good quality check shirt and denim jeans cinched at his waist by a beaded belt. His Spanish-style boots had seen a lot of wear but were maintained in good condition. The man had real presence. He smiled with big white teeth while Fellows gave him the thorough once over, then returned the compliment before thrusting out a big, calloused hand.

Fellows shook and said, 'Pleased to meet you, mister. Sorry, I missed the name. I'm Fellows, Marshall Fellows.'

'Tatawaw, Marshall Fellows, good to meet you too. My name is Askuwheteau, but please, if that's too much of a mouthful call me Watcher.'

40

Rawkins spoke up, 'We're lucky Askuwheteau was here giving a lecture and he asked if he could join us. He's curious about your story, Mr Fellows, and wants to study the campsite. He may be able to help us.'

'Yes. Sounds like you had a bad night. You must have been terrified.'

Fellows found a smile from somewhere. 'You'd be right about that.'

Watcher nodded. 'Takes a brave man to admit he was scared. Shall we go see what we can find?'

## 10

Worker and Chike arrived at the hotel a little later than planned, but they still had time to meet Medina in the bar before dinner. They were surprised to be joined by a thick-set, middle-aged man who introduced himself as Edward Louis. Medina explained that Louis had been helping with her research about Manitoba in general – and the eastern side of the Duck Mountain Provincial Park in particular.

The Flea invited Louis to join them for dinner and the group were shown to a table for four in an almost empty dining room. They talked easily while choosing their meals and selecting a brace of wines to suit.

Chike said, 'Always a pleasure, you know that Medina, but you evidently have something up your sleeve and we're just busting to find out what it is. What have you got to tell us?'

The wine arrived before the food, alongside a litre of cold tap water and a basket containing a selection of warm artisanal breads. Louis performed the honours and they all raised their glasses before taking a healthy sip. Medina took a second mouthful and then began to talk.

'I woke poor Edward up last night because I was screaming the place down. He heard me from down the corridor. Sorry about that, Edward.' He nodded sympathetically. She continued: 'I told him it was because friends of mine were in trouble and I was dreaming about them. And that was the truth.' She toyed with her glass before draining half its contents. 'What I didn't tell him was that these friends of mine are dead, and that some of them have been for quite some time. Sorry, Edward, but you seemed a nice guy and I didn't want you to think I was totally nuts on our first meeting. Even at three in the morning.'

She explained about the disturbance in the Realm of Light that coincided with the disappearance of nearly two hundred people from a spa complex in north west Manitoba.

'It was on the news this morning, and the connection clicked in my head like a light coming on. You know, a real light bulb moment.' She made a gesture above her head and mouthed *Bing!*

She looked hard from Chike to Worker. 'I've been asked to go to Manitoba and find out what happened there. The souls in the Realm are okay now, but the tormented spirits have been put behind a barrier because of the terrible noise they're making. I heard it for just a few seconds last night.' She shuddered. 'Terrible – you never want to hear something like that. The poor devils are going through Hell, quite literally, and the mentors can't help them. They can't get close enough to talk with them. The noise...'

She emptied her glass. Louis refilled it. No one else at the table said a word and Worker was aware that the few couples at nearby tables had ceased any pretence at private conversation. They were now hanging on the medium's every sentence. Her low, cultured voice had been trained in stage craft and she knew how to hold her audience, that much was obvious, but the tale she had to tell was riveting enough without need of artifice. The delicate, dark-haired woman wove magic around her and her huge amber eyes invited her spell-bound audience to believe in a place where ancient spirits resided in a Realm of Light – and that they might call upon an Earthly adept for help.

At that moment, their food arrived and Medina's entranced listeners nearly jumped out of their skins. They had to bring themselves back down to Earth long enough to work out who had ordered the fish and who the chicken, who the steak and who the fish pie. They tucked in. Louis opined around a tender mouthful that the food was edible without being inspiring. Worker agreed – he knew exactly what Louis meant.

Chike murmured, 'Competent without being excellent.'

Medina liked the food at the hotel. She was enjoying her fish pie and mixed vegetables. She wondered what kind of lives people lived to be so picky about something as simple as their dinner. *Enjoy what the day brings,* she thought. *We're a long time dead.* She knew that for a fact.

Chike asked what they could do to help the situation in the Realm. The medium became quite animated.

'As I said, I have to go over to Manitoba and find out what really happened to those poor souls. Edward has offered to go with me. He's researching the story for the Sunday glossies and will be on expenses, lucky thing...'

Louis protested that he would happily pay for her too, as a specialist consultant, but she waved him to silence.

'Yes, alright. Thanks, Edward. Either way I must go. But it would be best if I had some help once I got there, you know? Competent locals who know their way around and can point me in the right direction. Edward tells me the area falls under the remit of D Division of the Royal Canadian Mounted Police, specifically the squad based in a place called Dauphin, a couple of hours or so south of the park where the people disappeared. They might be able to help me and, hopefully, I'll be able to help them in return. But I'll need an official introduction because, let's be honest, who's going to take a

43

blind bit of notice of an Englishwoman who claims to be in touch with the spirit Realm? They'll think I'm a nutter and send me on my way with a pat on the head and a flea in my ear – sorry Felicity, you know what I mean – and who could blame them? And it needs to be a genuinely credible introduction, something they'll take seriously. And that's where I hoped you guys might be able to help. Do you know anyone over there you can talk to and introduce me as a viable, if a little unusual, witness?'

She poured more tomato ketchup onto her fish pie and forked some into her mouth while Chike and Worker looked askance at each other. They pictured the conversation that might follow such a call to a remote part of Canada.

Louis spoke up. 'If I may, I'd like to share a little background information with you. Dauphin is a city with a population less than half that of a town like Sutton. They claim to be very proud of their British heritage, but they also include French, Ukrainian and native American, or what they call "First Nation" people, as important and integral elements in their cultural diversity. Dauphin even has what they call a "prairie cathedral". Used to be a catholic church built by Ukrainians in 1939 and got itself declared a national monument in the 1990s. They justifiably take themselves very seriously, so we've got to be careful they don't think we're over there taking the piss. A call from a London DCI from the CID should be just the ticket. Smooth the path so to speak. Of course, we don't have to mention the spirit world just yet...' He glanced at Medina, who arched her brows. 'But we can say we have a specialist in the field of, oh, I don't know, say abductions and unusual phenomena. Someone who has worked closely with the Met and was happy to offer her help. I'll be along as the tousled boy reporter, a guise I wear very well as I'm sure you'll agree. I'll tell them I'm reporting on Miss Bishop for the national press. I can be quite impressive when I choose to be.'

He fetched out two of his business cards and handed them to the police officers. They looked blankly at them and then back at him.

He said, 'Sorry, look at the backs.'

They turned the cards over and saw the list of top newspapers.

'I've worked with every one of those and still contribute to a good number of them. I'm a journalist and a columnist as well as a photographer. I have every intention of producing some worthwhile copy during my visit to Manitoba, and might just write up a profile of the historic prairie city. It's got a lot to say for itself and somebody's sure to pay for it. Fair makes my mouth water just to think of it. What do you say?'

Chike said, 'We have to help. We owe Medina at least this much.'

Worker grinned ruefully. He had decided he might as well surrender. He was surrounded and outgunned. 'What time is it over there?'

Louis smiled. 'Six hours behind us. Makes it just after one-thirty pm.' He held out his note pad. 'And these are the numbers for the RCMP in Dauphin. The inspector in charge is called Cheryl Longknife. I bet that's a family tree with an interesting story to tell.'

DCI Page Worker sighed and opened his iPhone.

# [11]

'Real smooth ride.'

These were the first words Watcher had uttered since climbing into the eight-seater Mercedes. Fellows was sitting next to the driver to issue directions. Rawkins and her constables were chatting together at the back of the vehicle with an easy camaraderie. Watcher sat behind the driver and for the first hour had been gazing out the window to his left. Fellows turned and found the man's dark stare was now directed at him.

'Sorry?'

'I said real smooth ride. First time I've been in such a fancy rig. Professor's pay couldn't afford one of these.'

'You a professor?'

'Among other things. Professor of Anthropology at the University of Manitoba. Wrote my thesis about the Cree, the First Nations and the Algonquin language. It was very well received.'

'That must have taken years of study.'

'Not really. I just took my grandmother out for dinner and paid for the wine. Nohkômak, yeah, a great talker and she loved her nôsisimak as much as she loved a good meal with wine. She was always patient and strong. A good woman.'

'You must miss her.'

'Why? I see her every Thursday afternoon and evening. Still doing that research. She can't ride a horse anymore, and she would scare the whole county shitless if she ever got behind the wheel of a car. Her eyesight isn't so good these days, but she remembers the old times, and nihtâ-âcimow, she tells great stories. So, what do you do?'

The question was fired openly and bluntly.

'Me? I study rocks and make up stories about the minerals and oil contained in them. Got my Masters in Civil and Geological engineering from the University of Saskatchewan before spending a few years with the Canadian Special Operations Regiment, you know? Saw some time abroad. But now I just study rocks. Quieter. Safer. Or so I thought.'

'Married?'

'No.'

'Shame. Why not? Good looking guy. You gay?'

'No, I'm not. Why?'

'Also a shame. Really. You'd be very popular among the fraternity.'

Fellows was wrong-footed. 'What kind of fool statement's that? You gay or something?'

'Not yet. You interested?'

Fellows frowned at the man's lean, deadpan features. Something about him reminded the geologist of the Spock character from *Star Trek*; at the time when the Vulcan was undergoing the kolinahr in the first movie. He realised the man was pulling his leg.

He grinned. 'Who knows? Might be.'

The professor smiled back. 'Let's take a rain check. I get enough grief from being a Cree in a white man's world without being a gay man as well. And anyway, I'd have to ask Wikimak.'

'Who's she, your other grandmother?'

'No, no, she's my wife. Great cook. You should taste what she does with fresh walleye.'

'I'd like that.'

'Then maybe we should go fishing after all this.'

'I'd like that too.'

'You any good with a rod?'

'Don't know, never tried.'

Watcher slumped in his seat. 'We're gonna starve.'

'I've got some moose in my pick-up.'

'What's it like in a garlic saltine crust?'

The driver piped up with an edge of laughter in his voice. 'Sorry to butt in folks, but I need directions from here. Where do I go at the T junction?'

Fellows resumed his role as guide while Watcher returned to studying the passing terrain.

Behind them, Rawkins answered a call on her mobile. She spoke for several minutes, then came forward to stick her head between the Cree and the hunter.

'Just had a call from the chief. She tells me we've got a little help coming over from London. Some specialist from the CID's on their way, someone called Bishop. Sounds like a regular muck-a-muck. Chief says he's bringing along his pet journalist and researcher! I mean, give me a break. Why do I hate him already? They'll be with us the morning after tomorrow, don't know what time. They'll catch the midnight Perimeter special from Winnipeg and if they've got any sense they'll hit the sack as soon as they reach their hotel. How you holding up, Marshall?'

'Glad to be busy. Gut feels funny now we're getting closer. I can feel the place coming near the way I used to with some places in Afghanistan.'

Watcher said, 'I'm keeping an eye on him, Maelie. He's tough, he'll do, and he's no shit for brains red-neck. Good company.'

Rawkins nodded. 'High praise indeed. How long 'til we're there?'

Fellows answered, 'Forty minutes or so. We should be there around two-thirty and that gives us about five hours of daylight. I don't want to be out here in the dark.'

Maelie Rawkins gazed at the big sky and the line of the Duck Mountain Range to the west beyond the treeline. 'Sun goes down a little sooner around here in mountain country, but we'll be done long before then. We've got coffee in back, it's from a Thermos but not too bad. You want some?'

'Please.' Watcher nodded and the driver put his thumb up.

Fellows continued, 'We'll be coming off the road and onto a trail in about twenty-five, maybe thirty minutes. Going could get a little rough. You won't want to be sitting with hot coffee in your hands when that happens.'

'Good tip, thanks.'

He was right. Nearly half-an-hour later he directed the driver onto a rutted dirt track and the passengers were jolted around in their seats while the Mercedes' suspension laboured to deal with conditions way beyond the manufacturer's specifications.

With the breath pounded out of his lungs for the fourth time in as many minutes, Watcher groaned. He turned to the driver.

'Man, who taught you to drive? My grandmother?'

'Don't make me laugh. I'll bite my tongue. Ow, told you.'

Fifteen minutes later, Fellows barked: 'Slow down, slow down. Let me see, yes, yes, through there. See, the gear and camp fire? We're here.'

'Good,' said Watcher. 'When we're done can we go back and fetch my ass from where it got busted off?'

'That was brutal,' said Monk. 'Hey, sergeant, if we have to come back this way can we insist on a bigger wagon?'

Rawkins grinned ruefully and held up a palm tablet. 'Got this site on geo-location. We can fly here next time and save all our poor bones from the grindstone.'

Watcher held his hand up. 'Do you mind if I take a good look around before you Mounties go stomping all over any traces that may still be out here? That goes for you too, Marshall. Give me a few minutes out there on my own. That okay?'

Rawkins folded her arms. 'You're the boss, Askuwheteau. Okay guys, smoke 'em if you've got 'em but keep the stubs. The professor's taking a recce over the crime scene.'

The man of the First Nations was glad Sergeant Rawkins was in charge. She was everything he liked about a good police officer – someone with brains, respect and a sense of humour. She laughed like dirty water running down a drain, but she also knew when to take things seriously. He thought she should be offered as a role model for all young officers during training. Askuwheteau then took a deep breath and focused his mind before he climbed out of the vehicle and stepped into the crime scene. He moved like Kajika, the warrior who walks without sound. He was careful not to let his own footprints mess with any evidence.

He paused and raised his voice. 'Marshall, where were you sitting when it happened and where were your friends?'

'I was on that log over to your left; Tully was right in front of you and slightly to your right and Phil was at your two o'clock.'

'Thank you.'

He breathed gently and allowed his senses to open.

'Hey, Watcher, can you see anything? I want to stretch my legs, man.'

'Shut up, Pennink. Let the man work.'

*Thanks, Maelie.* He concentrated again. He was aware of the people behind him as if they were a cloud of white noise. Each of them was distinct and had unique features, but only Rawkins and Fellows had any density. He could also sense what the younger officers were thinking. They expected to be arresting Fellows before the afternoon was out. Classic scenario; the recipe for murder. Take three men out in the wild, add a few drinks, then throw in an argument that gets out of hand. The murderer tries to cover his tracks by reporting something totally wild. Wouldn't be the first time it happened. Won't be the last. But, is that what happened here? *Let the evidence be the judge.*

Askuwheteau crouched and studied the area immediately around the fire. There were the three logs the friends had been sitting on. Behind Fellows' log was a smear, deep impressions and distinct footprints, moving away. Not much heel but the toes were digging in and he was taking a long stride. In his mind's eye, he saw the man roll, scramble to his feet and sprint away from the fire. His eyes followed the steps the few yards to where Fellows had kicked up clods of dirt and there saw another smear. *Sudden stop when he reaches his rifle, then he turns and throws himself flat.*

*Okay, Marshall, just as you said it. But what happened then? Did you shoot your friends and dispose of their bodies? That's what the boys think. That or something like it.*

Askuwheteau turned his attention back to the area behind the other logs. He cleared his mind of all expectations, allowing himself to only see what was truly there. *Talk to me.*

'Can I get out, man? I'm getting cramp here.'

'Shut up, Pennink.'

Askuwheteau was in the zone. He couldn't be distracted. There was no evident disturbance as there had been behind Fellows' place. He walked closer, only placing his feet on virgin ground, barely breathing. His senses began screaming at him. What he was seeing was impossible – *impossible*! He heard the dry voice of Kestejoo, the idiot mind that shared his skull. It was muttering that he was looking at a staged scene.

*Surely even a blind idiot like you can see this is a set-up?*

He clamped down on the foolish words. He could see the scene enacted as clearly as if he'd been there. He made his mind up, circled the campfire in a wide loop, then headed west for several yards until he had reached the edge of the forest clearing. He examined the softer ground between the trees before scrutinising a jutting branch at the height of his mid-thigh. Then he straightened and stepped back to get completely clear of the trail he had been following.

When he turned back to Fellows and the group of police officers in the Mercedes he noticed that the one called Hayes, the driver, had lit up a filter tip. It was years since he had last tasted tobacco and the urge bit into him hard.

'Okay, you can get out now. But be careful where you put your size twelves. Hayes, you got one of those things for an old Professor who should know better?'

The constable fished a packet of Silk Cut out of his pocket and Watcher took another long loop around the crime scene to fetch it. Hayes lit the perfect white cylinder for him and he drew the smoke into his lungs.

He noticed how the non-smokers drew away slightly and he smiled. Side-stream cigarette smoke was going to be the least of their worries.

He blew some smoke out through his nose. 'This place is a crime scene for sure. Hard evidence proves that.' He took another drag. The younger officers moved in around Fellows, who didn't notice. He was too absorbed, listening to Watcher's words.

50

'Marshall,' he said, 'you have no idea how close you came to being a victim here. You moved just in time. One more second, maybe less, and you'd be gone like your friends. Now, who can tell me what lies between here and the mountains if you go...' – he indicated the tree line – '...that way?'

Monk drawled, 'I know the area pretty good. Head that way and I reckon you got some heavy forest, mostly pine, and then you hit the lake.'

'How long to walk there?'

'Not sure. Half-an-hour, maybe less.'

Watcher looked at the sky and then at Fellows. 'We've got time. Shall we go look?'

Fellows squinted. 'At what?'

'At where your friends went last night. At where they went under their own steam and without a struggle. At where they went when one of them gashed his leg over there on that tree, taking a thick scrape of skin, but didn't stop or yell because you would've heard it if they had. This is a real mystery, guys. Let's go see if we can find some answers.'

Monk held up a digital camera with an eighteen to two-hundred-millimetre zoom lens. 'Shall I take some crime scene shots?'

Rawkins sighed. 'Why do you think we pay you to lug that box Brownie around with you? We'll wait, but be quick.'

'I can catch you up, Sergeant.'

The black woman glanced at the Cree man. An understanding passed between them. She said, 'Just for the moment we don't want to leave anyone alone here. I don't know what happened last night, but somehow I don't think Marshall's friends were invited to a teddy bears' picnic. Do you?'

## [12]

Before the next twenty-four hours had ended, Medina's world would be turned completely upside-down. Yet it began so normally. When she went down to breakfast, Louis was waiting for her. Her scrambled eggs and smoked salmon on toast were particularly delicious. Louis chatted right the way through his full English breakfast, downing copious refills of strong, white coffee and buttering a pile of toast on the side. He talked so much, she wondered if the caffeine was affecting him.

Their WestJet flight from London Gatwick to Winnipeg was going to take just over eight hours. Louis told her he had booked two 'plus' seats at the front of the cabin for the extra leg room, and that their tickets included complimentary food and drinks. Medina opted for the window seat while her middle-aged companion was happier in an aisle.

'Better clearance to get to the loos fast in an hour of need.'

They would arrive at around six forty-nine pm local Canadian time. Take-off from Gatwick was scheduled for five-fifteen that afternoon. She had to take issue with part of her mind that kept insisting it would be less than a two-hour flight, but she was also fully aware that by the time she arrived at Winnipeg her body would think it was one o'clock in the morning.

*This had better be worth it.*

And then, when they arrived, they would have another five-hour wait before the Perimeter Aviation aircraft took them on to Dauphin's airport, named after World War One fighter ace Lt Col W. G. (Billy) Barker, VC. That was where they would pick up their U-Drive hire car and finally drive the last few miles to their hotel, The Canway Inn.

She might be in bed by two in the Canadian morning if there were no technical cock-ups, bad head winds or diversions due to drunken passengers trying to open the aircraft's doors in mid-flight.

*And that, ladles and jelly-spoons,* she told herself, *means that in real time I will finally be going to bed at eight o'clock tomorrow in the freaking morning.*

Louis had organised a cab to the airport. In the meantime, the two of them spent their last few hours in the bar enjoying a few drinks and a light lunch while gathering more information about Dauphin on Louis's laptop.

*It's a funny thing,* Medina mused. *You can research the guts out of a place as much as you want, but you'll never know what it's like until you get there.*

On Louis's advice, Medina had stashed some essentials in her bulging shoulder bag along with her tablet and a crime novel by one of her favourite authors. She had stowed panties and panty-liners along with a spare bra and a carefully folded brace of tops. She was good for at least two days if the journalist's dire warnings about luggage going missing during connecting flights proved correct.

She was already fast asleep by the time the aircraft cleared the Irish coastline and chased the afternoon sun north-west towards Newfoundland and Canada.

Her sleeping mind seemed to be floating in a warm, dark bubble. She became aware of a growing sense of wellbeing and lightness. The dark bubble gave way to brightness and her sight clarified in a peculiar way. It was almost as if her eyelids had melted away rather than opened. She found herself looking straight at the nearest cabin window. A smiling face looked back at her. Whoever or whatever it was waved. She waved back. The creature waved again and mouthed *Hello.*

She giggled and asked, 'Who are you?'

Into her mind settled a name: 'Fargo.'

'Hi,' she said. 'I'm Medina.'

'Medina Bishop, I know. I've been sent along just now to make sure you stay safe.'

She noticed the touch of an Irish accent and asked, 'Are you a leprechaun?'

It shook its head as if offended. 'Sure now, those are fanciful creatures. All pots of gold and rainbows and other such wishful thinking. Rare as lottery winners in Killarney they are. I'm an Earth sprite, and I'm just as real and solid as yourself.'

'Solid? Really? Well, I wonder. I mean, look at you out there. I for one can't fly.'

'Fly? Fly, is it?' The face looked down. 'Oh, shite!' And then it fell away and was gone. Medina suffered a sudden pang of anxiety, but before she could unbuckle her seatbelt and press her nose to the window the face was back again, its smile broader than ever.

'Caught you there,' it said in her thoughts. 'Fair enough. I'm an Earth sprite, which makes me an elemental, and I walk somewhere between just here and over there. Right now, and for the moment, I'm out here and you're in there. That's plain daft. You know the rules? Or maybe you don't? You don't? Right then. For me to come in there to you, you have to invite me.'

'Invite you? Invite you where? Oh, right, I see. Please, Fargo, please, do come in. You're very welcome.'

A slender figure appeared before her in all its antic glory. Crouched over her, it filled the narrow space between her knees and the back of the chair in front. It wore a long, sage-coloured jacket and tan trousers that reached mid-calf. Medina couldn't say what the clothes were made from. They had a plain tweed look about them. She guessed they might have been woven from herbs and grasses. The sprite smelled fresh like morning breezes and mown lawns, but there was also an earthy base note of cut turf and damp forests. Nothing unpleasant, but somehow more masculine than floral.

It wore neither shoes nor hose on its dark feet and its shirtless torso was finely muscled. She looked up into its green eyes and saw deep flecks of gold shimmer there. They seemed shockingly bright in its darkly tanned face, all under an unruly, silken mane of dark hazelnut hair. It smiled.

*My God,* she thought, *you're beautiful.*

'You're not so shabby yourself,' Fargo replied. 'If you weren't so dead set on hiding behind all that black nonsense, you'd make a very fine adornment for any gentleman's arm.'

The creature looked around the aircraft's cabin and shook its head. 'This surely isn't the best place for dancing or civilised conversation, now is it? Come on, take my hand.'

He reached out his long fingers and she took them, surprised at their strength.

'Are you a man?'

'Of course I am, after a fashion. Are you asking me to prove it? Perhaps later. Let's get to know each other a bit better first, shall we? Come on now.'

She couldn't remember unbuckling her seatbelt or rising to her feet, but she was suddenly spinning in Fargo's arms in a green place full of light and birdsong. Sweet and natural scents of the countryside were rich in her nostrils and a fresh breeze lifted her hair. She could taste salt on the moist air and felt the skin of her face relax. She hadn't realised how taut it had become. The processed and recycled atmosphere of the aircraft was gone, along with the dryness in her mouth and nose and the wit-stripping background hum of its engines' grinding their way west.

'This is wonderful.'

'You're welcome, Medina Bishop. Welcome out of that flying bucket. I couldn't stand another second in that pauper's bag of a place. Rather let

Mother Nature fill your lungs and wake your heart to glory. Do you know the Gavotte?'

'Is that where we are?'

'Never mind; let's make it up as we go along.'

He took her hands and grinned, the light of pure mischief sparkling in his eyes. And then they danced and they spun to the music of a whistle on the breeze and a duet provided by a blackbird and a robin. They danced across a carpet of mosses and cropped grasses within a glade of whispering trees. And all the while Fargo spoke to her in a language that sounded like music and she listened entranced without understanding a word.

Time ceased to weigh on her and it seemed as if her inexhaustible feet knew instinctively what to do. They danced using ancient, enchanted steps, and magic rendered them almost invisible to the outside world. An onlooker might just have seen a slight shadow weaving itself around a shaft of autumn sunlight. They danced the day away and then the night, and in the morning when the sun rose and sent the long-fingered light of dawn probing through the trees, he kissed her with a promise. Some cool and fragrant liquid passed from his mouth to hers and she swallowed it without fear.

He leaned close, said 'See you soon' – and was gone.

'Medina? Hello, Medina?'

She was back in the aircraft with its dead air and relentless droning hum.

'Well, you had a good sleep.' Louis was shaking her. 'Come on, girl, seat up. We're on final approach. You managed to sleep all the way to Canada – you lucky devil. And who can blame you! Those were eight bloody tedious hours. More re-runs of *Fawlty Towers* on the little screen, and the film was something with Meryl Streep. She was singing and dancing around on an island somewhere. Awful. I tried to sleep...' He held up a dark blue blindfold affair with a WestJet logo on it. 'Useless. This contraption didn't help, but of course they never do.'

She looked at him in a confused daze. He smiled at her, then said, 'Wherever it was you went in your dreams, it suited you very well. You look quite refreshed and, may I say, quite lovely. You must teach me the secret one of these days. I think we'll have the time. I always arrive looking like I spent the entire flight in the hold in a cardboard box. Still...' The plane bounced on the tarmac and flaps on its wings opened like steel flowers. 'Here we are.'

Medina's lips tingled. When she stood up, she discovered with happy surprise that her shoes were still wet with dew.

# [13]

It took just over half-an-hour before the small group finally caught the silver glint of water through the trees. Askuwheteau had found the tracking easy. The two men and their abductors had made no effort to hide their trail, blundering through the shrub and snapping branches in a fashion he described as 'like a drift of hogs in a panic'.

The forest was old and dense and the going had proved frustratingly slow, but Askuwheteau found a route that avoided the worst of the tangles. Hayes cursed when Pennink thoughtlessly pushed aside a whip-thin branch and let it lash back to catch the man behind him high on his cheek, missing his eye by less than an inch. Rawkins bit back a rebuke. She knew Pennink was an unpopular man. Word at Hedderly Street said he was harsh with his wife and daughter, a mousy pair of creatures who lived under the shadow of his alpha rat. Rawkins had a lot of time for her colleagues. She'd walk a long mile to find the best in them and had a naturally forgiving nature, but even she found it hard to like Pennink. She had seen how he behaved at the 'Family Invite' barbeque during the summer. The man watched everything his womenfolk did with mean, narrow-eyed possessiveness, while the shrunken woman had seemed cowed and the girl looked sullen and haunted. They didn't talk with others or to each other. They ate their food under their own little cloud of silent misery. She had wondered why they'd bothered to come at all.

Hayes was there, laughing with his pretty and flirtatious wife of Irish stock, and Monk canoodled and shared his food with his current, adoring squeeze, who never left the curve of his strong arm. And over there was her own dear husband. He was drinking beer and entertaining the usual crowd of listeners. She knew he would tell his stories so long and so loud and with such relentless humour that any donkey in the area would finally rip off its own hind legs and shove them in its ears in self-defence. She smiled at the memory. One big friendly family enjoying time off over a steak and a beer, all sharing the warmth. Except Pennink standing silently under his morose cloud. Him and his suffocated ladies.

She was brought back to her here and now when she noticed Pennink glance back at Hayes and spot the line of fresh blood on his face. She was sure she caught the man smirking. *Maybe he would be better working on his own,* she thought. And she wondered, not for the first time, if Pennink would be the sort of man who would fail his colleagues in a time of crisis.

And then they cleared the tree line and the placid lake stretched out before them. From there the Duck Mountain range looked much more like a tall cliff than it did from out on the prairie. She recognised the tallest mount, Old Baldy, straining up and away from its fellows as if one of them had farted and it was lifting its stubby nose to seek fresher air.

'Countryside is fine for those as like it,' she said out loud. 'But Mrs Planter's little girl grew up to sit on a comfortable chair, sleep in a bed under a solid roof and cook her dinner on a stove. Nobody ever got killed by a bear while they were watching TV, and there's no place safer than behind the door of your own sweet home. Baby, you can take that to the bank.'

Askuwheteau looked at her with wide eyes and his face wrinkled into a smile. She wasn't fooled by the smile. It looked to her as if his body was joining in with the joke but his mind was somewhere else, somewhere far distant.

He spoke dreamily, 'Maelie, this place is tame enough if you know how to walk through it. Treat it and whatever you find in it with respect and it will usually respect you in return – something officer Pennink might want to remember for the future.'

He turned and pointed down at a strip of soft, thick mud at the water's edge while completely ignoring the rat-like man's scowl and muttered threats.

He continued, 'They entered the water there. Look, do you see? You can see the men's prints quite clearly, theirs and whatever was with them.'

Rawkins couldn't let that pass. 'Whatever? Surely you mean whoever?'

'No, Maelie. No. I believe I'm old enough to say what I mean and mean what I say. Whoa, careful there! Try not to trample all over the evidence, guys. Hang back a bit.' He put his arm out to stop the posse from stumbling too far forward for a better look, and then held his flattened palm out to indicate what he was showing them.

'Look there and you'll see the boot prints of two men. Now look around them. What are those long, narrow marks? They all go into the water at the same point, but those are not the marks of human feet. Frankly, I don't know what they are.'

'Paralympians,' said Monk.

'I'm sorry?'

'Paralympians – those guys with no legs who run like greyhounds. You know, they run on carbon fibre blades and I bet they make marks just like that. The prints wouldn't look human, but a human could be walking on them. Great disguise.'

Rawkins and the Watcher took a long, slow look at Monk. Then Watcher gazed back down at the mud.

'At least five of them,' he said to the sergeant. 'And way too many legs.'

She nodded then turned her face up to the sky, squinting in the late-afternoon brightness. Monk and the other constables followed her eye-line, their eyes becoming slits. Eventually Hayes broke the silence.

'What are we looking for, sarge?'

She looked at him, her eyebrows raised and her expression blankly innocent. 'Monk thinks we're up against a gang of blade-wearing Paralympian kidnappers. I'm looking for a drove of flying pigs or James Bond in a helicopter, whichever gets here first. What do you think?'

Fellows and Watcher snorted into their fists. Monk blushed to the roots of his hair. 'Sarge! Hey. Come on. Don't josh with me.'

Watcher coughed. 'Imagination is a good thing, constable, a really good thing. But, you know, it's best to meter it with a little reality check. For now, let's just be happy with "don't know" until we have something a little more concrete to work with. Can we agree on that?'

'Sure, Watcher. I was just saying is all.'

Fellows nodded. 'Excuse me for butting in, guys, but the constable is right about how those marks look. I know the blades he's talking about and they would make those long spatula shapes. Yeah, just like that. But I saw something of those things last night and they weren't Paralympians. I'm telling you straight, they weren't like anything I've ever seen before.'

It was a warm afternoon, but his words brought a chill to the scene. Watcher turned to him.

'Marshall, could I borrow your Redfield scope for a moment? No need to unclip it from your rifle. But only if you don't mind?'

The geologist handed his gun to the Professor, who thanked him then brought it up to his shoulder. He sighted across the lake.

He grunted, 'They make a nice scope in Oregon; clear lenses, no sweet spot and sharp reticules. You're a man knows his tools, Marshall.'

'Thank you. I think I know what works best for me.'

The Professor walked to the tracks and spread his legs wide to straddle the footprints and strange marks. He placed his back precisely in line with the place where they had exited the trees and then aimed the rifle dead centre of the point where they entered the water. He screwed his right eye to the scope and followed a track upwards and then stopped.

'Thought so,' he muttered.

'Clever,' breathed Rawkins. 'Smart thinking, Watcher.'

Pennink whined, 'What's the smartass Indian doing that's so clever? He likes the sound of his own voice just a touch too much for me. A stunt is just a stunt when all's said and done.'

Watcher growled, 'Move over, Solomon. There's a new wise guy in town.'

Pennink made to take an angry step towards him and Hayes reached out to grip his shoulder. The man snarled like a cornered mink and lashed out at Hayes' injured cheek. Rawkins' voice cracked like a whip.

'What's eating you, Pennink? Suck it up and start acting like you belong here with us grown-ups and not back in the playground! You hear me? Grow up!'

Watcher put his eye back to the scope. While he studied the far shore, he spoke loud enough to be heard by everyone.

'He's scared, Maelie, and it's messing with his head. If he can't bully it or look down on it, he's frightened by it. Takes some men that way. Can't argue with a man's nature, he is what he is. I guess you just need to appreciate who you're dealing with.'

He stood tall and carefully extricated himself from his awkward position. He handed Fellows his rifle then walked slowly over to Pennink and looked him straight in the eye.

'I'll let you in on what I was doing, Constable Pennink. If you think about our track from the campsite where Mr Fellows' friends were abducted, you'll realise we have always been moving in a straight line. The strangers with narrow feet think like machines or Romans, Constable Pennink. They always look for the shortest distance between two points – a straight line.'

Pennink was panting with nervous hostility. He was blinking in the face of the Cree's ice-cold and level stare.

Watcher continued, 'With the help of Mr Fellows' most excellent Redfield scope, I stood in the middle of their trail and followed a straight line over the lake. I can just barely make out where they left the water over there on the far shore, but there's something there sure enough. Then I followed the line beyond the trees to the mountains, and there's an established walker's trail up there. Is it relevant? Frankly, I don't know. But I say we mark this spot and come back with a boat so we can go find out. I want to know just what the hell is going on here. What happened to those men? And why did they come here and walk straight into the lake with no signs of a struggle?' He looked around him again. 'And why did they hang around here on the shore for a while? The evidence says they did. What happened here? The evidence also points us over there towards the mountain. Why? I want to find out. Now I can do that with your help, Constable Pennink, or I can do it without you. That choice isn't mine, I'm glad to say. It's up to your sergeant. If she thinks you're worth the effort, I'll go along with her. She's a much wiser head than mine. But until she says the word, I'll thank you to treat *everyone* here with a bit more of the respect they deserve.'

Rawkins had known Watcher for several years and had never known him to be angry at anyone. Anyone, that is, except for one red-necked fool who spat on his wife and called her a filthy squaw bitch. That was when she had first met Watcher, the day she had arrested him for assault. He hospitalised the man; put him in a bed for two weeks. He was hurt so badly he was off work for more than a month.

Watcher's wife, Wikimak, explained everything that happened and pointed out that when the 'victim' was politely asked to apologise, he had turned on her husband with a tyre iron. He lashed out like a wild man before Watcher put a stop to him in self-defence.

'Maybe Watcher was a little hot-headed,' Wikimak said, 'but that idiot had it coming in spades.'

Rawkins had a word with the prosecutor and the Cree man got released with a stern warning. They had been friends ever since. She held up her geo-sat marker.

'This place is on the map, people. Let's go home. If Watcher will kindly show us the way once again, I'd be grateful. And Pennink, you take up the rear. You'll do less damage back there.' She gazed across the lake at the mountain range. 'We'll be coming back in the morning.' Then she cast a sidelong glance at the rat-like constable.

'Well, some of us will. Okay, guys, time's a-wasting, let's go.'

## 14

Medina Bishop and Edward Louis finally arrived at their hotel just after half-past one in the pitch-dark Canadian morning. He was more than a little grumpy. By the time they had picked up their hire car from a bleary-eyed young woman who failed to talk them into an upgrade and extra insurance, Louis was very tired and a little worse for the wine. He asked if she would drive the short distance to the hotel and then gaped at her in disbelief when she told him she didn't have a driving licence and had never even sat behind the wheel of a car.

'I daren't,' she explained. 'My talent can be a bit random, you see. Would it be fair to everyone else if I was bowling down a motorway and had a surprise visitation? It's a bit like epilepsy, I suppose, but without having to bite spoons. Please, Edward, I'd love to but I've never learned how.'

He was silent and concentrated hard for the few minutes it took him to drive to The Canway Inn. He didn't speak until they'd booked in and got their key cards and room numbers. Then he turned to her and smiled wearily.

'Shall we meet here at midday tomorrow? We can plan our strategy then. Give ourselves time to freshen up and see what we need to see in daylight. Sleep well, Medina. I'll see you tomorrow when I have a little more energy.' Then he whispered, 'And when I'm a little bit, you know, soberer.'

'Thanks, Edward. See you tomorrow. You've been great, really.' She reached up and kissed him on the cheek. Despite his dire predictions, Louis then trundled off to his room with his full complement of luggage.

Even at nearly four o'clock in the morning, for Medina sleep had been banished by thoughts of the beautiful earth elemental called Fargo. She had almost forgotten why she had come to Dauphin in the first place. She unpacked and took the opportunity to explore her room. She fell in love with its walk-in wardrobe, king-size bed and an enormous bathroom. She had the choice of either shower or tub, and so treated herself to a long and relaxing soak in her bath. Soothed and scented, she wrapped herself in a soft bath sheet and poured a welcome, albeit room-temperature glass of vodka and tonic.

She found herself to be filled with glorious energy. Dark and delicious warmth vibrated through her. And then there were her shoes. Some people might say her time with Fargo had been a dream. They might point out how long it had been since she'd last had a boyfriend – let alone a lover. It was all a dream.

But then there were her shoes.

After eight hours in the powder-dry environment of a modern passenger jet, her shoes had been damp with dew. And there was that fresh, wonderful taste in her mouth. Even after brushing and flossing it was still there. The taste of the wild wind, heather and snow, freshly cut hay. She had to stop herself from grinning like a fool and had found herself primping in front of her room's full-length mirror. He had called her an 'adornment'. She sighed.

'Medina Bishop, you got a crush, girl. Yeah, any fool can see you got it *real* bad.'

The speaker was Sable Hoskins, a handsome young black woman who had once been a slave in eighteenth century Jamaica. She had been given her name and her two children by the white overseer who ran the estate for an absentee Englishman. She wasn't surprised that as soon as they could walk tall and handle a machete the man had put his own flesh and blood out there in the hot fields. They had bled that self-same blood from their pretty, coffee-coloured fingers while cutting cane to make sugar for rich men's tables.

'He's an elemental, girl. He ju-ju you with nature voodoo.' Sable chuckled, a deep sound, richer than her short, hard life should have afforded. 'You kissed him! Is that why you turned into a frog? Is that why you spent so long in the bathtub? Ha ha ha. Move over, move over there! You other frogs make room on that lily pad. We got us a kiss-happy new frog in the pond now and she's dizzy from it as a kitten rolled down a hill in a fresh whiskey barrel.'

'Oh, shut up, Sable.'

The black woman's mockery was meant affectionately. She had been the first spirit to reach out to the newly orphaned Medina, calming her with a gentle word in those early, tearful nights. The tiny, dark girl had since grown into a small, dark woman who hid her prettiness and slender curves behind an almost Goth façade. 'Hiding herself in all that black.'

Medina had once convinced herself that she must have loved her parents too much – so much that they died. They had been taken away from her because of her heart's greed. Her punishment had been to survive and learn how to talk with other people's loved ones but to never hear from her own.

*Was that fair? Mum,* she thought, *Dad, can you hear me?*

'They can't, honey. If they could they'd never leave your side, you know that. They're good people but they've gone on. You'll meet them again someday, but until then you'll just have to listen to wicked old mama Sable.'

62

'You're not wicked, Sable. You never have been.'

'Then I probably shouldn't have killed that bastard Hoskins and got hanged for it, should I? But then he shouldn't have whipped his own kin over nothing. He was a real beast of a man. I bet by now he's a tree root in the marshland. He'll have to work his way up to being a sweet little frog like you.'

'Okay, Sable, I'm a frog. But it was worth it to be kissed by Fargo.'

A new voice cut in, 'Glad to hear it.' And he was there on her balcony.

Sable whispered, 'Talk of the devil,' and then fell silent.

Fargo stepped up to the balcony doors, hesitated at the carpet rail, and looked her over.

'You look better out of the black.'

Her fluffy white bath sheet reached from her armpits to her knees, but under his appreciative gaze she felt totally naked.

'May I come in? Or would it seem improper for such a charming lady to entertain a member,' he paused for effect, 'of the, ah... opposite sex in her rooms at such a late hour?'

'Get in here, you. I was wondering if I'd dreamt you.'

He sauntered in, sat beside her on the bed, and reached out his arm.

'Go on, pinch me.'

She gingerly reached out and squeezed the skin of his forearm.

'That's pathetic. Put some cat into it. Go on, *pinch* me!'

She did, with a vicious little twist.

'Ouch!' He leapt away. 'I definitely felt that in my teeth. You're awake sure enough, I can vouch for that. Cross my heart.' He made the gesture.

'And hope to die,' she finished the saying.

'What? Hope to what? Why would anyone want to say that? That's daft, that is. No wonder you people go around dropping dead all the time. You're wishing it on yourselves. Cross your heart is a promise older than the hills; well, the ones you can see from this window anyway. And it's a binding promise, made solid as gold with the old sign. Why do you think you draw crosses for kisses?'

He was like a glass of Champagne made flesh; all fizz, fun and bubble.

'Make yourself at least a little more decent will you, lass? My eyes are enjoying themselves so much I can't think straight, and I came here on serious business.'

She bounced off her bed and scampered into the bathroom. When she returned, she was wearing an expensive and brightly multi-coloured, striped linen bathrobe that had been her twenty-first birthday present to herself just over two years before. It had also been the only gift she received.

'Well, well! Weep, weep ancient Joseph! You are out-motleyed at last. Fits nicely where it touches too. Why do they call shoes like those mules? Ah, will you listen to me ramble like a moon-sick boy? Enough of that.'

His face tried to become grave and stern, then dissolved almost instantly into that of a laughing imp.

'I can't do the grim messenger bit when you're wearing motley. Forgive me, Medina Bishop. May I give you my message in my own way?'

She chuckled, her eyes bright. 'Tell me however you like, Fargo. What could you say that would wipe the smile from my face?'

He nodded and grinned. 'Very well. I will. Here goes... Now stop laughing or you'll set me off too. Are you ready? Right, this is it... Seriously now, you have a giggle like a dose of the measles. You'll have me catching it. Now listen,' he took a breath and then intoned, 'You must be careful in this place, Medina Bishop. Something here is active – or so they tell me. It's active and boiling out of the rock like a canker. If it touches you it will rip the very soul from your mortal frame and hurl it screaming into the light...'

Another voice entered her mind. It clashed and reverberated like great stones grinding together in a cavern.

It growled, 'We gave the sprite a task we thought he could perform, but the vessel is filled top full with frivolous foam. The bubbles always leak out. Medina, we need you to find the evil that continues to do this terrible thing to innocent souls. The barriers that contain the torment are stretching. Fargo's kin are doing their best, but who knows how long their work might last.

'But be warned. In seeking to discover the truth you may put yourself in terrible danger, not just to your mortal body but also to your immortal soul. Proceed quickly but with caution, Spirit Talker, and pray your guardian here can stop giggling long enough to be of value when you need him most.'

Then the voice was gone, and so was every trace of joy in the room.

Fargo offered a weak smile. He shrugged.

'What he said,' he whispered. 'He does it better than me.'

## 15

Hayes groaned. 'Aw no, where's Pennink?'

Monk looked back into the trees. 'You're joking. Has he gone off in a sulk? That man is the pits!'

'Pennink! Where the fuck are you, Pennink?' Rawkins bawled into the thickening darkness. 'Ah, man! Hayes, Monk, with me. Let's go get him. Will I lose my pension if I smack the man upside his fool empty head?'

Fellows looked at the sky. 'Sergeant, it's getting kind of dark here.'

Askuwheteau stepped forward. 'Maelie, I think Marshall's right. It is getting dark and I'm sure officer Pennink wouldn't just wander off in a funk. Not out here with no way home. And think about it, even *he* can't get lost walking in a straight line. Something's happened to him. Maybe we need to call for back-up.'

Rawkins looked at him, then at Fellows and then back into the trees.

'Hayes, you got the keys to the Merc?'

'Right here, Sarge.'

'Give 'em to Watcher. You guys wait in the vehicle while we search. If it gets too dark, turn the headlights on. Wait for an hour, after that light back to town and report four men down.' She handed over her geo-sat device and Monk's camera. 'Give it back to me when I come back, you hear?'

'Maelie, I'll come with you.'

'No, Watcher, you stick with Marshall. Pennink's an asshole and a bigot, but he's *our* asshole and *our* bigot. We got to go get him. Look, see, I made a promise to Marshall and I'm asking you to keep it for me, okay?'

Watcher nodded. Rawkins scowled. 'When we come back we might be running, so you be ready.'

'Born that way.'

'Where were you when I was looking for a husband?'

'Already married.'

She grunted and then turned to the trees, drawing her pistol. 'Arm up boys and try not to shoot me or each other. If you shoot Pennink, make sure it's a head shot. At least that way you'll do less damage.

The trees swallowed them.

Fellows said, 'I've got a very bad feeling about this.'

Watcher replied, 'You and me both, Luke. Let's get in that fancy pants Mercedes and do like the lady said.'

'Who's Luke?'

'Luke Skywalker. You know, *Star Wars*? Thought you were quoting.'

'No, no. I really do have a very bad feeling about this.'

'So did she, but she went anyway. Let's get the truck pointed at the trees, and... Marshall?'

'Yeah?'

'If I take the wheel, can you ride shotgun with that long piece of yours?'

'Yeah.'

They sat silently for ten slow minutes that felt like an hour. The sun dipped behind the mountains and twilight stalked the clearing. Watcher started the engine and put the lights full beam towards the trees. Something small was startled and scampered into the brush, then re-emerged and raced across the clearing. That was when they heard a pistol shot, then a second. Then there came what sounded like a brief fusillade. Fellows leaned out of the vehicle's window and took a bead on the treeline. He jerked the barrel upwards when Rawkins burst into the clearing. She almost stumbled and fell over the logs around the old camp fire. She cleared them with a leap and sprinted towards the Traveliner. Watcher slammed the Merc into reverse but held it on its brakes.

Behind Rawkins, Monk threw himself out of the trees, his face a mask of fear. He looked straight into the light from the headlamps and leaned forward to sprint, but something grabbed the big man from behind and lifted him clear of the ground before yanking him back into the shadows. His wild screams were almost instantly cut short. The sergeant threw herself into the minibus and fell headlong onto the floor.

She shrieked, 'Go, go, freaking go! Get out of here!'

Watcher hit the accelerator and the wheels spun for a moment, then bit just as darkness spilled from the line of trees and out into the clearing. Fellows began firing into the incoherent mass of inky bodies, joined by Rawkins who had grabbed a pump-action riot gun from a rack at the back of the bus. She was leaning from the same window as the geologist and when she fired, the hot barrel of her gun was so close to Fellows' ear he could feel his skin begin to blister.

The barrage of shells made the creatures hesitate for a moment in the full glare of the Merc's headlights. Fellows could see them clearly, but his mind skittered across them in confusion. *What are those things?*

Rawkins looked over her shoulder, yelled 'look out', spun like a matador and fired from the hip across the interior of the bus. Something insectile with too many limbs was blasted from the door she had left open in her panic.

Watcher had finally found the space he needed to manoeuvre the vehicle and tried to perform a handbrake turn, but the Mercedes' smart steering wouldn't let him. He almost stalled. Cursing, he spun the wheel the other way and accelerated onto the jolting ruts of the churned trail that led back to the highway.

Something hit the back of the vehicle hard and punched a hole through its rear window. A blue-black, barbed tentacle began to uncoil towards them along the aisle between the seats. Rawkins screamed and fired three times, shattering the window and knocking the beast out into the night. The tentacle whipped around inside the bus, slashing the seats, then its barbs caught in the fabric lining the Merc's ceiling. The tentacle stretched then held. Rawkins swore at full volume and stepped towards it. She pumped two shells into its taut, muscular flesh at close range, which shredded, splashed black goo across the rear seats and split like overworked leather. The tentacle – and whatever it belonged to – rocketed away into the darkness. Minutes later Watcher slewed out onto the tarmacked road and their bucketing journey smoothed to a civilised whisper.

He floored the accelerator and maintained a speed of well over one hundred miles per hour until he reached the dual carriageway leading back into Dauphin. He slowed to a pedestrian eighty.

Rawkins sat clutching her gun, her face working like she'd taken a bite of something she didn't want to swallow. Fellows was holding his rifle by the pistol grip, waiting for the barrel to cool. He had emptied two five-round magazines during the brief action, falling smoothly into the routine of aiming, pumping the bolt, firing, pumping the bolt, firing and then expertly swapping the dead mag for a live one. He had seen creatures fall under his fire and wondered if they had died. He hoped so.

Askuwheteau wondered what might have happened if they had been overwhelmed by the nightmare beasts. He shuddered. Then the scientist in him wondered what evolutionary niche they had been born to serve. First Nation teaching recognised the brotherhood of all creatures. Buffalo, bear, beaver, badger, sock-eye perch – they all had a single ancestor back in the primeval ooze and shared DNA with oranges, lemons and horseflies. They belonged here.

Those things back in the clearing looked somehow *other*, as if they had been manufactured in an alien workshop. They had a make-shift, clunky look that sat oddly alongside their magpie belly, blue-black weirdness.

Rawkins spoke up: 'Time, is it?'

Fellows checked his watch. 'Just after eight-forty.'

Watcher remained silent, lost in his thoughts. His mind itched as if it was touching the corner of something immense, but was afraid of pulling on it too hard in case it tore a hole in his comfortable world view. It was there for him. He just needed to open his eyes and he would see it, but his idiot Kestejoo slave mind insisted on waggling its fingers to distract him. It also kept singing the same phrase from an old song over and over, driving him nuts.

*Don't go changing trying to please me, you never let me down before...*

'Hey, Watcher. You falling asleep, man? You nearly went into that car!'

Fellows' shout brought him back to his here and now. He tightened his grip on the steering wheel and took a long shuddering breath.

'Sorry, I'm okay. Why are those cars flashing at us?'

He looked at his dashboard. His headlights were still on full beam. He switched them down. He checked his rear-view mirror and saw the black spray across the back of the bus.

*Of course! Now we got evidence. We can find out what we're dealing with.*

He caught Rawkins' eyes. They looked bleak. He couldn't blame her for that. She had left the station with three of her men and was going home alone. That was tough. Tough call.

She sounded exhausted. 'What do we do now?'

Watcher growled, 'We get that black shit all over the back seats analysed. We find out what we're dealing with and then we go hunting. Next time we meet those things we'll go properly loaded for bear.'

**[16]**

The ship called all its marauding units back to the cave. Something had gone badly wrong, and until she understood the situation she had decided to consolidate her position and draw in her horns. Using indigenous flora as the raw materials for constructing tools was standard procedure, but finding they could fight back had proved a terrible shock.

The kvult on her home world were powerful but mostly docile. Once caught, they surrendered to translation without a whimper. This place was very different, and some of those apes had somehow developed a nasty sting.

The ship had sent a collection party out in the breathless hours of the late afternoon and only half of them had returned. They reported the carnage caused by a barrage of unexpected projectile weapons. Later, in the heart of the night, she had sent out a pair of small, fast hunters to collect the lost core pods from around the clearing. Two of her crew, three tool units, a hunter and a climber had been lost. Two more had since died from their dreadful wounds. They would all have to be replaced, she knew that, but it seemed she needed to be more careful.

It was still a question of days or possibly weeks before the stone was completely cleared away from around her hull, even though she was making her tool units work at a ruinous pace. By then she would need to make sure her entire crew was in place. She told herself she had enough time to be cautious. Plenty of time. Then she paused in her ruminations – was that true? Did she have that much time?

She ran through her units' more recent sensor displays in the hope of finding clues to the level of threat she was facing. The upright apes seemed the biggest challenge. Were there viable alternatives?

During the early morning of the following day she sent her remaining hunters out in pairs to look at alternative life forms and to discover if they might be suitable for translation. Before midday she had called off that line of research. The creatures slow enough to be easily caught were too stupid to be of value; others were too dangerous to approach. One of her hunters had drawn near to a sand-coloured animal that seemed to be sleeping under the shade of a large birch. It looked to be an easy collect/translate. It wasn't.

The drowsy cougar had been startled awake by a strange, beetle-like object creeping up on it on sixteen triple-jointed legs. It was about three feet across and held what looked like an over-sized purple walnut in its jaws. The walnut sported a pair of eerily prehensile, thin antennae that probed hungrily towards the big cat's hide. The cat lashed out faster than the hunter could react. Its claws slashed deep and fatal gashes across the hunter's leathery carapace and sent it hurtling sideways into the tree trunk. It burst and splashed midnight ichor across the bark, which smoked hotly for a second. The twitching corpse remained splayed across the trunk for long sticky moments, and then its weight unglued it from the tree and it flopped bonelessly to the ground. By that time the big cat was several hundred yards away and still accelerating.

The hunter's partner recovered its dead companion's core pod from the wreckage and tracked down the one it had been carrying. It used six of its limbs to hold the two recovered pods against its back, leaving its own still gripped tightly in its fore parts. It trekked back through the pale morning light, cautiously keeping to the shadows wherever possible.

When it finally reached the home cave, it entered the ship and added its harvest to the sadly growing pile in a sheltered corner away from all the frantic activity. It then thrust its hindquarters deep into one of the craft's many relay cups. It made its report and received a frisson of pleasure in response.

The ship had been designed to provide an almost sexual relationship for its units. They neither ate nor drank, drawing all the energy they needed directly from her, but they could feel intense pleasure and that was their reward for a good job well done. The ship itself felt no need for anything so mundane as purely physical gratification, but intellectually she understood the value of it and was happy to provide her workers with their little thrill.

She added this latest hunter's report to her growing catalogue of alarming information about the denizens of the immediate area. She had begun to wonder how *anything* could survive out there. So many of this dreadful planet's native creatures had been designed to cut, hack, slash and tear apart their fellows – she wondered why the whole planet wasn't a waste-ground of rotting corpses. The entire population should have been decimated in a matter of months, even weeks, leaving the last bloody predator roaring defiance over the body of its final victim.

All she wanted was to replace her crew, cut her way free of her stone bondage and go home. A perfectly peaceful and understandable intent. But the minute she had started to put her plan into action she had come under attack from every quarter. A veritable army of fiendishly fast and wickedly armed creatures had been unleashed. And what of the strange, lethal sting of the apes? Where did that come from? What evil womb had birthed such a thing; what terrible mind devised it?

The apes had previously had no natural weapons that she could see. They were soft, fleshy things, which was why she had needed to replace them when they shattered or split while performing their menial tasks. But these latest outrages had seen her units punctured and torn by balls of hot metal, which expanded in their flesh with hideous effects. They made a small hole on entry but left a gaping crater on exit; doing so much damage in the process that the unit became useless and its tissues had to be recovered.

She would have been happy to begin a dialogue with whoever ran the madhouse, but her search through all available communication channels had turned up little more than gibberish or strange, acutely painful noises. She wondered if those were recordings of torture. They certainly sounded as if some poor creatures were being eviscerated while getting pushed through a curtain of vibrating wires. After a while she gave up. It was too disturbing.

The ship began to think of her prison planet as a place of danger and death. For the first time in its long, long life it was under attack, and in the process, it had also become the first of its breed to discover the true meaning of fear.

It was no longer so certain it would be able to survive the days that remained before it could leave the cave. And it had no core pod of its own from which it could be resurrected.

The ship realised it had to be cautious. Its units would never make it home on their own. It *must* survive, if only for their sake. The ship mind drew in its equivalent of a deep, resigned breath, and then began to plan its defence.

# [17]

Rawkins' emotions were in a state of utter turmoil. The day's events had driven her so far out of her comfort zone that her mental landscape had become unrecognisable. She tried to review what had happened back there in the forest – make sense of it.

They had found Pennink. He was standing stock still in the middle of the trees holding a baseball-sized, dark purple stone or nut to his chest. He watched them approach but remained silent, ignoring their shouted questions. Hayes ran forward and made to grab Pennink's arm, bellowing at him to 'get a freaking move on'. The rat-like man had just bared his teeth at him, a strange open-mouthed gesture.

That was when the black things surged from cover and grabbed at Hayes. Rawkins rattled off her first two shots, but there were too many of them. She noticed Hayes' face had taken on the same weirdly placid smile as Pennink.

Monk took a shot, then two more. She also loosed off a few frantic rounds, but it was hopeless. She grabbed at Monk's elbow and yelled, 'Run!' He didn't need to be told twice. Terror added wings to their flight. The tentative trail that had taken ten minutes to cover on their way in took just seconds to traverse on their way out. All around them, shadows flickered and moved.

Then she had been blinded by the headlamps and almost sprawled headlong over the logs by the old campfire, but she had made it. And now here she sat. Safe. The only survivor of her team. Pennink may have been a weasel, but he still supported his wife and daughter. Hayes, good old reliable Hayes. And his lovely wife – how long would that Irish smile last without her man? Monk may have established himself as one of the most active cocksmen in the city of Dauphin, but he was also a good, honest cop.

The bus was smooth on its wheels, but the wind blowing through it was deafening thanks to all the holes blasted out of it during that insane escape. Fellows had shut the door and closed his window, which helped quieten things a little, but it was still too noisy to talk at any volume below a shout. There was also a pervasive smell which she at first found impossible to identify, but eventually realised was coming from her bulletproof vest. It had been splashed by the tentacle's black 'blood'. She tore at the Velcro tabs and pulled the thing from her body, flinging it towards the back of the bus.

*Freaking vests hadn't helped the boys in their hour of need, had they?*

She thought back to the dreamy look on Pennink's face, that eerie smile from Hayes. She wondered if Monk now looked like that too. The bubble burst and hot, unstoppable sobs boiled from her chest. She expelled them like vomit, wracking, heaving sobs that almost strangled her. She gripped at her gun with hard, whitened knuckles, bent over it like it was the rail of a ship. Sputum dribbled from her open, distorted mouth.

Almost as if it was happening to someone else, she discovered arms around her and felt herself being rocked like a grieving child. Fellows took her in his arms and held her close. She should have been offended; after all, she was the police sergeant and he was the civilian. Who was he to do this, a virtual stranger? But after everything they had been through together they could no longer be strangers. They had become comrades in arms. She felt the painful, sobbing contractions begin to ease and gulped air back into her starved lungs. She wiped at her mouth and eyes with her fist and attempted a smile at the powerful man by her side. She raised her voice.

'They teach you that in the forces?'

He shook his head. 'My wife taught me.'

'I thought you told Watcher you weren't married.'

'Widower.'

'Oh. Oh, I'm so sorry.'

He changed the subject. 'You were really good with that riot gun, sarge. A wildcat. We would have had it if you hadn't got stuck in like that.'

'Yeah, well.'

And then the bus slowed for an exit ramp, and in a daze they found themselves navigating proper streets once more. Reality fell over them like a surreal blanket. They took in the change of scene like refugees escaped from a war zone, gazing dully at street lights, bars, shops and houses. People were walking in the streets without a care in the world. A voice in Rawkins' head wanted to shout at them, tell them to run and hide, warn them that childhood monsters under the bed were real and just a few hours away.

Watcher turned onto River Avenue and followed it to Hedderly Street. There were still lights on in the RCMP station.

Fellows said, 'Look, there's my pick-up. I bet that moose climbed out and walked home by now.'

Watcher grunted. 'I see nobody stole my old ride yet. I park it with the keys in the ignition just in case.'

Rawkins slid the door open and climbed out. Her body was a mass of scrapes, cuts and bruises. She saw the blood and didn't have the energy to care. She was too exhausted. She had left her sense of humour back at the old campsite along with her sanity and three men. She felt the weight of the riot gun in her left hand and thought about putting in down somewhere, then realised she didn't want to. *Not just yet. No, not just yet.*

The men stepped down from the bus. Watcher walked around it. He emitted a low whistle. 'Check this thing out. They really didn't want us to get away. They kicked the shit out of it.' The other two joined him.

Rawkins shook her head. 'That bus looks the way I feel.' She turned to look at the brightly lit doors of the station. 'Time to see if there's anyone in there I can make a report to, I guess.'

'We'll come in with you.'

'Thanks, Watcher. Appreciate it.'

The trio strode across the car park and up the steps. Rawkins paused at the doors and took a deep breath before stepping forward. The doors slid open.

The constable at the desk was checking something on his phone. She knew him. He was probably looking at the hockey results. He didn't look up.

'Be with you in a second.'

'Chief in, Parslow?'

'Sure, yes.' He looked at her. 'Shit, sarge! What happened to you?'

'Can you let the chief know I'm on my way to her office? And bring us three coffees, please. The good stuff, not that machine shit.'

The constable pressed the button to unlock the door to the station's interior and made a quick call.

'Chief asks can it wait 'til morning?'

'No.'

Rawkins led her party through the clean, smart corridors and along to a door that opened before them as if by magic. A slender and elegant yet hawkish woman stepped out with an annoyed expression on her face, an expression that quickly changed to one of alarm when she saw her visitors approaching and realised two of them were armed. Then she looked closer.

'Maelie, what's happened? You look like you've been through Hell. Askuwheteau, good to see you again. I'm sorry, but I don't think...'

'Fellows, ma'am. Marshall Fellows. I came in this morning to report two of my friends had been abducted.'

'Really? Maelie, will this take long? I have an important dinner engagement.'

'Chief, can we come in and sit down while I make my report? I think it best if you're seated too.'

Parslow brought the coffees some ten minutes later. When he took them into the chief's office he could sense the emotional charge in the room. The

74

three mugs were accepted gratefully. As he closed the door on his way out he heard his boss say, 'I suppose there's no way they survived the attack?'

He had been back at the desk for another ten minutes when Chief Inspector Longknife strode past with Rawkins and her guests in her wake. On his monitors, he saw her walk around the Mercedes bus and then step inside it with the sergeant. The two men stood patiently waiting. They were talking and pointing at the body of the bus.

*Something big's going on here,* he thought. *I'll bet a week's wages it's terrorists.*

His Chief Inspector came back in alone. She asked, 'Is Webb still here?'

'I believe so, Chief.'

'Don't believe, find out. Get him out there and tell him to bring his sample kit.'

Kit 'Spider' Webb was an amiable man who had a habit of chatting with those he called his 'customers' while he worked. He was lean and long with a startling mop of thick grey hair and disturbingly young features. His lanky body was unco-ordinated and moved around in a gawky, awkward fashion, but everything he did he did with exacting precision.

He was head of pathology for Dauphin and was most often called out for hunting accidents, but just recently he had been absorbed by the increasingly odd missing persons cases.

It was Spider who had made the call about the Duck Mountain Spa videos, observing that whatever had climbed out of that swimming pool was no longer human. And he suffered the mocking jeers from his peers. They told him in no uncertain terms that he was suffering from a dose of way too much imagination.

'A bit more fact and a bit less science fiction, Spider.'

Their comments didn't faze him in the least. It was true he would much rather watch the latest *Star Trek* movie than suffer some sticky love nonsense or well-meant social commentary. Working wrists deep in the corpse of a promising young French student, a boy whose body had undergone radical nervous trauma – and what appeared to be an explosive projectile bursting from his chest – was plenty of social commentary for one day. Philippe's body had reminded him of the victims in the *Alien* series of movies, an observation he kept to himself.

He gazed down at his latest customer. *Back to life,* he thought, *back to reality.* The naked corpse of a well-built, middle-aged man was stretched on his polished stainless steel examination table. Spider adjusted his overhead lamp. The man had suffered one of those traditional blunt force traumas so beloved of crime novelists. His hunting buddies swore blind that the spongy indentation in the occipital and frontal bone of the man's skull was the result of a bizarre hunting accident, and was, in fact, entirely the victim's fault. They said he had been tracking a fat pheasant and fired off both barrels when it flew directly overhead. He hit the bole of a heavy branch of an American elm which had been all but blown to splinters. What remained of the branch had swung down like a club and socked the poor fool across his head – allegedly. Dead before he hit the ground. He didn't suffer.

All three witnesses had signed sworn testimony to the account. They had even brought the bloodied branch in with them as evidence. If it hadn't been for the rumour among the medical fraternity that the deceased, a dentist, had been openly enjoying a torrid love affair with his nurse, well... who was Spider to argue? The fact that the dead man's lover was also one of the witnesses' wives, and that the dentist had only been invited to join the hunting party at the very last minute by that self-same and extremely insistent cuckold... Spider sighed. It wasn't much of a mystery to put before a man suffering from 'way too much imagination'.

'Should've maybe kept it in your pants, brother? Yah think? Or at least been a bit more discreet?'

His phone rang. He took off his gloves and answered it.

'Oh, hi, Parslow. Yeah, I'm here, I answered the phone, didn't I? The boss wants what? Where? Why? Really? Okay, I'll just put my customer on ice and I'll be straight up.'

While he cleared his table and stripped off his scrub suit, he said aloud to himself, 'So, what keeps the Chief working this late? Must be something awesome!' And he grinned. He liked awesome.

September sun had warmed the interior of the car to a pleasant degree and a good night's sleep had done much to improve Edward Louis's temper. So far it was proving to be a gold standard day. He had woken earlier than expected and breakfasted well, if alone. Then, while he waited for Medina, he had decided to become better acquainted with his hire car. He gleefully discovered that the Toyota had a built-in sat-nav which he had found simple to operate without recourse to the handbook. To add spice to his day, when Medina finally emerged she had somehow continued her transformation from introverted Goth to enchanting, elfin beauty. He felt inspired to comment on the fact.

'You look positively radiant this morning, if I may say so.'

'You may, and it's very nice of you. But I don't, not really. I'm just taking a good friend's advice and I've stopped burying myself in black. I almost forgot I had these old things in my case.'

Louis smiled and she grinned back. She knew she looked good. Medium heels had added a little height and her cream silk blouse worked nicely with a short, pleated terracotta skirt, which enhanced the length of her slender legs. Best of all, she had roughly teased her mop of raven hair out of her face.

Without so much as a trace of make-up she looked like a new woman; fresh and young and with a sparkle to her dark eyes that matched the teasing, enigmatic smile on her lips. If it wasn't for the fact that they'd arrived together early that morning and gone straight to bed, Louis would have been convinced the young woman had found herself a lover.

But then, he thought, perhaps she, like him, felt invigorated by this beautifully fresh September day.

Dauphin deservedly called itself the 'city of sunshine' and had two major passions – hockey and hunting. The first was served by its junior 'A' team, the Dauphin Kings, the second by several large hunting goods stores they spotted as they drove down the arrow-straight Main Street. The road was wide and busy and its buildings, a combination of clean residential properties and flourishing retail outlets, showed all the hallmarks of prosperity.

Medina began to feel as if she had been there before, which she knew not to be the case. There was something so familiar about the city's buildings, its roads and even its overhead traffic lights. Even the vehicular mix of pick-up trucks, family saloons and SUVs was ringing increasingly loud recognition bells in her head. *I know this place.*

On the sidewalks, suited men wearing neckties greeted friends in windcheaters and body warmers. Smartly dressed and ponytailed teenage girls flirted with denim-clad young men. Everything sparkled in the clear air. The city gave an impression of life, optimism and vibrancy.

Once they had passed Fifth Avenue the buildings gave way to trees, lawns and green spaces. A few minutes later Louis carefully turned left at the junction with River Avenue West and then almost immediately right into Hedderly Street.

The sat-nav chimed, 'You have reached your destination – on your right.' Louis eased the car into the car park and cut the engine. They spent a moment examining the red brick home of the Dauphin RCMP, D division. Louis ran his hand through his sparse hair and pursed his lips.

'It looks like a good sized public library. If it wasn't for the sign I'd think we were in the wrong place.'

'I suppose the row of police cars might be a clue?'

'Yes,' he chuckled. 'Unless the Dauphin clan of Mounties are great readers. Shall we go find out?'

Parslow was back at his post. He looked up with interest when an avuncular, sturdy looking man with thinning grey hair and a diminutive, fresh-faced and very attractive dark-haired girl came through the entrance door.

'Good morning, sir; miss. How can I help you?'

Louis answered. 'Good morning, officer. You are expecting us. Bishop and Louis. Specialist consultants sent by the London CID.'

'Very good, sir. Please, take a seat. I'll let them know you're here and someone will be with you very shortly.'

They sat on a bench under a board covered with notices. Medina experienced a sudden flash of realisation. She knew why Dauphin looked so familiar. The city was like so many she'd seen in American movies that it was almost as if she'd woken up on a film set. Clean and somehow very American despite being rooted in Canada. She decided to keep such thoughts to herself, reasoning that they might prove unpopular with the locals if she voiced them too openly.

Louis wasn't so considerate. 'I feel like we've walked into some kind of American detective film. I've had a strong feeling of déjà vu ever since we left the hotel.'

The inner door opened and a young, uniformed woman beckoned for them to follow her. 'The Chief Inspector will see you now.'

She led the way, chatting warmly about their choice of hotel, telling them it was the one they always preferred to book for their guests. She knocked at a door and entered, ushered them forward and then departed, closing the door behind her. A tall, well-made but distracted looking woman strode across the room and thrust out her hand to Louis.

'Mr Bishop, it's good to see you. I'm Chief Inspector Longknife, Cheryl Longknife.' She turned to Medina. 'And you must be the journalist, Ms Louis?'

A flustered Louis corrected her and Longknife coloured slightly. Medina could see the woman was wrestling with a fierce perceptual paradigm shift. Her eyes scanned the medium from shoes to crown and finally settled on her face. She gazed into Medina's eyes for a long, *long* moment, then nodded and smiled.

'Hoist on my own petard. All my professional career I've been fighting to overturn the sexual stereotyping that plagues us women, and then I go do it myself. Please forgive me, Miss Bishop.'

She thrust out her hand. Medina took it. An image sharp as crystal flooded the medium's mind and she heard voices egging her on. She held the Chief Inspector's hand a little longer than was entirely sociable and then said in a dreamy voice, 'There is a man called Askuwheteau. He watches. I must speak with him.'

Longknife looked quizzically at her and then across at Louis, who shrugged.

Medina released her hand, stood back and gazed up at her with her large, intelligent eyes. The Chief looked enquiringly at her. She saw the steel she had recognised earlier, but then she saw something more, something *other*. She became convinced those lovely eyes had seen things best left undisturbed. They made her think of death. Without knowing why, she felt a cold finger trace an icy path down her spine.

Then Medina smiled and it was as if a cloud had lifted. Longknife shook herself free from the sense of dread that had threatened to unnerve her.

She found her voice. 'What am I thinking? Please, take a seat.'

She gestured towards a cluster of deep chairs around a circular, polished wooden table on which was a tray containing a coffee flask, some milk, porcelain mugs, a platter of foil-covered biscuits and a bowl filled with small nuggets of sugar.

'We should drink the coffee while it's still fairly fresh. Those flasks keep it warm, but it soon begins to taste pretty disgusting, don't you think?'

They took their seats and Louis fussed around the coffee. He noticed the stack of wooden coasters and distributed them first before he handed around the filled mugs and offered milk and sugar. Longknife declined both, which didn't surprise him. He had rightly judged her to be a black coffee woman, and thought her quite handsome in a lean, hawkish way.

As usual, Medina had to wriggle to find the sweet spot in her seat. At first she had found the chair so large it drowned her, lifting her feet from the floor and swallowing her body in its depths. She couldn't relax, sit back and still reach her coffee on the table. And the biscuits were hopelessly out of reach. She fought her way out of it then moved forward until she could perch on the edge of its seat, a position she had learned to find comfortable enough over the years.

Longknife studied her. Even wearing medium heels, she was still just under five feet tall, but she was in proportion. Her legs were long for her height and shapely, and her gamine head was perched on a woman's body, not a girl's. *Really rather beautiful in an unaffected way.* Longknife decided she liked her, but wondered what her consultant speciality might be.

Medina was aware of the inspection. That was something else she had become used to. She had learned ways to take advantage of her height. She was a slight figure and could fade from view in plain sight, but when she wanted to she could project an arresting charisma that drew every eye in the room. It was a very effective tool when she wanted to be noticed. She brought it to the fore now and Longknife leaned forward as if entranced.

She said, 'DCI Worker from the London CID told me you had some kind of very special expertise that might help us solve a major abduction case. I'd be curious to hear what you can do. He spoke very highly of you, by the way, but he didn't go into much detail. Would you care to elucidate?'

Medina was certain it was the very first time she had ever heard someone use the word 'elucidate' in a spoken sentence. Its use spoke volumes about the speaker in a good way. She put down her empty mug and composed herself before offering her answer.

She said, 'A few days ago just under two hundred people died in sudden and terrible circumstances. The locus for the deaths was about a hundred miles from here in the Duck Mountain Provincial Park. Since that time a slow but regular stream of people have shared the same fate. I need to find out what's happening, and if possible put a stop to it. I believe we can help each other if we work together. That's why I asked DCI Worker if he would call you and introduce us.'

Longknife frowned. 'But... wait a moment. How can you possibly know about these things? Alright, the events up at the Duck Mountain Spa made it into the international press recently, I'm aware of that, but the others have only ever been covered locally. How can you know anything about them? I thought you'd only just arrived.'

Medina leaned forward, her expression serious.

'The dead told me.'

# [19]

Askuwheteau couldn't relax. His head was buzzing with events back at Duck Mountain. He had been talking with Fellows and Rawkins and they felt the same. It didn't feel real. Rawkins couldn't tell her husband what had happened because she feared he would insist she resign. Fellows wanted some payback. Just knowing those things were out there was keeping him awake at night.

'I tell you, man, I keep seeing those faceless heads.'

Askuwheteau told his wife he had some strange stuff he needed to think about. He promised he would tell her all about it when he had it 'properly set in his own mind'. At three that morning she had woken him from a disturbing dream in which he had been watching himself change to a blue-black monster. His muttering and twitching had woken her up. It took a while to find sleep again. That morning he should have continued work on some lectures specially commissioned for a local radio station, but he couldn't settle.

Finally, in a vain attempt to distract himself he went fishing. He watched his float bob gently on the water. It hadn't moved for more than ten minutes. He held his home-made bamboo fishing pole in one hand and a novel in the other. He had finished his lunch of cold chicken and threaded some of the bird's skin onto his hook along with a grouse feather lure. He was not a natural fisherman, but he loved the taste of fresh walleye fried in a garlicky saltine cracker crust – the way his wife cooked it. His mouth watered at the thought. But his brain was too engaged to be fully occupied with just sitting by the lake dangling a ten-foot pole over the water. The words in his book were just a grey blur. His mind was too busy elsewhere. He couldn't focus and the fish weren't biting.

Then the cork float bobbed harder and he tensed. It dipped. He put his book down carefully and got to his feet, feeling a tug on the line as the bamboo curved. He waited, hoping to feel the bite through his hands. Then it was gone. He lifted the pole and gazed at the lure. The chicken skin had been taken.

He drew the line in and this time tied a meaty bone to the lure.

*Steal that, you gypsy thief.*

It was only then that he realised a child was walking his way, her dark eyes fixed directly on him. As she drew nearer he had to modify his first impression. The slight creature was no child. She came into focus and he could see she was womanly enough, young but not a junior, and plenty easy on the eye. She smiled at him and he felt it in his gut the way he used to when he and Wikimak were still courting. Back when his wife had spring in her eyes instead of late summer.

'Mr Askuwheteau? Hello, I'm Medina Bishop.'

She held out her hand and he wiped his on his pants before taking it.

'Nice to meet you, miss Bishop. Am I meant to know you? I think I'd remember.'

'Sorry, no. But I've heard so much about you that I sort of feel as if I've already met *you*. Hope you don't mind.'

'All good, I hope? Sorry, I hate crap clichés like that. Heard about me? Who from? And don't believe all that shit about the whiskey.' He winked at her. 'Okay, believe it. But ignore that shit about me dancing with a grizzly bear. It was a black bear, not a grizzly. Grizzlies can't dance much as a rule, but show a black bear a good time and they'll pretty much dance the whole night away.'

He realised his mouth was running away with itself in the hope of another smile. He also found his ears calling for his attention after replaying her accent in his mind.

'You're not from around here, are you?'

'How can you tell? Is it the clothes? I haven't had a chance to go shopping yet and these were the only things in my luggage that weren't black or dark grey.'

'Britain?'

'London, yes.'

'Welcome to the City of Sunshine.'

'Thank you.'

'So, who's been squawking about me to pretty strangers?'

That earned him another smile and he felt that same intimately electric thrill.

'His name is Wematin, and he thanks you for remembering him with open eyes, honesty and affection. He also says sorry about the car, but it was your fault. You brought the damned rot gut. He just drank it. He had to drive, he says. He had no choice; he was too drunk to walk. And anyway, you were asleep. And snoring. Loudly. Then the tree jumped out at him. They do that. He blames the bastard wood spirits. Tricky devils, he says, but you know that.'

*His grandfather? She had been talking with his grandfather?*

83

She continued: 'He says I am to be Achachak Numees to you. And although you might be a scoundrel, you have a strong heart and you're an honest man. Even so, you don't deserve Wikimak. She's far too good for you. Oh, and please kiss Nohkômak for him. He misses her and is holding a seat for her. Please tell her that.'

He was speechless. *Achachak Numees? She was his spirit sister?*

He rallied. 'Lady, my grandfather's been dead a while. When did you ever get to talk with him? You don't look old enough to have ever met him, no offence.'

'None taken. He's standing there by your side. He also says the fish are smarter than you and you never learned to listen when he was trying to teach you.'

Askuwheteau looked to his right.

'He's on your left, one who watches. I can see you take after him. Fine looking, straight-backed man. Hair still black the day he died. By the way, he says, he was stupid enough to kill himself with tobacco and you're a bright boy so you should know to lay off the shit! And he means it.'

Askuwheteau wrapped his line around his pole and picked up his book. He placed it in his rucksack and pulled the straps over his shoulders.

'You like to eat fish?'

'Yes, very much.'

'So do I. Let's go buy some. And then I'll introduce you to the best fish cook in Manitoba. No, the world.'

Medina talked while they walked. After a while the Cree man sat on a bench and she perched beside him.

'I believe you,' he said, and rubbed his hands over his face. Then he told her about the black creatures in the forest. She watched the busy Main Street traffic and the people going about their day.

'You think these things are connected?'

He grimaced, then stood up. 'I think they have to be. This don't buy no walleye, and mystery makes me hungry. Let's go buy some fish and take it home to my very own genius chef. Get ready for a real treat.'

After a delicious meal, Medina joined Askuwheteau's wife in the kitchen where they continued the conversation they had started while the vivacious blonde was preparing thick fillets of walleye for the frying pan. She had learned Wikimak's true name was Charlotte, née Donovan.

'Wikimak means "wife" in Algonquin so that's what he calls me. Most First Nation names are descriptions. You already know his name means "he who watches". To understand him properly you need to know he's very proud of his heritage, but he's also a man of his time. He works in the past; he doesn't live there.'

Watcher and Charlotte had met at university. She was a professor of archaeology and had published several successful academic books around such subjects as human migration and the American pyramid culture – including the mysterious North American pyramid centres. She had proudly shown Medina their framed wedding photo. She was in traditional white and he was in full Cree wedding costume. Medina laughed out loud at another photograph of a wild-eyed Askuwheteau pretending to scalp his new father-in-law during the wedding breakfast – 'to save time'.

The man in the photographs was handsome in an almost Oriental manner, and the bride was beautiful with more than a measure of blonde Hollywood glamour. Medina thought they were ageing well and said so. Charlotte smiled with perfect teeth that spoke of orthodontic work as a child.

'He loves walleye,' she said. 'But if we ate it for every meal he'd get bored. He loves me, I know he does, but when he walked in with you he was like a mad puppy dog with two tails. He won't flirt and he always walks the line, but he has an eye for a pretty new face. It's mostly harmless.'

'Insult me with "mostly harmless" will you? How dare you? Who are you, Douglas Adams?'

The lean, dark man had entered the room with a half-empty bottle of wine.

'I thought you kitchen slaves might want your glasses freshened, and here I find you disparaging me behind my back! The master is displeased!'

He stood with his arms akimbo and took an imperious stance, then chuckled.

'As if I'd flirt with another woman with my grandfather watching. And anyway, Wikimak, I didn't marry a fish, I married you – and *you* are never boring.'

He turned to Medina. 'She overanalyses things, always has. Ask her why all the towels in the kitchen are white. Go on. Ask her. See what she says.'

Medina scanned the room and saw he was right. She turned to Charlotte with an inquiring tilt to her head. Charlotte sighed and adopted a rueful expression. She shook her head at her husband.

'He loves chewing this old chestnut. Okay, once more with feeling. When I was working my way through Uni, I was lucky enough to get a scholarship. My parents were doing okay financially, but I had two brothers whose education needed funding and there wasn't much left for me. The scholarship covered most things – you know, the essentials – but I took on bar and

85

restaurant work to pay for all those little luxuries that make life worth living, you know the sort of stuff. One of the best places I ever worked was called Vinitalia. It was owned by a Sicilian called Pippo Lillino. It was a great place. Pippo was an immense character with a heart nearly as big as his moustache, and his wife, who we all called Madonna Lillino, was like a lovely little mother hen clucking around looking after everyone.'

Charlotte smiled at the sepia memory, then continued.

'Anyway, one time I asked Pippo why all the towels in his kitchen were white when they would obviously become stained so quickly. Wouldn't coloured or even black be better? You know what he said? He said his was a clean kitchen and he served clean food and that was because he could tell from his towels if people were cleaning things properly. "White towels," he said, "mean clean hands, clean food and clean pots and pans." He was pleased I'd asked. He said, "I got the best corps de cucina in Canada because they're the smartest. Look at you, you'll be Professor Donovan one day. Martin over there is a mathematician. Audrey writes novels. Martinez wants to open his own place when he has enough money and he's learning everything he can. All of you, smart people, hard-working. Not a politician in the place." Then he grabbed up a towel and held it up like a banner and he said, "Look at this, spotless even on a busy Friday. I love you all." I've never forgotten that lesson and I'll always have white towels in my kitchen, and that's despite old mucky paws over there.'

'Hear what she calls me? I bought her some really nice towels with First Nation designs on them.' Askuwheteau indicated the walls. 'Look what she did!'

That explained the set of four framed artworks Medina had originally thought to be fine prints.

'They're really nice.'

'Yeah, well you didn't come find me to eat fish and talk about towels. Wikimak, Medina here is much, much more than a pretty face. She's already been over to see Chief Longknife and now she's tracked down the second most important person in town: me. You want to sit in on this? You'll find it eye-popping, I promise you.'

His jog around the lake had proved to be almost a half marathon and Razi was sweaty and starving by the time he neared its end. He hoped his girlfriend would have something tasty simmering on the stove. Unlike him, Bhatinda wasn't a slave to the track or personal fitness, but she was a magician in the kitchen. She could take the most mundane ingredients and conjure something magical. His stomach growled at the thought of the meals they'd shared. And she wouldn't even let him help in the kitchen, telling him 'not to be such a nosey parker'. He chuckled when he remembered her last words before he set off on his run earlier that day.

'You're such a smarty-pants! You'll learn all my recipes and then you'll be off cooking them for someone else. Forget it. You want to help? You can help with the washing up once we've eaten, so make sure you mop your plate clean. Now go run and keep that little bum of yours tight the way I like it. Leave me alone with my secret recipes that I learned at Hogwarts during potion classes.'

Razi enjoyed the freedom of camping, but didn't like slumming it. Their tent was substantial enough to have a solar-powered shower, a proper kitchen with a fridge-freezer, and satellite TV in the combination lounge/bedroom.

He had erected their chemical toilet at the rear of the tent and dropped a yeast tablet into it to kill the worst of the stink. He believed the smell of shit might attract bears, so it was better to be safe than sorry. Food waste went into a screw-down bin. Razi had thought of everything. He enjoyed his time in the wilderness, but saw no reason to go without civilisation.

He rounded a corner and saw the large, light green tent before him. He lengthened his stride and put on a turn of speed. Strange, he would normally be able to smell the food cooking by now. He hoped everything was okay. He slowed down and approached the kitchen extension with caution.

'Bhatti? Bhatti, love? Are you alright?' He pulled aside the tent flap and she was standing before him. She had a strange, almost vacant smile on her face. Her eyes were oddly wide and seemed to quiver, as if they were trying to register all of him at once.

'Bhatti? What is it, love? Are you sick?'

She stepped towards him with alarming swiftness and pressed her left hand against his chest. His last coherent thought was to wonder why she had her right hand inside her top as if she was holding something against her skin. Then the slave matrix buried in his DNA took over. Behind him the black hunter unit emerged from the shadows and led the docile pair straight towards the lake. Its triple-jointed limbs left a confusing blur of thin marks in the mud as it entered the water. Razi and Bhatinda dived in behind it and their core pods took what was needed from the lake to force complex changes in their bodies. Their human flesh stretched and chemically altered to become the characteristic, blue-black slave skin of the ship's crew and tool units. Musculoskeletal developments changed their physical design and tortured their bodies into a pair of six-limbed, arch-backed creatures. Their heads and necks were sucked back into their shoulders to become little more than muscular bulges that were hyper-sensitive to light, but could also 'see' into areas of the spectrum that were invisible to the human eye. Terrible, rending agony drove their screaming souls into the Realm of Light where they joined hundreds of others like them; their personalities ripped to shreds by horror, pain and disbelief.

The newly transformed crew members set their course straight towards home. Restored to operational levels of crew intelligence, they ignored the hunter as just another tool unit, little more than a clever – albeit almost insanely mobile – device. The hunter performed its job by following pre-programmed search criteria; the crew had to be smarter. They needed to be able to think independently, to make judgement calls. To follow orders without question.

A helicopter rattled overhead and all three units dived towards the bottom of the lake without altering course by so much as a degree.

'I'm sure I had faint heat signatures just then, but now they're gone.'

'What kind?'

'Not clear. To begin with I thought they were human... you know, people, and something a bit like a large dog. Then the signal went to shit and disappeared completely.'

'Longknife won't like that.'

'Yeah? Well she can come out here and look for herself. We've been here more than half an hour and it's the first time I've seen anything worth reporting. Wild goose chase. In fact, worse! Wild geese are easy. You want one? They're bloody well everywhere!'

'Don't shout at me. I didn't choose this place, Rawkins' geo-sat brought us here, and I didn't make your scanner go to pot. I just drive the egg beater. You're the lady with the brains around here.'

'They were heading over there. Should we go look see?'

The chopper veered to the left in a steep banking manoeuvre that pinned pilot and passenger back in their seats.

'There – there! What was that?'

'Shit, what? Where?'

'Right under our noses! Right under our freaking noses. Shit! Hey, you got the nose camera on record?'

'SOP. I'm in the air, I film everything back to the big old hard drive in the tail. Your infrared scanner has its own record channel too.'

'Hey, does it record everything we say?'

'Yeah, it does.'

'Oh shit! We take it all back, Chief. We love you really.'

'Shut up, for Christ's sake. Stop digging. You want to go back to base and check? See what we got?'

'No, no, not yet. Just had a thought. Follow this line a-ways. Let's see where it takes us.'

'It takes us up there, that's where. We're reaching mountain range country. See there, that's the end of the tree line and the beginning of climbers' tracks.'

'You've got good eyes. Hey, over there – what's that? Has there been some sort of rock-fall over there? Looks like a lot of fresh white spill running down the scarp.'

'Seen that sort of thing around a mine entrance once. There's no mines around here, are there?'

'Damned if I know. Wait, what's that?'

'What?'

'That! What's that thing? Fuck, look out, it's...'

The squat, blue-black creature had indeed been designed to clear away debris during mining, and had been hard at work ejecting spoil created by the stone clearing process. Now it performed exactly as the ship mind had hoped. From a rear end like a fat, short-nosed cannon, it fired a high-speed plug of compacted rock powder which smashed into the helicopter and wiped it from the sky like a swatted bug. The tangled mass of metal and glass spun away from the cave, torque from its twisting rotors wheeling it across the sky. It was over a mile from the kill site when it smashed into the trees. All that marked its passage were some torn branches and a slight rent in the forest canopy. The trashed helicopter never even reached the ground but hung pinioned upside down in the branches of an ancient oak.

The pilot and passenger were instantly translated to the Realm. There had been no time for a mayday and barely enough time for the fresh spirits to register their own deaths. They were shocked, dazed and confused, but they were still coherent. This made them two of the increasingly rare 'normal' deaths arriving from the Duck Mountain region.

Two gentle mentors came to them and listened to their story with wide-eyed incredulity. They were asked to repeat it. Memory melds were taken. At last the pair were taken to a conference with the Council committee overseeing the crisis in Manitoba.

The memory melds were shared with the committee members, some of whom were ancient beyond the telling of it – and wiser than silence. The pilot and his passenger had retained much of their human form, but the souls they were now confronted with seemed like creatures from legend. Their bodies had been redefined by time and purified by the Light. Their elegant physiques looked like antique bone polished and shaped by the sea, or sculpted ivory lace blended with the delicate skeletons of leaves, and the whole bound up with precious metals. They were huge, strange, vital and beautiful; awesome as a cathedral but gentle as a new mother's eyes.

One of them leaned forward and spoke with a voice like a soft breeze rolling from a deep cavern. Its breath smelt of sweet water and fresh snow. Its words were in keeping with its appearance – polite and formal.

'Your nemesis was as nothing we have ever seen before. It looked strange to the land, alien and ungainly. It could very well have been part of the nightmare that has been ripping innocent souls from life, and casting them into the Realm of Light. Those souls are so shocked, so demented, that we have had to contain them behind a barrier. Their screams are terrible to hear. But if that creature is responsible for the horror, how are you here? You both died complete – you're sane and responsive. How is that? There must be much more to this tale of woe. That fat, black bowl of a creature looked ridiculous, as if a water tub had mated with a cannon, but it was effective enough. It shot you from the sky. An evolved squid might be made to do something similar, but it would look much, much more elegant. Mother nature has never fashioned anything so ugly. It was an insult to the eye. But at least now we know *where* it is, and that might help us learn *what* it is. Understanding might help us find a cure for the poor damned souls we've locked behind that barrier.'

The passenger looked up into the bottomless crystal pools of the ancient's eyes and realised with stone finality that she wasn't experiencing a fever dream after all. This was real. She was dead. Her time in life was over and a new journey had begun. She wondered at her calmness in the face of such an immense transition. She spoke up. Her words, metered by shy formality, sounded strange in her ears.

'What can we do to help you learn more? Those of us here, we are the dead. Surely the world of the living is no longer within our grasp?'

'Not so. We have a voice among the living. She is listened to and trusted there. We shall speak with her and share everything we have learned from you. Now, we must let you go. There are many souls eager to see you again and they have much to teach you about your new world.'

Once the passenger and her pilot were gone, the ancient soul turned to its peers.

'We must tell Medina Bishop the news, and be sure to tell that impetuous elemental it must make doubly sure to protect her. We must preserve her. She is our strongest window into life. Without her we might have to wall those poor, demented souls away from the rest of the Realm for all eternity. That would be a terrible defeat for us and a horrendous fate for them. Unthinkable. Please, my friends, will you pray with me for guidance?'

Another voice rang out: 'Prayer can wait, my friend. First, Shimon, please, will you call the Talker with Spirits without delay?'

## [21]

The bell-like sound of children's laughter is music for the heart, but not when you hear it echoing in an empty room. Medina had been hearing such things for most if not all of her short life, but the sounds only started making sense when Sable first spoke to her from the Realm.

She supposed if she had a best friend it was the slave woman, dead for nearly two hundred years and hanged for murder, who had first whispered to her when she was six-years-old and alone in the world.

'It's okay, honey girl. It's okay to cry. Sable's here with you. You go ahead.'

Her aunt and uncle had welcomed her to their home and done their best for her, but they weren't gifted with parental instinct. They had already found everything they needed in life through their work and each other. Their emotional world had been complete without the complicated addition of a freshly orphaned girl during her most intense developmental stage.

They weren't cruel people and they always ensured she had intellectual stimulus, fun days out, good clothes and nutritious food. What was lacking in her life was something more fundamental, something every child needs for mental and emotional health – a parent's love coupled with that totally absorbed and fascinated delight in sharing everything Medina was discovering about her world. She lacked sharing her joy in climbing her day-to-day mountains and the important little triumphs she achieved. Her day was unimportant; her life lived in a vacuum.

Without knowing why, the little girl felt as if she was always in the way in her adopted home. A bit of a bother. She shrank back to a private place in her heart where she could feel wanted and loved and essential to somebody. Anybody. And then one night she realised even that place was empty. She was alone. Completely alone.

That night in her bed she wept as only a child can weep. She wept as if the world had come to an end and all joy leeched away, leaving nothing behind. She buried her face in her pillow to muffle the sounds of her tears because she didn't want to bother anyone. Her pillow became wet and she could taste the hot salt water drenching her face. Her stomach hurt and her little fists were curled into tight knots of emotional and physical agony.

And then the soft, strange voice spoke into her ear.

'Come on now, little girl. You cry out all that nasty poison in your poor tummy, and then we'll have us a nice little cuddle, shall we?'

Sable came into her life that night and never left. She fully opened the Realm of Light to Medina's talent and made it a place where the girl felt she had real value. Somewhere she belonged. It had been devastating to discover that she could hear and see the loved ones of strangers, but not her own mother and father. It was many years before she could finally accept that fact, and even begin to feel a burgeoning pride in her parents. They were such good people that they had bypassed the first Realm and 'gone on' to a place where she couldn't yet reach them. She had also begun to understood how very special she was. Only a talented few among the living could pull aside the grey curtain and touch the first Realm of the dead. Beyond that there were other places which she couldn't reach and one of those was where her parents had gone. She at first liked to imagine these other places as fitting together like matryoshka nesting dolls, but Sable quickly disabused her of that idea.

'I know the things you mean. I seen them. Dolls inside each other getting smaller and smaller like peeling an onion. Look like skittles or some such, don't they? Well, that don't work. You think the Realm is smaller than the world of the living? No way, honey girl! Nor is the next place or the next or the next or the one after that. And so, it goes on, like pouring fine flour through hundreds of riddles. Each riddle with a finer and ever finer mesh, just sieving away the dirt until finally the blessed soul is clean and fresh, and pure enough to be returned to the bosom of all creation. Each place is as near to the next one as a line drawn by a straight razor, but that skinny wall is tougher to punch through than trying to cut plate steel with a butter knife. People got to die to come here, and they sure got to be made of finer stuff to go on to the next place. And that's the truth of it. On and on and on to glory, or so they tell me. But your mom and dad must have been real special folks to jump straight through two walls at one time. Real special. Wish I could have met them.'

The spirit woman held tight to the childlike form of the woman she had grown to love over the years. They were silent together for a heartbeat, and then Sable brightened.

'But hey, sure! I know you, Medina. And that's a right fine thing too. The best of everything they ever were is right there, right there in you. You want to see your mom and dad? You just go take a good look-see in that mirror any time you like, and they'll be there. Looking right back at you.'

And there was Medina in her hotel room. She was looking in a full-length mirror and comparing herself with the framed photograph in her hand. There they were, her mum and dad: young, in love, and happy. And there she was with them, the white, carefully wrapped blob in her mother's arms. And here she was now, the unique Medina Bishop, Spirit Talker. Her career as a medium had started, almost by accident, in her mid-teens. And she had been kept busy ever since on her ever-widening circuit of small theatres and large churches. She had left school at eighteen with a fistful of the basic qualifications but, despite all her teachers' advice, had never thought of attending college or applying for a job. She had followed her vocation and while doing so learned her stagecraft from friendly, seasoned professionals.

The police work had also been an accident at first, but DI Felicity Chike and others had seen something different in her act that they liked. Chike had introduced Medina to the rarefied world of special CID consultants. By law nothing the medium saw or was told by her spirit contacts could ever be admissible as evidence in court, but her information helped set the tenacious policewoman onto the right path; and old-fashioned detective work would do the rest.

And now here she was in Canada surrounded by strangers who were only just learning what she could do. And they were evidently finding it hard to accept the truth of her talent.

Askuwheteau and Charlotte had already become firm friends, that was true, and Edward Louis, who she planned to join for dinner in an hour's time, was a stalwart. Longknife, however, had acted like a python trying to swallow an adult elephant whole. The woman knew she had a situation on her hands that she couldn't understand – and she knew she needed help – but she was reluctant to involve herself with a talent she couldn't comprehend. Medina wasn't yet on her list of go-to people and 'medium' wasn't listed in RCMP guidelines as a useful occupation. Never mind. Her strange life had given Medina a thick skin when it came to rejection. A Canadian cop with her head up her arse wouldn't leave her crying in her soup, just because she'd been told to go away and let the woman think for a few days.

'Earth colours suit you. They make you even lovelier. Let me cast off these humble robes that I might bathe in the beauty of thine eyes.'

'Fargo! I didn't hear you ask to come in?'

'You already invited me, don't you remember? Once invited the door stays open, at least for here. And anyway, the door to your heart has been properly unlocked by these, me unearthly charms. Much as the key to my love glisters deep in those lovely orbs of yours.'

He came over and examined the photo, taking the hand that held it into his own.

94

'Is that your ma and da? Fine looking couple. You take after your da, but your ma was a real head-turner true enough. May I steal a kiss?'

She chuckled and shook her head. 'I'm going to dinner shortly and I want to shower and get changed. I need a few moments' peace.'

Fargo spun away like a ballet dancer and perched exquisitely on her bed. He laid his right ankle across his left knee, placed his elbows in his lap and folded his hands together before resting his chin on them. He fluttered his long eyelashes at her.

'Please,' he smiled. 'Don't let me stop you.'

She gazed at him for a long second, and then took off her shoes. She stripped slowly until she was naked and then walked into her bathroom. She didn't lock the door. Her shower was large and made of glazed bricks. She entered it through a doorless, L-shaped arrangement and turned on the water. Every inch of her body was quivering with anticipation. She rinsed her hair and added shampoo. She wondered if he needed to be invited into the bathroom and was on the point of crying out when she felt strong slender fingers in her hair.

'Let me do that for you,' he said.

And she could feel his heat. She turned.

...

'You've got your blouse buttoned up all wrong. Are you alright? You look a bit flushed. I like your hair like that, by the way. You look the positive gypsy.'

Edward Louis was on his second drink by the time Medina finally joined him in the bar. The ice had melted in the vodka and slimline tonic he had ordered for her half an hour earlier.

'I lay down for a moment and fell asleep. Sorry, Edward, I'm still a bit woozy. Naps always do that to me. Excuse me a moment.'

She scooted into the powder room and straightened her clothes, realising in the process that she had omitted to wear a bra in her hurry to get ready. She hoped Louis would be a gentleman about it. She judged him to be one of the old-fashioned sorts. She grinned and touched the blush of her cheek. What would he say if he knew? She felt like an alley cat in heat and thought about the last hour with Fargo. Her nipples stood proud and plain against the fabric of her blouse. *This wouldn't do. This wouldn't do at all.*

She took a deep breath and started going through her times tables in her head. She was chanting 'eight eights are sixty-four' before she felt able to rejoin her companion and take a welcome draught from her now room temperature drink.

Louis took her elbow. 'They're holding the table for us. Shall we go?'

They were chatting amiably enough through the meal when Medina realised that Louis was behaving in an unusually strained, distracted fashion. He was making a concerted effort to only look at her eyes, his glass or his plate. It was as if a barrier had been created to steer his vision away from every part of her body below her chin. She smiled. *Bless you, sir*, she thought.

And then she clearly heard the chill voice she had heard before, and she almost dropped her glass of wine.

'Spirit Talker, there has been a development. May we speak with you?'

'Soon,' she said aloud.

'Soon what?' Louis looked baffled.

'Something's happened to "you know where",' she replied. 'And it sounds important.'

'Do you need to go back to your room?'

'No, let's finish our meal and then I'll go up. They say there's been a development. I'm curious of course, but it can wait. Nothing can happen before the morning, no matter what they say.'

She raised her glass. 'Cheers, and by the way, thanks for being an honest to God gentleman. It matters.'

'Cheers and, ah, I couldn't possibly imagine what you mean.' He blushed crimson before offering her a sheepish smile.

## [22]

Cheryl Longknife sat in the driver's seat of her BMW and gazed across at the entrance to her workplace. For the first time in her career she was reluctant to go in. She wanted to go home and make it up with her husband. That morning they had had one of their rare rows – and what was worse, she knew she was in the wrong. Today was their twentieth wedding anniversary. They had made plans for the day, and none of them included her sitting in the Hedderly Road car park while trying to control the stress headache that pounded behind her eyes and threatened to overwhelm her.

Darren, her husband, was a placid, pleasant man unless riled. He was riled that morning. He very pointedly told her he had booked a table for lunch at the 'High Harvest', and if he tried to cancel now they would take twenty-five dollars *each* from his credit card. He had specified the exact same seats by the window overlooking the lake where they had been sitting when he had proposed. He had booked flowers to be brought to the table. What was he meant to do now?

She promised she would do everything in her power to join him.

'I'll be there,' he said, eyes blazing. 'If our marriage means *anything* to you, you'll join me.'

Her marriage meant everything to her. She quivered with frustration and could feel tears sting at her eyes. Her breath felt hot in her mouth. She looked at her watch: eight-fifteen. The table was booked for one-thirty and it would take her twenty minutes to get there from here.

*I don't care if the Lord High Commissioner himself comes in for a chat. I'm out of here at one, sharp.*

But she knew she had to be there, at least for the morning. She had to set wheels in motion even if, for the moment, she didn't know where to point them. And that was the problem. *What was going on?* Since the mass abduction a steady trickle of people had been disappearing from Duck Mountain Provisional Park, including three of her officers and now a helicopter and its crew. There had been no mayday call, not even a squawk, and the several square miles of ancient forest where the A-star 'squirrel' had vanished was off the radar. Literally.

*What is this?* she wondered. *An episode of* The X-Files?

She hadn't slept much the night before. A cascade of nightmare images had flooded through her mind. She had always been praised for her active imagination at school and got good marks for her essays. But now she was a Chief Inspector in the Royal Canadian Mounted Police and imagination had no place in her day. Or her nights.

She squared her shoulders. Something had declared war on Manitoba. Okay, she understood that. But even during war there must be time for lunch and flowers. She had already ruined Darren's surprise, she accepted that, but she was not going to let her work ruin the whole day. She sighed and climbed out of her car.

The entrance doors slid sideways and she strode into the lobby. Parslow smiled weakly at her and then tilted his head across to the long bench on the opposite wall. She turned her head. Inwardly she groaned.

The elfin Bishop, portly Louis and rock-hard Fellows cut their conversation and got to their feet.

'Somebody want to call this meeting to order?'

She looked over her shoulder at the sound of his voice and saw Askuwheteau duck his head in greeting as he entered the station.

'Hi, guys,' he continued. 'Glad to see you.' He walked to her shoulder. 'Chief, ah, look. I'm sorry to a pain so early in your day, but can I steal ten minutes of your time?'

She studied him, then the other three. She took a deep breath, sighed, then straightened the line of her suit jacket.

'Parslow, I'm taking conference room A until twelve-thirty at the latest. Organise coffee and biscuits please. Pastries?'

She fired that question at the small group. Everyone shook their head.

'No? Fine. No pastries. Now I know you guys aren't secretly undercover cops. Is sergeant Rawkins in yet?' This was directed at the desk officer.

'Yes, ma'am.'

'Good. Ask her to join us, please.'

She moved to the door and held it open while the four filed past her.

Askuwheteau said, 'I know the way. Okay if I lead?'

'Please, Watcher. By the way, help yourselves from the water cooler. It's not much but it's wet, and it's all we've got until the coffee gets here.'

Rawkins had met the constable in the corridor and she brought the coffee tray into the room. From somewhere Parslow had found a plate of doughnuts. They remained untouched throughout the morning.

Longknife took a seat and crossed her arms.

'I'm leaving here today at one o'clock. Unless you people have come to tell me there's a missile strike due to hit the High Harvest by the lake at one-thirty I'll be gone in... four hours. I've got some questions myself, but they can wait. Okay. Who's first?'

Medina said, 'Mr Fellows was already here when we arrived.'

'Me first? Right. Okay. Chief, I've been thinking about what I've seen. Those things nearly got me twice and, you know, I've seen some good men go down without a fight. Really good men. I'm sorry to say this but I think we're out of our depth here. I think we should be talking to CANSOFCOM. Watcher's here to back me up on this. I went to see him last night and we had a good talk about the situation. Now, we all know the Dauphin RCMP is an excellent group of men and women when they're pitched up against something normal, but what's up there isn't normal. It's nothing like normal. Special needs call for special solutions and we believe you need to call in Special Operations.'

'Very well, Mr Fellows. I hear you. You agree, Watcher?'

'I do, Chief Longknife. I hate to see it that way, but I think Marshall here has a point. We need help.'

'I see. Ms Bishop, Mr Louis... can you bear with us for a brief while?'

They nodded their assent.

'I think it would be useful to find out a little more about just what we're dealing with. Sergeant, could you ask Mr Webb to join us, please?'

Ten minutes later Spider Webb loped into the room and shook hands with everyone before folding himself onto a seat. Introductions over, he sat like a fidgeting child. His chair seemed too small to support his long limbs.

'Mr Webb, I was wondering if you had any results back from the Mercedes bus?'

'I'll say. That spiky tentacle thing in the ceiling was still moving. I had to pin the bastard to a board to stop it thrashing around. It's safely in a bottle now, nice and tight – screw-top lid.' He blinked rapidly. 'Drowned it in formalin. It's stopped wriggling now.'

'Thank you, Mr Webb. And what were your results?'

'Inconclusive, I'm afraid. Apart from the DNA profiling of course.'

He sat quietly twitching, while everyone else craned forward.

'Yes? And?'

'Oh, sorry. Ah, right! Of course, yeah, you don't know. Stupid of me. I haven't written my official report yet, have I? Dumb. Trying to work it out, you know? Thing is, ah, well... it's human, yeah, human. Male, actually. It's been modified somehow, but that's what it is alright. *Quelle surprise* huh? Who would have thought it?'

Longknife squinted hard at him. 'Human? Did you say human? Are you sure?'

'Ninety-nine-point-nine followed by a long tail of nines. I'm not even *that* sure about some of my customers, but I'm dead certain that's a sample of human boy tissue we took from the bus. I've got some good people looking at it right now, which is why I've been a bit, you know, quiet. Specialist guys. They want to know which circus I got it from. Two of them identified it as yeti, yeah? And they don't even work together. Birds of a feather I guess. Hmm?'

As Webb returned to his basement 'parlour', the group sat quietly to collect their thoughts. Longknife looked at her watch. Eleven a.m. already – where was the morning going?

'Very well, food for thought there. It's going to take some digesting though. Ms Bishop, what shocking revelation are *you* going to share with us this morning?'

Medina stood up, which made little difference to her height but gave her an ounce more confidence.

'Well, Chief Longknife. We wondered if you'd like to know what happened to your helicopter.'

## 23

The Chief kept to her timetable. After she had left the station in a marked hurry, the four new comrades in adversity were happily joined for lunch by Rawkins, who told them she knew a place within walking distance where they were certain to get good eats without breaking the bank.

The place she took them to was clean and comfortable with big windows overlooking Main Street. Plain wooden furniture was enlivened with red and white checked tablecloths, and white stucco walls held large framed townscapes that looked distinctly Mediterranean. It was already busy and the air was filled with a pleasant hubbub of voices that was the sure sign of good food and contented customers. Aromas from the kitchen were spicy and mouth-wateringly tempting. They asked if they could have a table for five and admitted they hadn't booked in advance. They were told they were in luck.

The strikingly pretty waitress who led them to a table for six was patently intrigued by the cultural diversity of the group. She cleared away the unwanted set of cutlery before bringing them their menus and a complimentary jug of cold water, all the while looking from one face to another. In the end her curiosity got the better of her.

'Excuse me?'

They looked up at her expectantly.

'Sorry,' she giggled. 'Are we being filmed for something?' She almost stumbled over her words. 'It's just that if we are... well, you see, I need to know for... you know... my class and all!'

Louis responded in his most sparkly, avuncular fashion. 'And what class is that, my dear?'

She beamed at him with her perky, talented smile.

'Juliette Messé's School of the Liberal and Dramatic Arts. You know? Juliette Messé? The actress? Anyway, I'm just starting my second year, you know? We've been, you know, *told* that if we had even the smallest chance of getting in front of the, you know, camera, we should be sure to talk about it in class afterwards. And this would be so, you know, *cool*, to be filmed with you, ah, you guys. You know? Oh, this is *so* cool.'

She made a happy little bouncing motion with her knees together. Under her well-fitted, traditional waitress outfit of white blouse and tight-fitting black pencil skirt, her curves performed their own little bounces in evidently firm and very diverting sympathy.

Fellows asked, 'What gave you the clue? That we were, you know, being, ah, you know, filmed?'

Both Medina and Rawkins fought the temptation to kick him under the table, while also fighting the broad grins that tugged at their mouths. The girl stifled a shriek and hastily looked around, then performed another of her trademark bunny hops. She put her fingers to her lips and made a zipping motion.

'My lips are *so* sealed. But it's, you know, brilliant! You guys just *so* fit the bill. And you look *so* natural together, you know? *So* cool. I'll be back. *So* cool.'

Askuwheteau looked at Medina, who was shaking with silent laughter.

'You know what she's on about, don't you? Somebody told you.'

'Yeah, her grandmother. She loves her dearly, but also calls her "the prettiest air head who ever learned to walk, talk and breathe at the same time but never learned to think while doing it". She should do well in the chorus. Apparently, she can do the vertical splits. I'm told there's quite a call for that sort of thing in the legitimate theatre.'

'So, what the hey was our future Gypsy Rose talking about?'

She told them in a giggling whisper, and the resultant shout of laughter drew some queer looks from other tables.

Medina's theory proved right. Their waitress was very attentive and (you know) charming, but had obviously not been able to keep her (you know) exciting news to herself. During their meal, random members of staff and diners shuffled to their table and asked if they could take selfies with the ensemble. Medina had enjoyed a taste of the celebrity life while on tour, so she was unfazed. The others kept looking at each other with wild smiles on their faces.

And then a narrow-shouldered, black-coated young Hasidic Jew, complete with beard, hat and payot side curls, hustled into the restaurant with a girl in tow who was carrying a state-of-the-art digital camera mounted on a Steadicam. With them came a Muslim youth in traditional dress. The odd trio made a bee-line to their table and the two young men grinned knowingly at the group.

The Muslim said, 'If you want to properly represent Dauphin's diversity, you need us in there too. Do you mind?'

Without waiting for an answer, one crouched down between Medina and Askuwheteau and the other between Askuwheteau and Rawkins. The girl began filming, recording them talking, smiling and embracing. Their waitress gave them almost constant attention, and her smile found the camera with unerring accuracy.

Once they had finished their meal, which was excellent, Fellows asked the waitress for the bill and everyone shook hands with the Jew and the Muslim – who then strode out arm-in-arm under the lens of their camerawoman. That was when a massively fat, bald man, who smelled strongly of cumin and Hugo Boss aftershave, appeared at their table. He held up their bill before their eyes.

'*I* – I am Vasyl,' he announced to the room. '*This* – this is my restaurant, and *this* – this is your bill.'

He tutted and shook his head with an exaggerated gesture that set several chins into energetic motion.

'What shall I do with this bill? It is a quandary, a problem. For, you see, your money is no good here today. No good at all.'

With a dramatic gesture, he tore the narrow sheet of paper in two, then again, and again, and a third time. He continued until he held a handful of paper scraps and then threw them into the air. Paper rained down on the table like a brief shower of confetti. A small, dark woman with a large camera worked her way through applauding diners until she was at the end of their table. She caught every pose as Vasyl placed his bear-like arms around first Medina and then Rawkins. He kissed each of them on the cheeks and then shook each man's hand in a two-fisted grip. He indicated the photographer.

'Please meet Alyona, my good lady wife. Like me she is Ukrainian... and now, please. Is there a Chinese person here? Or will we have to send out for one?'

He laughed at his own joke. A tiny grey wraith of a woman pushed her way to the table and bowed gently, before punching the restaurateur hard on his arm.

She snarled, 'Watch it with the racist cracks, buster! But I'm in.'

'Then we are complete. Please, madam, would you join with us? And can everyone else please do their best to get behind us?'

There was a melee that lasted several minutes, following which Alyona took several shots. Vasyl held a different pose for each one. He stood beside each of them and made a point of kissing the Chinese woman before, at last, the ordeal was truly over. They fought their way to the exit through a barrage of handshakes, hugs and kisses, the big man behind them every step of the way.

When they finally reached the outside, Vasyl stood on the sidewalk to wave them off. He seemed to float on the paving stones like a happily tethered, giant balloon. He remained rooted at his post, arm high in the air, until they had turned a corner and, with a final wave, vanished from his sight.

Askuwheteau smeared tears of laughter across his cheeks.

He said, 'Last night I thought we were living in a nightmare and now... now I don't know what to call it.'

Louis offered, 'Do you think I might get some of those photographs from Mr Vasyl's wife? This would make a great story for the London free papers.'

Fellows chuckled. 'You think? What would you call it? "Restaurant fooled out of lunch bill by five con artists"? Maybe we should play it down.'

Medina grinned and shook her head. 'Too late, Marshall. As soon as those guys with the camerawoman came in, we were doomed. They're obviously a pair of semi-professional self-promoters. And somebody's going to get paid for the tip-off. We'll be all over YouTube by now, posted on social media, you name it. It'll go viral in hours if not sooner.

'Okay. Our waitress, Rosa Lee by the way and that's her real name I kid you not, thought we were a stunt for Cultural Diversity Celebration week. Is there such a thing? No? Well, I bet you there will be by tomorrow. Did we tell her that's what we were? No. Did we ask for all the fuss? No. Is Vasyl going to complain if his place becomes more famous than Las Vegas for the next week? Of course not. Will Rosa kick off about her cute little bod getting splashed all over the internet? No way! She'll have a fan club by Friday. But never mind. We really needed something to lighten the mood and that was a peach of a way to do it.'

Askuwheteau sobered. 'You're right. We needed a bit of time out. But those things are still up there on Duck Mountain and you tell us they're still killing people. We have to put a stop to them somehow, anyhow!'

Fellows shrugged his powerful shoulders. 'Chief said CANSOFCOM will be here tomorrow. If Canadian Special Ops can't swing the deal, I say it's best if we all get the hell out of Dodge. But that won't happen. I know what those guys can do. That bunch of alien weirdos'll be just a bug smear no more than an hour after they land. You mark my words. Whatever they are, those things are toast.'

## 24

Of all the spirits in the Realm, two ranked high among the wisest. They had once been a man and a woman, and although their time on Earth was separated by centuries, they were related by blood. Deep concern weighted the woman's gentle voice.

'They fear the barrier is failing.'

'Then it has to be reinforced somehow. We cannot afford for it to fail. The entire Realm will be driven insane by that terrible noise from those poor devils.'

'Come and see for yourself. Perhaps you'll be able to advise the elementals.'

'Advise them? I would as lief tell a miller how to grind wheat or a baker how to bake bread. Tell me, have you ever been to their city?'

'Scytaer Faehl? No, but I hear tell it's quite beautiful.'

'If we find answers to our current problems, you must go there. I will take you. "Beautiful" is too clumsy a word. Scytaer Faehl is more than beautiful, much more. Try to envisage how a city might look if it was built by ancient, wise creatures who are masters of all the elements at their command. No, sorry, don't even try. It would be pointless. You're an intelligent woman, I know, but the task would be beyond even your imagination. I've been there, spent time there, and I struggle to find words to describe it. We need a new language, something finer and purer. Our tongue is too crude; it becomes ashes in my mouth. It's too coarse and unwieldy to describe a place so, so... it's no good. You'll just have to see it for yourself. See how that race of insane geniuses brought together earth, fire, water and air to build a city where everything works in perfect harmony to create such exquisite...'

The harsh planes of his face softened as he remembered.

'...Scytaer Faehl is a poem come alive in the place between worlds. The sun warms it by day and the werelight of the Realm colours its nights with silver. Some people think of the fey elementals as mischievous clowns, but that's an illusion. They're so very easy to misunderstand. They are an ancient, noble people, and they see all existence as something to be nurtured and cherished. But they also see the humour in it. They are not like us. Even that playful lunatic Fargo has an awareness of creation that would render me a drooling imbecile, and he has command of many rare powers honed over long, though admittedly lively, millennia.'

He offered his companion a rare smile. 'They enchant me, Maryam, and fill me with awe in equal measure. They are like the finest music made flesh. Or whatever you call that fabulous stuff they use for flesh. Enough of this. You say we must go? Come on then, call swifts. We have no more time to dawdle. Let us see for ourselves the failings in this wall of theirs.'

A pair of elegant shapes swooped from the sky at Maryam's call, winged creatures fashioned as if from the air itself. The ancient called Suleiman ben Duwad settled himself onto the seat between the shoulders of one of them, crossing his legs under its pommel with practiced poise. His companion did the same, demurely arranging her skirts. They pulled the layer of elastic tissue stretched between the beasts' shoulders up over their knees and gripped tight with both hands. The swifts took to the air with a few powerful beats of their transparent wings and, long necks straining forward with the sheer joy of flight, wheeled high above the landscape of the Realm of Light.

As they gained height, the land unfolded and spread out below them. They could see right to the curving rim of rainbows that marked its distant boundaries. If the outer skin of planet Earth with all its lands, seas and mountains had been peeled and laid down like a rug within the Realm, it would take up less than a tenth of its surface. And most of it would blend in very well, but not all. Polluted urban scenes of traffic-bound chaos could never find a place in that garden of peace. The thick stench of fossil fuels would never foul its air. In the Realm of Light, first circle of the dead, nothing had ever died to provide oil or coal. There were no plastics. Life for the dead was simple and rich, dignified and full. Even among the thick rooted dwellings of half-formed mud things in the mangrove swamps, there was loveliness to be found for those who had eyes to see it.

Suleiman marvelled at the breath-taking vista – as he did during every flight.

Excepting Scytaer Faehl, he thought it the most perfect place he had ever seen. Every mile of it natural and richly painted with crystal colours under a sunless, silver sky. It was an endless tapestry of fresh greens, limpid blues and glowing white snows on the mountain tops. The Realm was the kind of landscape the very best of Earth might aspire to, and it was a place genius poets might hope to visit during opium-induced dreams.

His heart swelled with emotion. He loved this land. Then the swifts banked to the left and ahead of him he could see the shining wall enclosing the poor, demented souls. It was a swirling cylinder, seemingly constructed from mother of pearl streaked with complex veins of bright platinum. The width of a vast arena, its base circled the peak of a steep hill in an area of simple savannah, and it lanced up like the haft of a spear into the sky.

Suleiman yelled across to his companion. 'Must it be so tall? The pressures on that wall must be immense. It looks like an axle between the wheels of a world.'

She shouted back, 'The demented enter the Realm from every direction and at every level without rhyme or reason. The mentors must direct them here as swiftly as possible, no matter what height they arrive. It has been made as tall as the Realm because it has to be.'

Closer to, the containment looked less like a spear and more like an immense length of marbled gut, pulsing with a slow peristaltic rhythm. The swifts circled around and down the length of it and landed with a complex flurry of wings. All the way down, Suleiman became aware of a growing sense of nausea which seemed to become stronger as he got closer to the construction. He gazed around, but failed to identify the cause. He stepped down from his swift which made soft, contented noises when he patted its neck and thanked it. Then both lovely creatures were gone, spinning away as if gratefully accepting the freedom of the sky. Suleiman clasped his hands to his midriff in discomfort. Maryam nodded.

'Sorry, I should have warned you. Are you feeling sick?'

'I don't understand what I feel. Some kind of vibration. It feels very odd.'

Maryam indicated the slow-moving material of the containment barrier.

'They say micro fissures in the fabric of the barrier condense and concentrate the sounds from in there. You can't hear it, but the whole sky around here is screaming like an Irish Banshee.'

A fresh voice said, 'You're lucky you can't hear it. A Banshee makes good dancing music by comparison. Real toe-tapping stuff. Old school.'

A woman walked to their side. The russet and rich earth colours of her clothes and her wild mass of auburn hair told Suleiman exactly what the newcomer was, but he didn't recognise her.

He bowed and spoke formally. 'I thought I knew all of the fey working on this project, and I feel I should know such a fine example of the elder race, but your name escapes me. Forgive the poor memory of an old soul. And, may I say, you are very lovely, my lady.'

'And you are very gracious, Suleiman ben Duwad. I'm told you also appreciate the finer points of architecture. But tell me now, why have you not Sublimed?'

The sudden question caught him out and he was momentarily lost for words. Then the elemental woman put a hand to her temple. A frown creased her fine features and her eyes narrowed in pain.

'Please, will you walk with me?' she said. 'I can't hear myself think for all this pesky shrieking. There's a shelter in the lee of this hill where perhaps I can collect what little wits I have left to me. And hopefully your poor belly will settle as well. You too, Maryam, daughter of Imran. Let's get ourselves out of this imperfect storm.'

It was a calm, still day with just a refreshing breath of a breeze, but the elemental bent her head and shoulders as if forcing herself into a full gale.

'Not much further,' she spat through gritted teeth.

And then Suleiman felt it happen, a great release of tension as if a weight had been lifted both from his guts and from behind his eyes. He found he could breathe more easily. Maryam blinked and sighed, drawing a hand through her hair.

The earth-coloured beauty sat on a kind of grassy bench set in what looked like a natural, shell-like contour in the side of the hill. She grinned.

'That's a relief. My teeth were fair set to cracking, I was grinding so hard. You know something? You people surprise me. Especially you two and others like you. You could Sublime and get yourselves away from all this shite any time you like, but you choose to stay. Now why is that? My name's Rowan, by the way. I believe you knew my dam, May?'

The pair muttered assent. They were finding Rowan's blunt way of speaking a touch unnerving.

'Look at the pair of yez. You've more of jewellery in you now than human, lovely though ye are. You could Sublime to the next circle any time you like, so you could. So tell me – why don't you?'

Maryam looked at Suleiman, her glowing, golden eyes large under a haze of misty silver hair. Her face held an expression of gentleness, love and compassion. His was a steely aspect of almost pure intelligence. Dark brows frowned over ebon eyes that gazed out from an intense face. His profile was all flat planes and his mouth set in a firm, thin line while he pondered the question.

'We don't walk away from problems. We work until we find solutions.'

Rowan studied him closely. 'Well find a solution to this problem then. We built the barrier with everything the Realm could offer – and a few things it hasn't got – and it isn't enough. It's beginning to leak. Those poor demented souls in there are literally screaming the house down, and when those walls finally go we won't be able to raise them again. So, Suleiman the wise, what do you suggest we do about it?'

The man stayed mute for a long second, his eyes veiled in thought. He was thinking about millers, bakers and the aching perfection of Scytaer Faehl. And then he squared his shoulders. His face reflected his resolve.

'We must find a way to strengthen the barrier,' he replied. 'And I think I know just how that might be done.'

## 25

'Marshall? Hey, little terrier! That you?'

'Sergeant? Sarge! It's you! Hey, Klosky, you beautiful old mutant. How you doing?'

'Not so much of the sergeant, dude. It's Captain Klosky now. See the pips?'

'No.'

'Exactly! But you could always see the stripes!'

The two burly men pounded at each other's shoulders and shared a hug of genuine affection.

Klosky said at close quarters, 'You still walking around with rocks in your head?'

'Yeah! And you're still eating that Polska garlic sausage for breakfast!'

'Growing boy. Healthy appetite.'

Captain Klosky topped Fellows by at least eight inches and his shoulders had athletic width to match his height. He was muscled in a hard-trained fashion and looked exactly what he was: strong and fast. They had seen action together and learned they could depend on each other. Fellows couldn't stop grinning.

'How are the other guys from our SOF?'

Klosky grinned back. 'Quiet as ever.'

The troops of CANSOFCOM were known as the *Silent Professionals*.

'This op's an S.O. Arrowhead. What the hell you been scaring up in them thar hills? Something's got CSOR Petawawa so fired up they had to fetch me out of bed and pack me into the back of that nasty old whirlybird bucket of a Griffon. Had me a good book to read too, and I had to leave it behind. Don't know now if I'll ever find out if Amelia will discover Lord Rupert's true feelings for her. What if she settles for that cheating bastard of a love thief, Matthew? What'll happen to her poor old widowed mother then?'

Canada's Special Operations force still used the Bell CH-146 Griffon helicopter, which was claimed by independent observers to be under-powered, under-armed and plain uncomfortable, but was regarded by the ground troops with a degree of affection. It could take a great deal of punishment and the crews of three were claimed to have ice water for blood.

The SO troop's motto was *Viam Inveniemus* – "We will find a way", but the Griffon crews reminded them (after a post-operational beer or two):

'Yeah, but we're the ones who have to get you there and bring you back afterwards. On a stretcher if we have to!'

Two olive drab helicopters had quietly flown into a reserved section of the Lt. Col. W. G. (Billy) Barker, VC airport just before ten in the morning. Marshall, Bishop, Askuwheteau and Rawkins were among the reception committee as the best witness consultants available. Bishop had been invited on the strict understanding it was only on a temporary and honorary basis – and subject to her proving herself sane; a subject Chief Longknife was taking a rain check on for the time being.

Louis had been dragooned into continuing his research in the city library, despite his eagerness to 'mix in with the fray at the front line'. It had been decided he would 'just be along for the ride' on a mission where it was best to 'keep it neat and petite' and to 'cut the flab to the bone'. He wasn't told any of that. Bishop had left him to his breakfast after wishing him well with his research and planting a kiss on his cheek.

Rawkins was happy to share what little she knew, but wouldn't be tagging along on the mission. She debriefed to Klosky and suffered his long quizzical stare when she described their attackers. She defused an awkward situation by asking, 'Hey. How come a fine, big black man like you ended up with a name like Klosky?'

He shrugged. 'Guess my momma married a man called Klosky. I grew up calling him Dad. My sisters take after him, but I take after mom. Especially the moustache. How come a fine, upstanding black woman like you is wearing a police uniform?'

'My husband likes me to bring the handcuffs home at the weekends. And you know something? The uniform comes right off.'

They high-fived each other.

Marshall was told to leave his gun in the pick-up and was handed a C7A2 assault rifle.

Klosky commented, 'No need to ask, man. I know you know how to use it.'

Then he turned to the First Nations man.

'What you packing?'

Askuwheteau walked over to his car and fetched his weapon from under a blanket in his boot. He brought it back to the captain and handed it over.

Klosky smiled. 'Nice piece. Ruger American Rifle Magnum. Stop a moose with a single shot. How many rounds?

'Three.'

'You ever handled an assault rifle?'

111

'I could tell you, but I'd have to shoot you.'

He rolled up his sleeve and Klosky admired a slightly faded tattoo of a feathered tomahawk with a scroll across its handle. The scroll contained the legend *Viam Inveniemus*.

'Good enough for me, soldier. Put the piece back and grab a C7. By the way, why a tomahawk?'

'I'm Cree! What would you expect, a basketball?'

The big man was still grinning when he turned his attention on Medina Bishop. Even after squatting down on his heels, they still weren't quite eye-to-eye.

'Well,' he said, 'you must be the new, individual, Weight Watchers-sized portion. I'm Klosky. Who you, little lady?'

Medina leaned closer to his muscular face. 'I'm the little lady who has three things to tell you. One: I know precisely where the bad guys are and I can lead you to them. Two: Red Babs says you still can't tell a book by its cover. Three: I can fire a C7A2 when lying down. Standing up, I tend to fall over backwards. Not enough mass. Name's Medina Bishop, but you can call me Ms Medina Bishop for making stupid sizeist remarks. I won't take a poke at you for being gay and you don't take a poke at me for being small. Neither fact matters a damn in the real grown-up world! Deal?'

Klosky sat back on his butt as if pushed.

'Whoof! Girl, you manage to punch above your weight and below the belt at the same time. I guess I'd rather have you in my tent pissing out than outside pissing in. Glad to meet you. How d'you know about Babs?'

'You two didn't get on. You never thought women should be at the front line, not even as medical personnel. You changed your mind when you heard she'd been killed by a roadside IED. It wasn't the bomb that killed her. She was speared by a long leg bone blown out of her driver. If she hadn't thrown herself over the patient in the back of the ambulance, she would probably have been okay. The patient survived, the doctor she was working with survived – another brave woman by the way – and even the driver survived, what's left of him. Only Red Babs was unlucky enough to be killed by that stupid bomb made from cat shit, compost and tin cans held together with string. But she's alright now. She sends her best and says she'll see you soon. But hopefully not too soon.'

Fellows leaned down and offered his friend a hand. He tugged him back to his feet and dusted him down. The giant glared at the tiny woman in confused silence.

Fellows explained, 'Medina's unique, big fellah. Whatever it is she does and how she does it, well frankly... I just don't know. She's famous over in Britain. People pay good money to get a helping of what she just did to you. They queue up for it. Hey, but hold on there. What she said just then. You really gay?'

'What of it?'

'Nothing. Hey, Watcher, you still trying to resolve those sexual issues of yours?'

'Nah, Wikimak told me I'm straight and who am I to argue with her? We've been married nearly twenty years; I guess she ought to know.'

Klosky shook his head and sighed. 'Okay. Let's get this job done and get out of this madhouse. Watcher, Marshall and Ms Medina Bishop, you're with me. Henderson, Lou and Perry with us. The rest of you guys, you're in the other bird. Let's go get it done.'

Medina stopped him. 'You seem worried about the kind of guns people are carrying. Are we going in on the ground?'

The big man pointed at a brutal looking weapon mounted to the front of the helicopter's big side door.

'Ms Bishop, I'd like you to meet a man's best friend. That there piece of ordnance is a Dillon M134D Gatling gun, and that makes it just about the finest small calibre defence suppression weapon available to a working stiff like me. It's a six-barrelled, electrically-driven machine gun chambered with 7.62mm NATO and it fires at a fixed rate of 3,000 shots per minute. Gatling guns typically feed from a 3,000 or 4,000-round magazine. They are capable of long periods of continuous fire without threat or damage to the weapon, making them an excellent choice for defensive suppression.'

'It shoots stuff up, yes?'

'I seen what it can do. Yeah, it shoots shit up and chews it to tiny little pieces. We'll use that from the air if we can, but I believe it's always best to be prepared.'

He showed her his bracelet. What she had at first taken to be charms she realised were small pieces of polished metal.

He told her, 'Each piece comes from a different vehicle that tried to either shoot us down or was being a bully in the playground. We kicked their asses and I like to keep souvenirs.'

'Wonder what you'll get this time?'

He helped her climb up into the Griffon. 'Ms Bishop, I honestly don't care so long as I get home afterwards. I just got to find out what's happening with that fool girl Amelia! You know how it is.'

## 26

For the first time in four hundred and forty-five million years, the ship's thrusters had finally been prised free from their stone prison. The shell of rock directly overhead was almost but not quite thin enough for break-out, and the process of loosening its belly from its petrified bed was nearly complete. For the first time since its burial in the seabed, the ship's mind dared hope it might soon be released.

Soon it would see the open sky again, and the stars. Soon it would be free to go home to the vast, emerald continents and forest cities of Inigaia. Inigaia where it had been born and where the ship had been grown around its infant mind so long ago. Inigaia, the memories of which had buoyed the ship mind during the worst of its terrible incarceration in the lonely darkness. It would hear once more the haunting call of the kvult in the emergent forest canopies, high above the civilised levels. It would see the slender, blue-black elegance of its creators, the Inigaian people. It took a few moments of personal time away from monitoring the labours around it and soaked itself in fond memories of home.

The ship's current crew and tool units were but crude approximations of the dominant race on its home planet. The Inigaian race had evolved from an ancient lizard-like creature. They had long powerful legs and four skilful tool-using limbs, which depended from delicate yet strong shoulders. From wrist to wrist and down to the ankle on each side of their bodies stretched a sensitive layer of tough and flexible skin, supported by extremely long fifth fingers on all four hands, each of which had a thick, curved talon at the end. These allowed Inigaians to take long, gliding flights around their arboreal home and cling to branches like bats.

Those forests had once been alive with birdsong, and many brightly feathered species had flickered through the branches across the great continent. No longer. Although most of the long-tailed avian species had easily overmatched the dark Inigaian fliers with darting, aerial flair, they had eventually been hunted to the point of extinction. Only a barely viable breeding group had been husbanded, kept alive under spacious skynets for the sake of their colour, their song, and to serve as the main course during rare celebration meals.

The art of flying had become vital to Inigaian culture. They mated in the air and performed important rituals there. When their leaders became too feeble to fly, they would be shepherded into one of the large and strong yet super-light kernels of the kraavel nut, which were kept polished to a deep ruby shine for the purpose. They would then be ushered into the air above the canopy, escorted on their final journey by a phalanx of their strongest aides. And there the Ka-Anit ceremony would be performed.

To a song of celebration, the aged personage's veins would be opened with great reverence and their blood given back to the forest. When the final drop of blackness had spilled, the kraavel nut kernel was flipped over and the corpse let fall. It would crash like a broken tool unit to the forest floor, twisting and bouncing through the thick limbs and foliage of the layered canopy – down into the looping vines and roiling insects of the dank understory. If it wasn't caught up by branch, bough or vine the body would eventually strike the soft, friable soil and matted debris at the base of the mighty tree trunks.

Ground level was a hot, dry, sunless place, and bitterly sour smelling. The air was thick with a choking miasma of decay. The corpse would arrive like a spinning missile and pound into the ground, driving a deep crater in the dead leaves, fungi, mosses and soil. Its final reward after years of service to its people would be to end up shattered at the bottom of a hole; discarded in a twisted tangle of broken limbs, torn wings and ruptured thorax, its bloodless organs flung out and exposed to the rank air.

The forest floor was home to herds of fat praxel stock, a bloated, pallid and almost blind wormlike creature which provided the principal source of protein in the Inigaian diet. The praxel was a noted vegetarian, except when it got the chance to gorge on carrion meat. Praxel farmers would often find a herd of the creatures happily snuffling around near the distinctive scar of a Ka-Anit crater. When praxels were about, the crater would invariably be empty. This was the traditional sign that the personage had been accepted as worthy and subsumed back into the fabric of the forest. The fact that the praxels' snouts were smeared with black fluid and that shreds of chewed wing leather might be found wedged between their big incisors was ignored. Farmers also accepted that praxel meat from any animal harvested from around the fall site after a Ka-Anit ceremony would taste all the sweeter. This was considered a tasty gift of gratitude from the forest.

The planet had no factories. Homes, tools and even spacecraft were grown using sophisticated arboreal technology. Inigaia was mineral-poor and centuries had been devoted to creating ships that could travel off-planet, survey other worlds and bring back the mineral wealth they found there.

The people of Inigaia had no desire to personally explore space. They loved their home and the rich lives they enjoyed there. They even regarded their planet's great oceans with deep distrust. Life under the salty waves might just as well have been in an alternative dimension for all it meant to the city dwellers. Space was a far more attractive option; it was merely an extension to the art of flying. So long as no Inigaian was required to visit there.

The next great development opened Inigaian eyes to a whole new universe. Called the Way Station project, components for a great hyperspace portal were grown in the forest and then assembled off-planet by remotely operated tool units. It was designed to be the key tool in a new initiative that, if successful, would increase the planet's mineral wealth by opening new pathways to ever more planets. It would take advantage of a purely theoretical phenomenon Inigaia's most advanced physicists described as 'spatial branchways'.

Once complete, the Way Station was anchored firmly within the gravity well of the home system's star and activated by the crews of two elderly mining ships. Both ships instantly disappeared and then re-appeared a few hours later. They returned with tales of strange new worlds and distant star systems. It seemed the theorists were correct: the universe at large was now open for business.

When the ship crash-landed on Earth it had been a brand-new, state-of-the-art craft. Smarter and larger than its predecessors, it had nearly exhausted the planet's mineral reserves. At its heart was a mighty storage facility in which it was hoped she would bring back five times her own weight in precious metals: iron, copper, gold and silver, lead and titanium. So much depended on her.

Even now she would not be going home empty-handed. On her way inwards she had mined tonnes of metal from the belt of tumbling rocks further out from the system's white dwarf star. If only she had ignored the intense blue orb of Earth and remained out in the harmless vacuum of space, she could have escaped hundreds of millions of years of misery. But all her sensors had lit up like spark flies on a rare moonless night at first sight of the blue planet. And she just had to take a closer look. Had to.

With a sudden shock the ship mind realised the exact parallels between her fall from the sky into the clinging seabed and the Ka-Anit ceremony. This alien world had attempted to subsume her! It had tried to leech away her precious minerals and keep them for itself – and it had failed. She was made from infinitely superior stuff to this foul place of mud and water.

Hers was an emerald world of leaf and wood – a world of tall ancient trees with trunks hundreds of feet thick grown by custom into dwelling places and workshops; a paradise woven by Inigaian ingenuity. Through her crew's eyes she had seen the stunted, infant growths around her cave and regarded them with disdain. Mud, water and shrubs. Such a sickly place. Even indigenous slave materials were no match for her home planet's kvult beast. They were made of stronger, superior stuff too. She was alive because this planet couldn't devour her. She was too rich a morsel for its puny stomach.

With a sense of growing pride, the ship mind called her crew back to their posts. They clambered over and around the buttresses and stanchions of her interior and slotted themselves deep into their work stations. She made them run through full systems checks. The Finder sent her a short message of greeting. It told her it had already calculated the route back to the Way Station and from there – home. *Home*.

In the cave, tool units were clearing away stone and polishing her sensors ready for flight. A thrill of joy coursed through her which was picked up by crew members and tool units alike. They were all brought to an exquisite peak of pleasure the like of which none had ever experienced. Some became bedewed with a salty exudate which excited the interest of those around them. They were poised on the cusp of a spontaneous orgy of mutual enjoyment that might hold up the ship's project for hours if not days. She upbraided herself for her stupidity.

And then she sensed two large clusters of precious metals flying straight towards her hiding place at high speed, and her heart sank. This looked very bad. Very bad indeed. Her voice lashed out and stripped away her minions' burgeoning lust. Chastised, they meekly accepted new orders.

# [27]

The flight to Duck Mountain took just over twenty-five minutes. Medina was strapped onto the centre of a canvas-cushioned metal bench which was designed for a bigger behind than hers, and seemed intent on grinding away her pelvic bones. She was wearing a huge helmet which made her look even smaller and more frail, and she was talking into a microphone that fed directly to the chopper crew and troopers.

She was channelling precise directions from Zack Willis, the dead pilot of the crashed A Star 'Squirrel' police helicopter. Those who could both hear and see her kept casting bemused glances towards her diminutive and evidently female frame. The voice on the comm, however, was calm, precise and very male.

All three civilians had been seated on the inside of the Griffon, a soldier seated either side of them. Askuwheteau and Fellows were wearing bullet-proof body armour; Medina wasn't. It didn't come in 'petite' as Perry, the task force armourer, had informed her.

'If any firing starts, sit on your helmet, curl your legs up on the bench and make yourself as small as possible – no offence intended.'

'None taken,' she'd replied.

And now her eyes were shut and she was deaf to the jolting rattle of the Griffon's flight. Her eyes and ears were those of a dead man killed more than twenty-four hours earlier.

'You're looking for a thing like a big black pot. It's like a witches' cauldron made from some weird material that looks a lot like leather. I didn't see it very clearly before it shot me down. It packs one hell of a punch.'

Zack was still explaining what the waste-clearing tool looked like when the two choppers cleared the lake and roared over the tree line. The cave was directly before them.

The pilot blurted, 'There's nothing there.'

Zack shouted back, 'There has to be. Be very careful.'

The lead chopper suddenly folded around its centre as if hit by a massive hammer. It spiralled from the sky. There was no sound of weaponry and no hint of a warning.

In Klosky's craft, everyone remained silent, eyes straining. Then Henderson shouted and pointed.

'There – fuck me! There, there it is.'

118

Perry, the gunner, saw the strange creature in a clearing and instantly opened fire. The waste disposal unit-cum-Howitzer and the two smaller tool units frantically trying to reload it disappeared in a hail of shattering cannon shells. They were torn to shreds. Then, as if obeying a silent signal, from all around the clearing fleet black shapes scampered from the shrubs and raced for an almost hidden cleft in the rocks. Perry at the M134D hesitated long enough for Klosky to scream, 'Fire, damn you, fire!'

Perry concentrated his fire around the cleft, which began to disintegrate. The last tool unit, a hunter, was scattered across the landscape in a welter of black blood, bone and leather. Cannon shells poured like deadly rain into the entrance of the cave.

The ship issued an emergency recall. A flood of multi-limbed workers surged from all around it, abandoning their tasks in their haste to escape the chopper's firepower. Shells ricocheted around them and some took hits – none fatally. The ship waited until the last was inside and then sealed itself. Time had run out.

Klosky's pilot was barking into his comm trying to raise the other chopper. The wreckage had vanished into the trees and he was searching for it while also holding his position steady to support Perry's concentrated fire. Peripherally he caught sight of the mountainside bulging outwards, apparently rising to meet him. His body reacted before his stunned mind could accept what it was seeing. He automatically kicked the Griffon into a steep banking turn away from the new threat, rolling it sideways and down towards the lake. In the body of the chopper, everyone's breath was pounded out of them. Bishop suffered most because she had never experienced anything like it before. While she clung to her straps in terror, she was thinking about Zack's last moments and wondered if she would soon be talking with the dead pilot face-to-face.

The pilot slewed around to face the mountain sideways on. He was ready to open the throttle and race away at his craft's top speed of one hundred and sixty miles an hour. His nerves twanged with adrenaline and his mouth was dry. He longed to take a drink from the bottle of water in the holder by his left leg, but daren't take his eyes from the mountain or his hands from the controls.

He heard Perry yell, 'Holy shit!' and then the M134D opened fire in a fusillade of shells, uselessly knocking sparks from a welter of erupting stones. They watched spellbound as the mountain seemingly exploded into a rising dome of soil, shrubs rock and boulders.

The landscape geysered skywards, throwing out a fountain of boiling dust and debris. Just before they were blinded by the thick wall of finely powdered stone and dust rolling towards them, they saw the massive disc of a glittering craft shake itself free and soar at an incredible rate towards the sky. The air was split by a loud double boom.

Perry repeated, 'Holy shit!' and then shouted, 'Look out!'

The cloud hit. The interior of the Griffon filled with choking, bitter dust. The flight crew were glad of their breathing masks and goggles, but troops and civilians could only cover their faces with their hands and hold their breath. The pilot was blinded and prayed he was holding the Griffon steady while trying to wipe the dust from his lenses. At last it was over, bar the hacking coughs and choking noises. Perry cleared his nostrils into the palm of his hand and wiped it on his pants, leaving a wet smear. He spat bitter bile towards the lake.

Klosky shouted, 'You okay over there, Ms Medina Bishop?'

'Been worse.'

'Care to tell us what that thing was?'

'How would I know?'

'I thought you were the girl with all the answers.'

She was quiet for a moment as if thinking, and then an ice-cold male voice emanated from her.

'That device was not of Earth, and no, Medina Bishop does not have all the answers. Other minds much older than hers have also never seen such a thing before. We are just as keen to discover more about it as you. However, we *can* tell you that some of your colleagues in the other helicopter are still alive. Your priority for now must be to aid them. Zack Willis says there is a suitable landing point near the crash zone. He will guide you.'

The more familiar voice of the pilot replaced the stranger and soon they were landing in a broad clearing untouched by the chaos of the ship's launch. As soon as they touched down, the chopper's crew set to brushing out the dust that had coated everything before clearing the filter in a partially blocked air intake. Everyone else walked away downwind and hastily beat the fine grey powder from their clothes. And then, on Medina's advice, they brought two stretchers with them when they followed her into the trees.

She led them to a crumpled mass pinioned between the branches of a splintered elm and a neighbouring redwood. The hot metal of the Griffon's ruined engines was making a ticking noise as it cooled. Klosky asked Askuwheteau to wait with Medina.

He said, 'Ms Bishop, you may talk with the dead, but maybe it's best if you don't see how they got that way. I'm sure you agree.'

She shook her head, releasing a fine cloud of dust. 'No, I don't. I'm trained in first aid and I have direct access to some of the finest medical minds ever known. I can triage and dress wounds. I'm going to help and so is Watcher here. We're going to be more use to you over there than hanging around in this bush. And I know what I said, but call me Medina. You're making me feel old with all that "Ms" bullshit. After what we've been through, I reckon we're on first name terms.'

'Cool, fine. You can call me Klosky.'

'I plan to.'

The wreckage showed where a plug of compacted rock had ploughed into the starboard side, crushing the rear of its passenger compartment and gouging through one of its engines. Its rotors had either been smashed away or rendered useless. It had fallen belly down into the trees, landing on its armoured underside, and that may be what saved some lives. There had been six troopers and a flight engineer in the passenger compartment, a pilot and co-pilot in the cabin. Lou carefully climbed up to the wreck followed by Perry. They gazed mutely into the tangled mess for a few moments, then Lou tested its stability by leaning all his weight on the sill. It creaked noisily but stayed firm.

He shouted down, 'Nobody conscious I can see. Two gone for sure.'

Klosky shouted back, 'You certain?'

'Yeah, pretty much. You want details, sir?'

Klosky flicked a glance at Medina. 'No, no need.'

She spoke loudly with a clipped English accent: 'Private Lou, is it?'

The soldier poked his head out into the open, his face a blank mask.

Medina nodded at him. 'I'm afraid you have three dead and two very severely injured. Both pilots can wait, they're just stunned, as is the flight engineer and Lieutenant Birkin. Pavel is bleeding internally. He needs immediate attention. And one of Kocher's lungs has collapsed, which means he's drowning in his own body fluids. Luckily there are no broken bones, so they can all come down on tethers, Kocher first then Pavel. Jump to it.'

Lou looked first at Klosky and then straight at the tiny woman gazing up at him.

'Izzat you, Captain Wilson?'

'Of course, yes. I remember you now, private Lou. We've done this sort of thing before, haven't we? Get on with it, would you, please? There's a good fellow. Kocher can't wait for long.'

Perry turned to Lou and said quietly, 'Someone you know?'

'Yeah, good bloke. Medic, or he was right up until he had half his head blown off during Operation Enduring Freedom in Afghanistan.'

'You know something? Today's Friday. I woke up this morning looking forward to my fish and fries for dinner. I never thought we'd be doing shit like this before I got to the catsup.'

They mounted the tether pulleys into place and got to work.

## [28]

Medina attended to the injured men as soon as they had been brought down and placed on the stretchers. Kocher was breathing more easily after she'd finished, but Pavel was turning grey. Henderson was officially the team's medical field technician, but he could clearly see that the work she was doing was way out of his league.

'Henderson, you're a good chap. I hate to do this to you after everything else today, but I need you to lie for me.'

He didn't know whether to call her sir or ma'am, so he simply responded, 'Why?'

'Pavel here is in a very bad way, I'm afraid. He can't survive the trip unless I open him up and tack a few sutures in place – field surgery sort of thing. Problem is Medina has no formal medical training. If anything goes wrong she could be in all sorts of trouble. If it goes right, we save the poor bugger's life. See the problem?'

'Yes, yes I do.'

'So, is it alright if I go ahead but, hmm... you say *you* did it?'

'I... what?'

'You say you did it and I assisted. It's the only chance he's got.'

'I... I...'

'Come on, man, yes or no? He's got minutes at best.'

'Oh, God. Okay, yes. Yes, go on. Do it.'

'Good man. Let's get ready.'

Askuwheteau wandered over to see what the pair were doing at the stretcher. He quickly turned away and almost walked straight into Klosky, who was glaring at Medina and Henderson.

'Are they doing what I think they're doing?'

'If you think they're trying to save that man's life, then yes.'

'She's cutting Pavel open.'

Watcher looked back over his shoulder and then up at Klosky. He said nothing.

Klosky spat the words out. 'She's got no medical training beyond first aid, you heard her. Henderson can bandage and splint, suture a wound, all basic stuff. He wouldn't try that. She's cutting Pavel open, out *here*. It's not exactly sterile, is it? Fuck! This is too fucking weird. I've seen some shit but, man, this is out there.'

'So, what are you going to do about it?'

Klosky turned and looked up at the men lowering the survivors from the crashed chopper. Flies were beginning to gather around the dead. Fellows had been back to their Griffon to fetch body bags. The co-pilot and flight engineer came back with him, carrying four more stretchers between them. As soon as all four stunned men were safely on the ground, the dead would be bagged up in the aircraft and then lowered.

Two of them still had their identity tags; the third had ceased to exist above the waist. He had been directly impacted by the projectile and his upper body had been sliced away and then rammed through an engine block. Recovery would have to be carried out using a cotton bud.

Medina appeared at their elbows. 'Henderson's done all he can. Pavel needs the hospital, but at least he should survive the trip now. His colour's improving. Kocher's breathing fine now – he should be okay – but Wilson says you need to get both to care ASAP. These other guys need x-rays and examination for concussion.'

She watched what looked like a half-empty body bag coming down on a tether.

'Nicholls never even saw it coming...'

'Okay, enough now! Enough!' Klosky rolled his massive shoulders. In his confusion, he bent down and grabbed the wisp of a woman by her arms. Perhaps he did it harder than he meant to. She gasped.

He landed with a jolt over ten feet away. The wind had been painfully knocked out of his massive body and for a moment he thrashed about in the dust trying to work out what had just happened. He had once been thrown during a martial arts demonstration by a seventy-three-year-old South Korean man. The man was a little taller and perhaps a touch heavier than Medina. He had seen what the man was going to do before he did it, but was helpless to stop him. This was different. This was as if the air itself had picked him up and flung him away. Bishop hadn't twitched so much as a finger in self-defence.

The woman spoke to the air. 'No, Fargo, he wasn't going to hurt me. Leave him. Leave him alone.'

A dust devil began to swirl faster and faster then moved towards Klosky with obvious intent. Askuwheteau strode to stand in front of the felled giant.

He yelled, 'Achachak Numees, you must stop it!'

Medina shouted, 'Fargo, for my sake, no!'

And then the spinning column fell to the earth and was gone. Fellows came to Klosky's side and helped him to his feet.

He said, 'Man, this is getting to be a habit. You okay, boss?'

Klosky dusted himself down and stood for a moment with his head bowed.

He spoke quietly, 'Medina, I'm sorry. I lost my head and acted like a fool. You've been amazing ever since I met you and I've been an idiot. I don't get what it is... how you do what you do! I mean, okay, you're freaking me out, but that's for me to deal with, not you. Are we okay?'

The elfin woman smiled impishly and walked to stand in front of the giant. She said nothing, but beckoned for him to bow down to her level. When he did so, she put her arms around his massive neck and kissed him chastely on the lips. He was so surprised, he stood upright and took her up with him so that she dangled from his neck, her feet in mid-air.

She looked at him. 'Could I have a hand back down, please?'

He put his big hands around her slender waist and then bent to place her gently back on the ground, just as a heavy clod of dirt whizzed precisely through the space his head had occupied scant moments before. The tiny medium stamped her foot.

'Fargo, you stop that! You're here to protect me from harm, not hurt my friends. Stop it or I'll get you replaced! And I mean it. You hear me?'

A fine ripple seemed to pass under their feet, like a mini quake; a narrow crack opened in the soil between Medina and Klosky. It widened. She leapt the crack and took the big man's hand in hers. To Askuwheteau she almost looked like an angry child. Almost.

She yelled, 'Go on then. Go on, I dare you!'

There was a sound on the breeze like a howl of rage and the soil slammed shut with a puff of escaping dust. Somewhere on the mountainside they heard a sudden rock-fall cascade down into the trees.

Medina chuckled. 'He'll be okay. He can get a little temperamental sometimes, but he's nice really. He forgets himself.' She looked archly up at the astounded Klosky. 'You know what I mean?'

The big man ran his fingers through his short, dense curls. 'Yeah, I guess I do. Hey, lady, you told me you can fire a C7A2 assault rifle lying down. Why did you ever bother to find out? You're already one of the most dangerous creatures I've ever seen on two legs *without* any hardware. Much respect to you, Medina Bishop.'

'Thank you, mister Klosky. However, Captain Wilson is getting quite insistent about getting these injured men out of the field and into care. Shall we get on with it?'

Medina stayed behind with two of the unconscious men and the body bags, while her companions took four stretchers back to the Griffon. She calculated she had perhaps twenty-five minutes before they returned.

'Fargo? Fargo, are you there?'

The elemental appeared and turned his back on her.

'Who wants to know? I don't know you any more, missy "kiss me quick". Is any poor mortal safe, I wonder? She's insatiable now, isn't she? Got a little taste for the naughty have we, missy "hug me right here, right now"?'

She ran at him and grabbed him around the waist. 'Yes, I have. Right here, right now, and with you, my lovely, lovely, jealous man.'

If the stretcher party thought they would find Medina in any way unnerved by her time alone in the forest with three dead men and two supine pilots, they were wrong. When they reached her, she was gazing out towards the lake with bright eyes and a satisfied smile on her bruised lips.

Askuwheteau studied her with a raised eyebrow. *Kitty got the cream,* he thought, and then nearly burst into laughter when she looked directly at him, grinned, and slowly licked her index finger. Suddenly all trace of the little girl was gone. A vital and beautiful woman stood proud in the sunlight.

## 29

The ship felt the thinning atmosphere ablate away the last scraps of rock and soil clinging to its hull while it climbed through the blue sky towards the blessed blackness of space. Its integrity had been slightly compromised during its premature break-out, but its tool units were already at work sealing the few micro breaches. Just a few more days would have been optimal for clearing and thinning away surrounding stone, but under that terrifying barrage of missiles it had no choice but to muscle its way free.

Five of its tool units and a hunter had been lost in the attack along with their core pods. Another hunter was missing, believed dead. It hurt to lose any of its units, but things could have been a lot worse. The little pile of purple pods was safely tucked away in its hold ready for resurrection by Kvult, and all its crew were slotted firmly into their stations. It was ready to make straight for home once the route to the Way Station was completely clear.

Not yet. Forward-facing sensors were reporting a confusing array of metallic clutter directly ahead, and for a long moment a major part of the ship mind ached to add some of it to the trove already in its hold. It almost hesitated when it drew near to one of the larger satellites and eyed its precious metals hungrily, but the mere thought of spending any more time in that despised vicinity drove it on.

Below it the landscape of Earth had changed almost beyond recognition since the time of its crash. The great continent she remembered had broken up and the pieces had moved around in the blue oceans. The skies and the lands now swarmed with mechanical movement and organic life, while the planet's volcanic activity had reduced from great storms and sheets of exploding lava to a few thermal flutters. Much must have happened while the ship was sealed in the mud. It didn't care. That was all behind it now.

It accelerated into position when Finder posted a viable course to the Way Station and then paused waiting for final clearance. It ensured all crew and tool units were slotted into their places. The ship's route would take it in a great arc, outward bound from the white dwarf star at the centre of the alien system and on through the belt of asteroids beyond the Red Planet. Her sensor crew reported aggressive, hard light probes slashing at her hull at the precise moment Finder chimed 'clear space ahead'. She opened her thrusters to full flow.

Several curious Earth agencies had begun tracking the incredibly fast-moving, unidentified ship, and when it stopped moving they began hitting it with spectrographic analytical lasers. They witnessed a sudden blip of acceleration and then the trace disappeared from their screens at speed that seemed completely impossible. Such acceleration would create brutal G-forces, forces violent enough to wreck anything known to man that was not solid state or at least encased in a thick layer of protective gel. Organic material – such as a human body – would have been instantly pulped and left as little more than a thin protein paste smeared against the rear walls of the spacecraft.

The shape of the Inigaian ship's exterior had been developed from that of the aerodynamic kraavel nut kernel, meaning she could fly equally well in vacuum or atmosphere when under power. Her interior, however, was more cellular in structure, which was why the young woman called Melba – one of the earliest victims and since transformed into the Finder – had found it so difficult to navigate around it in the dark. It had no kinship with human logic.

While the ship could fly perfectly well in atmosphere, its interior had been designed for gravity-free space. It was constructed much like a honeycomb. Careful cushioning and buttressing – even down to the molecular level – ensured that once her crew were fully embedded in their work stations like seeds in their casings, they were cushioned against the savage stresses and flexions of even its most gruelling acceleration.

Tool storage was designed in the same way. Once acceleration had stabilised to a constant speed, no matter how fantastic, the tools could begin to move around the ship once more and carry out their tasks, but while it took place they all remained safely cushioned in their sheaths.

When the ship crashed, it was the sudden and catastrophic *deceleration* that had killed her personnel. When she was swiped from the sky and ploughed into the sea at several thousand miles per hour before arrowing down into the seabed like a rock, the forces were too violent. Nothing had ever been designed to survive such treatment. Very little had. But now she was free again. She was going home and she had a story to share that would set Inigaian ears alight. Or so she thought.

After hundreds of millions of years of solitary confinement, the ship mind was no longer entirely sane. While she had languished in the boredom of her dark and lonely tomb, memories of her birth planet had been iterated and reiterated so frequently they had become polished beyond all recognition. In her mind's eye Inigaia's emerald forests had taken on a lush and perfect greenness that no reality could match, and its blue-black denizens walked abroad with the elegant grandeur of dark angels. Her desire to return home piled illusion upon illusion until even the praxel stock beasts – little more than giant, protein-rich maggots – took on a silken, muscular magnificence.

And she thought herself to be part of the beauty. She was one of the divine fruits born from Inigaia's transcendent purity. Weak and watery Earth with its pathetic, tender shoots had benefited greatly from her presence. She had given them a brief sight of her superior form and then whisked it away before they could be blinded by fear and awe.

She chose to ignore the tracking and targeting probes she had escaped at the very last moment. She believed herself the very pinnacle of art and design and at last she could return to the hands that had fashioned her. Only they would be fit to reap her rewards and glory at her wonders.

And then the coin flipped and she began to fret and gnaw at her situation, a syndrome from which she had been suffering for many millions of years. Buried in her tomb for so long, even at her lowest level of awareness, the ship had begun to react to her situation in a classic bi-polar fashion. When she wasn't high as a kite and painting insanely beautiful pictures of herself and her creators, she hit the depths of despair and blamed herself for her plight.

Surely the volcanic fist that had struck her into the sea could have been avoided? If not, then perhaps she should have been faster in deploying slave matrices to the creatures on the seabed? Surely even such poor material could have been made to work harder and with more purpose if it had been brought to her aid earlier?

She remembered the clinging silt sucking her hopelessly down and further still; dragging her to a crushing, lightless hell of a place and draining away all hope. Her only remaining physical ability had been to keep herself balanced on an even keel. Blind, and with most of her sensors useless, she had eventually become lost to an overwhelming sense of claustrophobic dread. Ship minds like her were formed from newborn Inigaian females; they were considered stronger and better able to cope in a crisis. But her designers had never planned for the nightmare she had endured – they would have been astonished she survived.

The ship's architecture was a miracle of metabolic bonding and material purity. Its engines could reach out to any energy source and utilise it with incredible efficiency. Solar energy, background radiation and even gravity were meat and drink to them. Her crew could perform their tasks with almost unimaginable precision. But at the heart of all this perfection was the ship's mind, and underpinning her every thought lay the time-rotted foundations of a creature driven mad.

Only the Finder had concerns about the ship's mind. It had to suffer the droning monologue of thoughts, memories and observations coming from the bridge because its duties required it to remain permanently linked with the mind. And there was another problem. Like all the crew elements it had no conscious concept of how much time had elapsed since the crash. But unlike them it could estimate the time scale by studying the positions of the stars, and since reaching clear space its findings were looking increasingly impossible. It had boasted it had a clear route to the Way Station's branchway portal, but now it had been forced to revise its calculations. It was faced with the mammoth task of trying to position the ship correctly, a task made all the harder by that distracting voice constantly whispering in its ear. *What was it saying now?*

'Out of the dark and into the night, the stars shall witness our glorious flight. But soon, soon to be home. The traveller to the hearth shall come. They will think me their greatest child of all. It has been so long. Too, too long to be away from the emerald forests. They shall be brighter with me in them; I shall shine so bright they will cover their eyes to shield them from my glory. But what if they say it was all my fault? What if they put me back in the dark and cover me up and forget about me? What if they've already forgotten me...?'

In a few hours, they would reach the Way Station portal, meaning the Finder had to focus on their approach. And then, if it was right, would come the final transition to Inigaia's system through the spatial branchways. Even so, a feeling of cold doubt had settled in its mind. If Finder's calculations were correct and the incredible time scale proved true, the maddened ship mind could well be right and the home planet might have forgotten them. What would happen then? What kind of welcome would they receive if they arrived out of the blue, not as returning heroes but as strangers? Strangers arriving unlooked-for to a strange land might get a very chilly reception indeed.

## 30

Klosky, Fellows and Askuwheteau stood in line. They were playing witness to a masterclass demonstration of Medina's stubborn resolve in the face of a direct order she had no intention of following. Every line of her body spoke unyielding volumes. Her voice was flat and implacable.

'If anyone should go with them, it's got to be Henderson. He's the medical tech on the team and he needs to debrief the hospital types. I'm just a civilian adviser along for the ride. You've got to admit it, gents. Come on, you know I'm right.'

The other troops were faking disinterest while sitting several feet away on the benches that had been removed from the Griffon's passenger compartment so the six stretchers could be loaded on board and strapped down. The three members of the flight crew were standing by the helicopter's nose, smoking and waiting to be told they could begin the round trip back to Dauphin. It was getting late in the day and they needed to get to Dauphin, unload the injured, then return to pick up the living – and the dead.

The captain stood side-by-side with Medina's friends. They all believed she should return to safety as quickly as possible. They had all seen the mysterious disc launch itself into space, but there was no guarantee that some of the murderous, blue-black beasts might not still be in the area. To them it was a no-brainer to send her back with the casualties – at least get her out of the combat zone before sunset.

She was having none of it.

She stood with her legs apart and her arms folded firmly across her chest. Her eyes glittered dangerously and her face was flushed a fine pink. To Askuwheteau she looked magnificent, like a wildcat about to pounce. Klosky could barely take his eyes from her, but he was also glancing around, warily poised to dodge flying clods of earth. Then the young woman held out her hands and tried a different tack.

'Look, Zack Willis and his passenger are hooked up in a tree somewhere nearby. We can't leave them up there to rot! We can't, can we? I know where they are and I can take you to them. Their chopper has recordings of the beasts in a hard drive that should still be undamaged. While we're waiting for the boys to come back, we can go get their bodies and collect the hard drive. It's the only decent thing to do! What do you say?'

Klosky breathed down his nose like an angry bull and glowered at the diminutive figure before him. Then he seemed to slump a little.

'Okay, listen to me everyone. Perry, you and Lou grab two more body bags, a pair of stretchers and a gear pack with water and rations, just in case. Henderson, when you get to Dauphin, let me know on the sat-tel and stay with the injured guys. I want regular updates, hear me? Right, let's get going. We don't have all day.'

Within five minutes the Griffon had lifted away and headed south, its starboard side sparkling bright in the orange rays of the lowering sun. Klosky watched it leave.

He sighed ruefully, 'On days like these, you know, I wish I'd taken my mother's advice and stuck with the ballet. You meet a much better class of person in the ballet.'

Fellows went along with it. 'So, why didn't you?'

The giant lifted one of his huge feet. 'Couldn't find a pair of pointes to fit. Then CANSOFCOM told me they had a pair of boats they weren't using, they fit and I got sucked in. Shame. My *pas de deux* was pure poetry, a thing of beauty.'

He turned to Medina. 'Right then, spirit sister, or whatever it is Watcher calls you. Let's go get your friends, shall we? While they're still mostly fresh.'

She chided him, 'You do know Zack can hear you, don't you?'

'Whatever.'

'I'm just saying.'

Six armed men formed an impromptu honour guard around the medium in the gathering twilight. They reacted guardedly to every noise in the undergrowth. They had lost colleagues that day and they were keen not to lose any more through being caught unawares.

After more than fifteen minutes Klosky whispered, 'When you said "nearby" you meant "nearby", not just "somewhere in Manitoba", yes?'

Medina whispered back, 'There.'

Klosky looked up and groaned. 'Aw no, great. Does anything hit the ground around here? Is everything up a freakin' tree? Okay, Perry... Lou... time to practice your tree climbing skills again. And make sure it's safe. We don't sacrifice the living to rescue the dead. Sorry you had to hear that, Zack.'

'He agrees with you. Says be careful, he really appreciates this. And so does Miss Bianco.'

'Who she?'

132

'Coffee Bianco, his passenger.'

'Great name. Okay, guys, up you go.'

The A Star Squirrel had jammed firmly between two big redwoods. It was completely upside down. A cloud of flies and midges clustered around the figures dangling in their straps.

The woman was nearest. Perry hit her buckle release and she slid the short distance to the roof of the machine. Lou strapped his pulleys to a stout branch, fed through the tether and ran the loop at the end under her armpits. She had a large, firm bosom, and the loop caught securely underneath it.

Lou couldn't get enough purchase to jolt it free, so they agreed to lower her with the loop where it was. That was a mistake. As soon as they threw enough weight on the tether to pull her free of the helicopter, Coffee's blouse burst open to expose her amply filled, 38D Victoria's Secret scarlet lace brassiere, and the smooth chocolate skin of an exaggerated cleavage.

'Sorry 'bout this, Miss Bianco,' Lou said. 'It weren't deliberate; I can promise you that.'

'And I can vouch for him, Miss. He's lots of things, but he's no pervert.'

When her body reached the ground, Klosky hissed up at them, 'Hey, can you comedians send Zack down without pulling his cock out?'

'It was an accident, boss.'

'Yeah, well see if you can send him down with his clothes and his dignity still intact. Hear me?'

The pilot was retrieved without incident. He was lowered gently and the two troopers followed him down a few minutes later, after they had recovered the hard drive from the tail. The last of the light was fading from the sky by the time the party left the trees. It was even darker by the time they returned to their campsite and respectfully placed the two fresh body bags with the three originals.

Klosky came off the phone to Henderson. 'Slight delay before the Griffon gets back. The engineer caught his foot in one of the stretcher straps and went down real hard. Twisted his damn fool ankle and he's being treated with ice packs. They'll have him strapped up soon and then they'll be on their way. By the way, Henderson is being commended for his brilliant work on Pavel and Kocher.'

He grinned at Medina. 'I don't even know who I should be saying thanks to, Ms Bishop or Dr Wilson. Thanks to both of you, and especially to you, Medina for sticking to your guns. The rest of the injured guys are good too, responding well to treatment. Wish we had a glass of something to celebrate with.'

Askuwheteau said, 'I don't know about drink. We got any food? I don't want to sound callous, but I'm starving. I can't even remember when I had my last meal.'

Perry grunted, 'You're right there, dude. What kind of hosts are we? My ma would chew me out for leaving a guest hungry.'

He rummaged around in his pack and fetched out a bottle of hand gel. He washed his hands thoroughly then handed the bottle to Medina.

'Everyone get their hands clean and I'll dig out some chow.'

After several minutes of studious palm-rubbing, everyone received a cardboard box containing a foil sleeve which had a combination plastic fork and spoon attached to it under a sterile film cover. They were then handed an MRE – 'Meal Ready to Eat' – food pouch. Perry showed Medina and Askuwheteau how to put the MRE pack into the foil heating sleeve, pour a little water in to get the self-heating process started, and then fold the sleeve over and slide it into the box. Twelve minutes later the packages puffed out and felt warm to the touch.

Medina asked, 'What is it?'

'Well, it could be meat and potato stew, meatballs and pasta in tomato sauce, chicken curry with rice, or kleftiko. There's a vegetarian option in a packet with a green tab, but I'd never hand that to a guy with an assault rifle in his hands. Sometimes it's fruit crumble or stewed prunes with custard. There's a numerical code on the package that tells you what it is, but where's the fun in that?'

'Is it good?'

'Hmm, try it. At least it's hot.'

She dug out the inflated pouch and peeled away the strip at the top. Wisps of steam escaped along with a vaguely savoury aroma. She carefully spooned some of the hot food into her mouth.

Perry asked, around a mouthful of his own meal, 'Well, what d'yah think?'

'It's not bad.' She offered her package to him. 'Which one is this?'

He sniffed, then sniffed his own. He shrugged. 'You know I never have been able to tell, and I've been eating this shit for years.'

The assault when it came was sudden and swift, and Medina discovered just how capable the men she was casually eating with were. The target, Askuwheteau, was standing to one side and calmly eating his meal one moment, and then he was down and rolling away from his assailant. Almost instantly he was back on his feet and using his rifle like a club. His attacker reared away and was poised for another strike when it was hit from four sides by short and effective bursts of rifle fire. It crumpled, twitched twice, and lay still.

## 31

The hunter had become completely confused. During every second of its existence the quiet voice of the ship mind had been there in the background, telling it what to do. It had been a key element in the creature's mental landscape. It had been a happy, stringless puppet, directed through its waking hours by invisible and welcome fingers – and rewarded by an almost sexual glow of gratification when it performed well. And now that voice had gone, along with the ship, the cave and every familiar thing it had ever known.

In the scattered rubble where the ship had been, it had found four core pods and collected them. It placed two on a flat slab of rock where it could easily find them again, took one in its sucker-like proboscis, and used two of its limbs to hold the fourth securely against its leathery carapace. It was no longer receiving direct instruction, so it decided to continue following its most recent orders. Tool units and crew had to be resurrected and the hunter's job was to find the most suitable donors for transformation.

When it first saw the group of people they were alert and watchful, pushing their way through the twilit forest. It remained back in the shadows but dogged them, hoping one of them would lag behind. It weighed their value. There was one very small one that would have proved easy prey, but donors that size tended to split during transformation, so it wasn't fit for purpose.

Another looked too large and may have become a hybrid during the change. Those tended to become unhappy, half-made creatures, neither one thing nor another. They lived briefly in abject misery and suffered from wrenching agony. It was best if they were dispatched quickly and mercifully. The other four all looked viable. It decided to take whichever of them came close enough first.

The prey reached their camp and put down their burdens. Before very long they had prepared and began to eat their food. The hunter knew this would be the perfect time for its attempt. Donors became distracted when they ate – it was one of their fatal weaknesses. The tall, lean creature with long black hair was walking around with its food in one hand and an eating utensil in the other. He came closer and closer until he was almost within reach. The hunter could smell the hot food it was spooning into its face.

It leapt from the shadows with the pod pressed forwards, and that was the last thing it ever did. The target dropped his food and threw himself to one side. He rolled out of reach and then took the barrel of his gun in both hands. Legs braced wide, he clubbed at the hunter before the core pod could be brought to bear. It reared and rolled and bunched its muscles, unsure whether to try for a second attack or make its escape.

Before it could twitch another muscle, it was almost shredded by four streams of high velocity 5.56x45mm NATO cartridges. Its complex tangle of legs jerked twice and then were still. The men formed an outward-facing ring and surveyed their perimeter. When they were convinced there was nothing else in their immediate vicinity, they turned back to study the slaughtered creature by the light of small but powerful LED lamps. Perry kept watch as Klosky crouched down and reached out with a curious hand.

'I wouldn't do that, captain.'

The giant looked across at Medina. He withdrew his hand, stood up and took a cautious step back.

'You haven't made a bad call yet, spirit sister. I'm listening.'

She drew closer to the ruined alien thing then pointed towards its bulbous head and snout.

'You guys reacted so fast I wondered what I was seeing, but I'm sure this thing was trying to hit Watcher with that purple ball there. And it has another one there, see? On its back.'

They craned forwards. Perry hissed, 'Those fuckers are still alive, see that?'

He shone his lamp so everyone could see the glistening, yearning threads of the core pods' antennae. They all took an involuntary step backwards. Something primeval clutched at their hearts. For some reason, they knew to fear the touch of those eerily searching, whip-like feelers.

Askuwheteau was the only one who had seen the film of events at the Duck Mountain Spa, when nearly two hundred teenagers and young adults had marched down that hill to the pool. He remembered how each of them was clutching one hand to their breast. He was certain he now knew what they were holding in that hand.

'Achachak Numees, you told me there was a problem in the spirit realm. Tell me again. I think our friends here need to know what you've learned, and then maybe it's my turn to speak. I think I'm beginning to understand the true extent of the nightmare that visited these mountains, but please, you go first.'

When she answered, Medina's voice had changed to that of a cool, calm male. 'Spirit Talker has allowed me to borrow her tongue. I am Suleiman ben Duwad and I show respect to you. You are true warriors.' She bowed low and gracefully. And then the man explained about the tormented souls in the Realm of Light and the great cylindrical tower that had been erected to contain the sounds of their agony.

'The sound of their screams has been silenced, but they are still tormented in their prison. The sound they make is terrible. It would rend your hearts and burst your ears before it tore away your sanity. We had to contain them – had to in self-defence. We had no choice. But we still pity them. Something truly dreadful broke those poor souls' minds when they died, and now they exist in a state of madness and despair. If we can understand the cause we may yet find a cure, otherwise they will be doomed to suffer for all eternity. We are at a loss, and we asked the Spirit Talker to be our eyes and see what she might find in the world of the living. She has brought us here, to this place and to you.'

Lou almost whispered in awe, 'Am I hearing right? Are you saying you're Solomon the son of David?'

'Yes, I am. You have heard of me?'

'Well, yuh-huh. It's like, you know, I'm Jewish. Of course I've heard of you.'

'That is most gratifying, but it will not provide a solution to our problem.'

Askuwheteau spoke from the gloom, 'I think I may have part of the answer, and it lies here at our feet.'

He walked over to the benches from the Griffon and sat down.

'Join me, guys. Take a load off. Damn, this is crazy. I'm beginning to feel like Alice in Wonderland talking to the Queen. I'm being asked to believe a bunch of impossible things and I guess I'm way out of practice, but I remember how the Queen told Alice she had learned to believe six impossible things before breakfast. I guess I need to take a leaf from her book. And then there's Sherlock Holmes. He said that if you study the facts and take away everything that's impossible, whatever's left – no matter how improbable – must be the truth.'

Everyone made themselves as comfortable as possible to listen to the man of the First Nations. He gave a wry chuckle.

'You can take the lecturer out of the lecture hall, but you can't take the lecture hall out of the lecturer. Listen to me, I'm like a starving dog circling a porcupine. Hungry enough to attack, but afraid to get too close. Okay, okay. Some facts. Let's start with the first impossible truth.' He pointed at the smashed, sixteen-legged hunter. 'Marshall and Medina will back me on this. That – that *thing* is made from human tissue.' He raised his hands at the sounds of protest. 'Don't shoot me, I'm only the messenger. The original message was written by the pathologist back at the RCMP station in Dauphin. Guy called Spider Webb. He's weird as a sack of pink squirrels, but very good at his job.

'We had samples from something that got its ass shot off trying to attack us, much like our friend here. Spider told us how the samples tested as one hundred per cent human. In fact he could even tell us they were from a young male. But how? Yeah, how? Well, right now I think I know, and I think it all started in a spa facility a few miles from here. That brings us to impossible fact number two.'

He told them about the CCTV recordings of people going from room to room in the spa and then seemingly settling down for the night before the mass exodus down to the pool at first light.

'I don't think they were sleeping. I believe they were waiting for the dawn. I'm thinking the process that turns one of us into one of those... those *things* requires three elements before it can take place. And that's impossible fact number three: it needs one of those purple balls, sunlight and water, the trinity of nightmare, to make the horror happen. And then, when all the ingredients come together, we change. There must be something in us that triggers it, I have no idea what, but there it is. One, two, three, bingo! And somebody's son or daughter is running around on more legs than is rightfully decent. I think those purple creatures' feelers are used to latch onto the victim somehow. They look pretty active, don't they? And once you're infected and the sun comes up and there's water around you, you've had it. You change.'

His voice became cold and his eyes glittered in their shadowed sockets.

'Chills me to the bone to think of those poor kids thrown out of their own bodies in so much pain and terror that even their immortal souls have been driven mad.'

Then Solomon's words struck at them like fists from the darkness.

'There never was a Hell in the Realm of Light before, but it seems there is now. What you tell us dooms those poor souls, but it also damns all of us who barricaded them away in that terrible place. They are harrowed by madness and we are tortured by guilt. If what you say is true it means that for the Realm, the time of eternal peace has ended. An eternity of torment has only just begun.'

139

## 32

Five human bodies, the remains of one mystery creature, and three pods which had been packed away with a level of care normally associated with dangerous radioactive waste were piled behind the rear bench in the body of the Griffon. The third pod had been spotted by Lou when the hunter was being pressed into a body bag and had been extracted from the spoiled body with immense care. The helicopter was going to be overloaded for its trip to Dauphin, but the captain refused to leave any personnel on the ground a second time.

'If we come back here we come in daylight. So, let's do like the shepherd said and get the flock out of here. I got me a good book to read and a bed with my name on it.'

The injured flight engineer had been given the job of covering the campsite while they prepared to leave. He scanned the area using a powerful lamp attached to the Dillon M134D and eagerly ranged the six-barrelled cannon backwards and forwards across the clearing, looking for something, *anything*, on which he could open fire.

Klosky reached up and held the wavering barrel of the gun.

'Garcia, we're about to go home. If you shoot me, even by accident, I'm gonna come back as a dose of gonorrhoea, infect your wife, and then laugh while all your friends get sick. You hear me?'

'That's okay, captain. I don't mind you making fun. Just don't infect my girlfriend and I'm happy. Deal?'

'Always the one with the snappy answers. Hey, is that safety on?'

'What safety? This peashooter has a safety? All these years an' how come nobody told me about it? Shee-it! I tell you, man, that could be freakin' dangerous.'

'Foolish of me. Forget I said anything. Okay?'

He patrolled the perimeter and met Askuwheteau stepping out of the shadowy shrubs. He was buttoning his fly.

'Not good, Watcher. I wondered where you'd got to.'

'I wasn't going to risk my bladder in that bone rattler, not even for half an hour.'

'Yeah, man! But you ducked out of sight of your troop in a hostile zone. You know better than that.'

'Yeah, but I also know better than to piss in front of a lady.'

'She would have turned her back.'

'You so very sure of that?'

They both turned and regarded the busy little silhouette which seemed to be flitting around like a weightless bird.

Klosky grinned. 'Amazing little creature, isn't she?'

'Yeah, captain, she's all of that. Cute too. I tell you, I'm glad my wife's a real beauty or I might just have fallen for that girl, you know? Just a little bit. She's got a wild kind of fire about her, a touch of magic. You know what I mean?'

'Yeah, magic. I'd say so. She's got some kind of genii throwing rocks at anyone who annoys her, and for some reason the target always seems to be me! And what was with that crack in the ground? I'm telling you, man, I reckon there's more than just a touch of magic there. It's more like a whole bucketful and then some.'

They heard Perry shout, 'Captain, we're ready to go here!'

'I hear yah – just completing the final perimeter check. Making sure you girls didn't leave your guns behind in the bushes along with your pantyhose snagged on those nasty branches.'

'Damn, is that where I left them?'

'Ask the boys to get the egg beater started. We're on our way over.'

The two men crouched low and ran as the helicopter's rotors began to spin and downwash kicked up the dust. Within a minute they were buckled in and the Griffon lifted heavily away into the darkness. Apart from a few marks on the ground which were largely eradicated during take-off and some traces of urine in the bushes, special ops ensured they left nothing behind to indicate they had been there. As soon as possible the crashed whirlybird in the trees would also be recovered.

The gruesome spray of black blood in the centre of the clearing was covered by a fine layer of swirling dust. When the clattering sounds of the helicopter's flight finally subsided to the south, a fox crept out of the trees and made a slow approach to the place where the hunter had been gunned down. It sniffed at the dust and whined low in its throat before it cocked its leg and sprayed copious amounts of urine over the patch of mottled earth. It then squatted and defecated. When it had finished, it kicked dirt over the spot then scampered, tail high, back into the trees.

All over the mountainside, animals reclaimed their territories in the same fashion, spurning and scent-marking the fading traces of the ship's minions. But none entered the hollow place left by the ship's departure. The stink was too pervasive there. It haunted the soil.

The hunter had been the last of the operative alien lifeforms on Earth, but two more indigenous lives were lost after it was killed. The two remaining core pods left at the cave site claimed a raccoon and a very young lynx before the week was out. The animals were taken on different days, each in daylight, and almost instantly they scurried down to the lake. Each threw themselves into the water and began to change shape. There was insufficient body tissue in both cases and the transformations failed, tearing each donor's body tissue into strips of blue-black skin and sinew, while clouding the water with rank, dark fluids.

The smell drove away all marine life in the area. Even insects gave that sector of lake a wide berth. The creatures' malformed skeletons crumbled like discarded science experiments and became lost in the mud and matted weeds of the lake bed. The pods also fell into the weeds. There they would remain: active, ominous booby-traps sitting passively in wait for the slightest touch of the unwary.

Medina sat next to Askuwheteau. She took his hand and looked up into his face. Her beautiful eyes were bitter with anguish. Part of him wanted to take her up in his arms as if she was a child and squeeze all the bad things out of her memory. He wanted to lie to her, tell her everything was alright, kiss her until all the monsters disappeared and then rock her to a peaceful sleep. Another part of him was all too aware of her womanly heat against his hip, but he chose to ignore it. At least he tried to. He blamed his Kestejoo idiot mind for the thoughts he was having, the seductive things he was imagining. He told himself they were unfit and beneath his notice, but silken lures still dragged his eyes to those lips he ached to kiss. He wrenched his head away and gazed out into the inky blackness. Ahead an orange glow told him the city of Dauphin was getting closer.

She said something, but the sound was stolen by the helicopter's roar.

'I'm sorry?'

'I said I've heard them. Heard the tormented souls. They sound like knives scraping down ice, like millions of fingernails scraping down chalkboards but amplified until it becomes truly unbearable. The sound petrified me. It was so loud, so shocking that it paralysed me. I curled up in a ball. I couldn't move, couldn't breathe. We can't blame the Realm for wanting to protect itself, but they asked for my help and I've failed them. Watcher, I've failed them. I feel terrible. What do we do now? What *can* we do now?'

He put his arms around her narrow shoulders and hugged her as well as he could in that confined space.

'I don't know,' he admitted. 'I don't know. But we don't give up, okay?'

'Okay,' she said, and gave him a sad smile that stopped his heart in mid beat. He smiled back.

'I promise,' he said. 'I promise. Somehow, we'll find a way.'

## [33]

The Finder calculated its final approach to the Way Station's portal while trying to block the sing-song sound of the ship's mind. It wondered if she knew she was speaking aloud. The words were increasingly disjointed and swung like a pendulum from mad delusions about her Messiah-like return to Inigaia – in which she believed she would be worshipped by her own builders – to abject misery at her failures as a mining and survey vessel. During these latter moments, she openly voiced her fears that she might be decommissioned and even subsumed to reclaim her valuable raw materials.

Whatever was going to happen when they got home, getting there safely would depend on Finder ensuring the ship made the correct approach to the portal of the Way Station's spatial branchway. Unless the angle was exact to within just a few degrees – and final approach had to be contained within very precise parameters – its sensors would be unable to find the artificial breach in time and space, let alone enter it.

Behind Finder's blank oval of a face, an armoury of sophisticated alien calculators and sensing technology had been created from what had once been a young woman's brain, eyes and ears. It retained few of her original sensibilities. For example, part of it could still appreciate some forms of beauty in what it was 'seeing'. Despite its transformation it had preserved a crude understanding of the aesthetic, but little of its overall consciousness would be wasted on such petty diversions. It was first and foremost efficient and capable, designed to be the best at what it did, and neither idle thoughts nor the wittering of the ship mind would be allowed to side-track it from its job.

Finder filtered out the sounds of the relentless monologue and focused its prodigious capabilities on the task at hand. It was thinking in four dimensions, the last of which required its most precise calculation: time.

The estimated time scale since its original inception into Earth's system was staggering, but not impossible to manage if it refused to be distracted. It needed to calculate the portal's movements over hundreds of millions of years and position itself directly in front of its current predicted location. Once the ship entered the portal it would automatically travel back along the spatio-temporal branchway to its home system, collapsing the artificial sinus behind it as it went, but leaving a trace in case it wished to return. But first the Finder must find the portal.

144

All other crew and tool units had become subservient to the Finder at this critical time. It could dip into any other crew mind, order any manoeuvre and demand instant obedience.

Its task was immense. Finder had estimated more than twenty-two thousand potential rendezvous points – all of them calculated to exist somewhere within a globe of space more than fifteen light minutes across. Each point had been carefully factored and given a percentage likelihood of being correct – and at that moment the ship was just seconds away from the most probable.

It was feeling an enormous amount of pressure. The slightest and most subtle imperfection in its calculations might doom them to a future spent hunting around the solar system, searching desperately for the Way Station's spoor.

And then the ship mind began to shriek in despair. The Finder's concentration jolted away from its task for just a fraction of a second before it hastily reeled its mind back to its calculations.

It performed a vast number of systems checks to ensure it was still on course, but knew in its heart it had been seriously distracted and was now trusting to pure luck. The creature had no spleen for anger or even mild chagrin, but it wondered how the ship could possibly be operating at full efficiency when its mind was so evidently unhinged.

And then a pearlescent cloud rolled in front of its massive forward viewports. The cloud was invisible from the sides and had no apparent dimensions in real space, but it seemed to sweep away to infinity when seen directly head-on. Finder fiercely and suddenly stopped any of the ship's lateral motion, which sent some of its tool units rattling sideways to fetch up against the ship's interior bracing stanchions. There the portal was, almost exactly where it was calculated to be.

At this point Finder was required by long-standing protocol to request the ship mind's permission to proceed to the Way Station. It took a second to listen to its commander's raving chatter and decided it had better make an executive decision. It ordered the ship's complement to their stations and waited until all had reported as secure. Then every erg of energy that could be teased from the ship's main thrusters was unleashed.

Space was almost instantly empty once more. The portal winked out.

Earth scientists spoke of wormholes in space, but the more arborescent Inigaians did not think in terms of worms. They imagined the branches of a great tree, snaking out from the original Way Station's firmly anchored locus. With the right tools, space could be twisted and manipulated; made to act like a fluid, a gas or a form of energy, but it couldn't be directed. When the branches flared out from the Way Station's 'bole' and formed its massive crown of potential routes to new worlds, they did so in a random way, flaring out like a hyper-immense discharge of electricity. It had used an unthinkable amount of energy.

For a nerve-jangling moment after the Way Station was activated, the Inigaians' sun dimmed in the midday sky and its creators held their collective breath. They numbly wondered if they had accidently triggered the destruction of their civilisation. Then the star regained its light and warmth once more, and they breathed a deep sigh of relief before they began to celebrate in earnest.

In theory, anchoring the device to the Inigaian star helped ensure that the ends of its many branches would be naturally attracted to – and anchor themselves near – similar stellar objects at the heart of distant systems. The branches would, theoretically, use the shortest possible tempero-spatial routes, distorting and compressing time and space in the process.

The ship delivered to Earth was just one of many sent out in a spirit of optimism, hope and greed. They were expected to find mineral-rich systems and plunder them, then return with their bounty so that more ships could be built, and then more, and more, until Inigaia had placed itself at the centre of an empire of worlds; all held in durance to its material needs.

And now the ship was returning along its branch, following a precise pathway from which it couldn't deviate by as much as a thousandth of a degree. It was following the sinus it had created on its way outwards hundreds of millions of years before, and travelling at a fantastic rate relative to real space. Its home world was part of a system many thousands of light years from Earth, but in branch space the ship would only need to travel for a matter of light hours.

It would re-enter real space after just a few days, and all the while it was bathed in the unchanging, creamy purple light of pseudo space. This light was unique to its environment. It was not the kindly glow created by stars, but a shockwave of radiation thrown out by distorted dark energy. This strange light could only be seen while squirting at fantastic speeds along an interstellar gut torn through the fabric of space itself. It told Finder it could relax for a while. It had done its job well.

But what should be done about the ship's mind? In fact, what *could* be done about it? Finder was at a loss. At that moment, the mind had begun to sing a song of childhood, a bitter sweet lullaby lamenting the loss of a dead child cradled in its mother's arms. In the song, the mourning mother rocked her baby and sang to it as if it was only sleeping, 'but its sweet eyes were closed forever to love and fortune'.

It was too much. Finder had to escape and somehow find respite from the madness. It allowed its subtle senses to drift out into the silent void beyond the viewing ports – out into light created by stricken dimensions. It could imagine itself as an outsider looking back towards the fleet beauty of the ship.

In its mind's eye, it watched the ship racing through the thick purple light of branch space surrounded by its blue-white aura, an aura created by atoms too sluggish to slide around the sleek hull getting smashed to ruin against its ultra-dense skin.

Rapt in such beauty, the transformed creature suddenly felt itself to be very alien and very far from home. Finder had no eyes from which tears could flow, but somewhere deep inside it a forgotten girl began silently to weep.

## [34]

The big window beside the glazed balcony doors in Medina's hotel room was north-facing and had a deep wooden surround. The landscape she could see through the glass seemed too perfect – a framed fragment from a lovely dream.

Her viewpoint from the hotel's second floor meant she could see out over the buildings of Dauphin and across the fields, plains and lakes towards the mountains on the horizon. The sky was a mighty bell of blue torn only by rare vapour trails carved by what appeared to be impossibly tiny aircraft. They glittered like cheap silver trinkets in the light of the early sun.

She sighed with guilt at the pleasure she was feeling, then sighed again as Fargo moved deeper inside her with long, powerful strokes. When it started, her orgasm was a sweet and familiar surprise, a bloom of warm pulsations which drew a soft groan from her lips. Her lover spilled heat into her in urgent, hard jets, his neck corded with the intensity of his passion, his belly hard against her yielding softness. Her body found release, but it wasn't enough to break her mood. The sadness remained.

Afterwards he helped soap her in the shower, cupping and pushing against her tender flesh in an affectionate and yet strangely possessive manner. *This flesh is mine to care for*, his hands seemed to say. *Mine to touch, to hold, to cradle and love. No other hand must loiter here. Put away your card. I have marked every dance.*

She wondered if their lovemaking was his way of scent-marking her. Even when she was alone she was very aware of his distinctly bright musk on her skin, and washing only intensified the intoxicating perfume. Edward Louis had commented on it over dinner the night before.

'I thought you used Ô De Lancôme.'

'Yes, yes I do. Why?'

'Oh, that's strange, how very odd. I've always prided myself on my nose, I could have sworn... please, don't get me wrong. You smell lovely, my dear. Enchanting. Like a fresh sea breeze blowing across autumn heather, but not like Ô De Lancôme. Nothing like it in fact, nice as it is. You remind me of a window opened onto a stuffy room and when sweet air brings the promise of spring after rolling across meadows and a cool, freshwater lake. Your perfume is lovely, whatever it is. Lancôme would do well to follow you around and make notes. Sorry, listen to me. I've embarrassed you, silly old

148

duffer. Forgive a frustrated poet with too much love for words and perhaps a touch too much of this excellent Cabernet.'

Medina had felt the flush come to her cheeks while the man talked, but it wasn't due to embarrassment. Louis was describing the way she thought Fargo's scent could brighten a room. In her secret heart, she thought he smelled the way the Scottish Highlands looked – wild, free and potentially dangerous. His fresh musk heightened her desire as much as the sensation of his big hands on her breasts, or the way his gold-flecked eyes searched her face as if he wanted to remember every feature in minute and loving detail.

Their relationship was about more than sex. They had danced naked in his magical glade by dawn's early light; visited sacred, painted caves older than elder memories. She held her breath with enchantment when he showed her badger kits playing by their sett under the moon's watchful eye. He had spun her world into a net of playful magic and she knew he was trying to impress her with his wizardry.

She let him unleash his wonders and she wanted to revel in them, but sometimes, as had happened that morning, he would be making love to her and her mind would stray back to the mountains and the fate of the tormented souls murdered there. Her heart felt congested by sad darkness an orgasm couldn't disperse.

...

It had been nearly a week since the survivors brought their dead back to Dauphin. Nearly a week since Medina had heard anything more on the subject. Marshall and Askuwheteau shared her frustration. The people of the Realm wanted to know what was happening so they could find ways to help the demented spirits, and she'd had to report that the living had no further apparent interest in assisting the dead. Chief Inspector Longknife had thanked them all for their 'invaluable assistance' and told them that the case would be pursued with 'utmost and extreme vigour'. Rawkins contradicted all of that as 'total BS'.

'It's embarrassing for them is what it is. They don't like aliens and spaceships and all that Roswell, Area 51 shit. I bet you that all your samples are in a warehouse somewhere by now, all under secure lock and key. I'm telling you, Spider had to surrender everything he had, *and* all his notes. They even took his laptop, and that was his own personal, paid-for property. The one he got back was almost identical except it was brand new and had the latest software.'

She grimaced, 'All the details of the black thing and the test results were gone. Not erased, you know, just never there, and a bunch of suits went over his place like a white tornado and vacuumed everything and everywhere those scraps of black stuff had been. I tell you I want those guys' names. Job they did there I'd *pay* to turn them loose on my house. Spotless. Even the Mercedes bus has been replaced. The old one's gone for "forensic research" and we got a brand spanking new one, just eight miles on the clock. It's got so crazy I keep thinking I'll wake up one morning and see a mushroom cloud where Duck Mountain and the lakes used to be.'

They were sharing a quiet beer in a bar where they could find a shadowy corner and avoid the furore of lunchtime at Vasyl's place. The other patrons were watching the Dauphin Kings in an important junior league hockey game. Short of firing pistols at the TV set, they would be completely ignored.

Rawkins sipped her Labatt Blue and sucked her lips back against her teeth, shaking her head.

'I'm even surprised I'm still seeing you good people here, you know? I thought you'd have been shown the courtesy door by now. "Here's the way out. Thanks for the help, but you've got other places to be I'm sure. Little black creatures? Why, what are you talking about? Where's the proof?" Ha, where's the proof? Bastards, I'll tell you where the proof is! You buried it, you bunch of fuckers!'

She said this last a little too loud and a few heads turned in their direction. When they saw the uniform, they went back to the match. Hockey was much more interesting than a foul-mouthed cop.

Fellows was equally nonplussed. 'I tried to get in touch with Klosky and the guys and I've been told they're not available. Not that they're away or something... just, you know, *not available*. I know they're the silent professionals, but I thought my time in the service might cut me an inch of slack. Nah, no deal. You won't believe this, but I promise it's true. I asked if I could go along and attend the funerals for the guys we lost, you know? Pay my respects. I got told that no personnel had been lost on any recent missions and I was thanked for my concern. Thanked for my concern! I told the stuck-up little bastard he was suffering from a severe head/ass interface and asked to be put through to someone who could talk like a human being. You know what he said? "This interview is terminated." And he hung up. Little shit! I wanted to reach through the phone and grab him by his throat and squeeze the truth outta him.'

150

His hands balled into claws as he mimed just how much he wanted do it. Askuwheteau looked down at his empty glass. He needed a break from the misery, just a few minutes' respite.

'Who wants one? I'm in the chair.'

Medina followed him to the bar. The crowd around the TV looked like they needed cheering up too. There was a palpable air of gloom in the place.

He placed his order and the barman set to work. While they waited, he searched her face.

'You okay?'

'No, not really.'

'Yeah, I thought not. I could tell. We First Nation people are very empathic like that. Ask Kevin Costner.'

He looked back at the group around their table. He could hear Rawkins sounding off.

He sighed. 'Listen to that. And who can blame them? They feel betrayed, I guess, but once they've had a chance to let off steam they'll be fine. Day-to-day shit will start to become important again: work, play, bills, family. Whatever must be dealt with, it'll have to get dealt with, you know? But it's not like that for you, is it? This is what you do. You're involved. You can't walk away, can you? Tell you what, come to my place tomorrow, say ten. Let's go for a walk around the lake. Take the pole so Wikimak thinks we're fishing. Then we can have a real talk, spirit stuff. What do you say?'

'That would be nice, thank you. I'll buy the fish this time.'

They took the drinks back to the table.

When she hadn't shown by eleven the next morning, Askuwheteau rang the hotel. He was told she had checked out due to some medical crisis at three after midnight. He asked to talk to Edward Louis and was told the man was being interviewed by the RCMP in Dauphin. It seemed the journalist had created something of a fuss at the reception desk after asking if they might call his friend in her room to find out when she would be coming down for breakfast. When he was told she had been taken to a clinic, he became quite heated and demanded to see Miss Bishop's room. When he was refused, he became loudly abusive. The manager called the police and Louis was taken away, swearing and promising to 'bring down the very letter of the British press on the heads of everyone involved'.

Askuwheteau felt as if a cold fist had gripped his guts and squeezed. He put the phone down and looked at his wife. His voice was a shocked hiss.

'The bastards have taken Medina. They've taken her.'

'What? Who? What are you saying? Who's taken her?'

Galvanised, he rushed to grab his jacket.

'I don't know. But first I'm going to go bust Edward Louis out of jail.'

The troops of CANSOFCOM may have been nicknamed the 'silent professionals', but Perry couldn't keep his story to himself. He had to tell someone. He was back in CSOR Petawawa, going through an inventory of equipment used and lost during the mission with his superior officer in the armoury. Once the official business was out of the way, they drank espressos made using freshly ground beans from the major's private store and drawn from his Rocket Espresso Giotto Evoluzione coffee machine. It was a ritual moment and a rare treat.

The major, a fanatic, talked as he always did about places he had drank amazing coffee, and where he sourced the best beans. Perry was glad the man didn't insist he tried a revolting sounding brew made from what the major described as 'the legendary beans from the wild kopi luwak of Northern Sumatra'. Perry didn't want to drink anything that had passed through the gut of a cat, even at twenty dollars for just fifty grams. Good old plain coffee, full of flavour, strong and black, was just fine for the sergeant. And then Perry told the major about Medina's extraordinary powers – the way he remembered them.

'You know captain Klosky, the really big guy.' He indicated the man's size with his hands. 'Well, I'm not kidding, sir, but she whupped his big ass without laying a finger on him. She's like some kinda *Jedi* or something... really, and don't you smile like that, sir. I know what I saw. And she ain't no more than a bite-sized morsel neither. Sure, she's pretty enough, mind. Yeah, I'm saying she's gorgeous, you know what I mean? Kinda pocket-sized but all woman. She's a babe, not a child.'

Major Franke had more than a passing interest in both women and the paranormal and the fact that it was Perry telling the tale, a man he knew to be a solid pragmatist, piqued his curiosity. He pressed for more details and was soon treated to a description of Medina splitting the very earth itself and how she talked to the dead. He learned how she had channelled a dead pilot, a doctor and 'some guy called Solomon ben something'.

Franke wondered why, if she was that remarkable, they hadn't heard about her before. Perry explained that she was English and over in Canada to work with the Mounties. He thought she was staying at the Canway Inn in Dauphin.

'She's on her own over here apart from some old guy who's also from London, England. I haven't met him, but I hear tell he's a newspaper guy. Yeah, oh, and she's also hooked up with a native American guy called... ahhh, what was it? One of those great names. Askuwhoohoo? No, hang on. Yeah, Askuwheteau. He's a professor or something and used to be in the forces himself. Nice guy. Oh, yeah, and Marshall Fellows, remember him? One of us and very capable. Was with us over in Afghanistan and can still handle his shit like a pro, you know what I mean? Good people. Right handy in a tight spot.'

Later, Major Franke shared Perry's news with some friends in the Officers' Mess. He told the story around a rare steak sandwich, curly fries and a bottle of decent Merlot. His friends loudly derided him for being so gullible, but he insisted his source was 'Kosher'.

'No, honestly, guys, he's okay. The real deal. If Perry told me he'd been abducted and gang-raped by topless supermodels, I'd ask him where it happened and go stand there with a week's supply of condoms in my pocket. Man's a gem. Honest as the day's long.'

'What was the girl's name, Hermione Granger?'

'No, you idiot, it was Medina Bishop. Miss Medina Bishop. And from what I hear she's a real pocket princess. Tiny, sure, but a top-class honey. You could wrap her legs around your waist and run up and down the stairs all night without breaking a sweat. Little girl like that might be grateful for a touch of military meat in her diet, you understand what I'm saying?'

He shut his eyes and made an unpleasant sucking noise. The drink was getting the better of his famously limited social graces.

'Hah! Might just pop over to Dauphin and hang out in the bar at the Canway Inn. See if I can buy the little lady a drink or two.'

In the face of his colleagues' relentless jeering, he decided to shut up and fill his mouth with the order of now cold curly fries and then finish his wine. As usual he decided to start his diet the following day. He ordered another bottle of Merlot and signed the docket. While he did so, he noticed a woman he didn't recognise heading for the bar's exit. He tracked her progress and carried out his customary mental audit. She was walking briskly while talking urgently into her cell phone. *Bony-assed, narrow looking bint*, he thought. *Nice hair, auburn, and good tailoring on the green suit. She has decent legs but there's no sway to her hips – the rest is all sharp corners. A man could cut himself on a woman like that.*

Audit complete, he dismissed her from his mind and chewed some more fries.

The time was nine-thirty in the evening. Just over two-and-a-half hours later there came a sharp rap at Medina's hotel room door.

Half asleep she called out, 'What is it? It's midnight. What do you want?'

'Hotel security, Miss Bishop. We only need a second. There's been reports of an intruder and we need to make sure you're safe.'

She sleepily opened the door and blinked at the pair of suited men who towered in the doorway.

'There's nobody here, I can assure you...'

One man pinned her arms, put a hand over her mouth and pushed her back into her room as if she was a rag doll. The other took a prepared syringe out of his pocket, removed the cap from the needle and pressed it home. Within moments she was unconscious.

It took fifteen minutes to strip away Medina's pyjamas and redress her in outdoor clothes before roughly pulling her arms into the sleeves of a heavy coat with a hood they took from her wardrobe. They performed their task as if the woman between them was a manikin. Their hands roamed and pulled at her body in a fashion both intimate and careless, but also cold and impersonal. They then packed the rest of her clothes and gear into her suitcase and cabin luggage, grabbed her shoulder bag and left.

The room behind them was spotless. They carried the girl between them, each taking an arm in one hand and a piece of her luggage in the other. They pulled the hood over her lolling head. When they passed through reception at some speed, the night porter called out, 'The lady alright, gentlemen?'

The larger one answered, 'Give us a minute, will you?'

While his partner strapped Medina into the back of their car, the one who had spoken went back into the hotel brandishing her card key.

'Miss Bishop's been taken very ill. It's a chronic condition. We're from the clinic. Specialists. We need to get her to a monitor station and a nebuliser and the clinic's over fifteen minutes away. Here's her key – is there anything outstanding?'

Bill settled, the big man with the bland face and the cropped grey hair bade the porter goodnight and was gone.

'Poor little mite,' said the porter to himself. 'Nature can be such a cruel bitch sometimes. And she looked so healthy too.'

He scratched at his bristled chin then returned to his spy novel, wondering why things that happened in the book never happened for real. He yawned.

# [36]

Her eyes opened like dusty shutters at old windows and she blinked slowly. She felt her lungs fill with air and then empty again. There was music to it. Everything around her was happening very, very slowly, but in incredibly fascinating detail. She watched a dust mote spiral on the merest breath of a breeze and saw the incredibly fine hairs on her forearm glisten under clinical, white light. The thin white counterpane on her single cot was full of subtle shades, thousands of variations on the theme of grey. Grey and white like snow, but warm and sleep-inducing. She was lying in a landscape made up of warm snow – *warm snow*. That was quite funny, but she was too tired to laugh. Funny, but she was also too alert to sleep. What a joke. She allowed her eyes to drift and roam across the counterpane. So many miles of warm snow for that single mote of dust to cross. Poor, poor little mote.

Her mouth was dry and she would have liked a drink, but with so much going on it was difficult to work out when she would be able to fit it in. Too busy. Her dance card was full. Fargo, yes, sweet Fargo. He had taken all her dances. It seemed very sad to think that all her dances were gone. Her tongue moved lazily in her dry mouth. It made a slow, rasping, smacking noise. She passed her tongue across her lips and it felt strangely thick and numb. Her lips felt scaly. She wondered if she had become a monitor lizard. Was that why everything around her was so slow? Was she a big old lizard now?

'Miss Bishop.'

*Not now, not now.* Her mind was too crowded for idle chit-chat. *Go away. Leave me to my warm snow and my little mote of dust. See, see it fly. There it goes across the edge of the soft, warm glacier.*

'Miss Bishop, I can see you're awake. I'm sorry, but we had to administer a little tranquiliser. It's harmless enough, but you might feel a little dizzy for a few moments. It was done for your own safety and security. I'm sure you understand. For your own safety. And security.'

No, Medina realised, she was wrong. *She* wasn't the lizard. It was her, the narrow, green-eyed woman in the green suit and the green silk blouse who was sitting across from her in a straight-backed wooden chair on a shiny black floor. She *definitely* looked like a lizard. Medina had a sudden urge to see the woman's tongue. She was convinced it would be long, forked and blue. The woman had a long and narrow jaw. She also had thin lips and long, narrow eyes. An exercise in long and narrow things.

Medina studied the woman's legs and hands. *Yeah, thought so. Long and narrow.* The lizard woman evidently spent a lot of time on her light auburn hair. It looked very full-bodied and the styling was probably very expensive. She resembled a green-stemmed rose. Long and narrow stemmed rose. Medina wondered if the woman used perfume. Would it be floral or something flintier? Something that smelled of flint and desert dust? Something that smelled... her mouth felt drier just thinking about it. Scratchy, dry. She badly needed a drink.

'I'm thirsty.'

'There's some water in the jug on the cabinet beside your bed. It's been there a while and might not be cold. I can get you some fresh if you wish.'

Medina turned to the bedside cabinet and focused on the jug. *Ooh, pretty shape like a glass balloon.* No, that was wrong, not a balloon. More like a bloated frog just about to croak. The frog had a tumbler perched in its open mouth. She sat up, reached out, took the tumbler and poured water into it from the frog's mouth. The water overflowed and the wet, slapping sound it made as it hit the floor was so amazing she let it continue for a moment. Then she remembered she was thirsty and she drank the water like a greedy child, gasping and breathless after draining her glass in one long draught. It was delicious. She poured and drank more. And then a third time. The third glass of water was disappointing. It was warm and tasted of dust and grey Friday afternoons backstage in provincial theatres; or maybe those rooms in churches where they stored prayer books, the rooms where she was invariably told she should change before her performances. That seemed sad too. She wanted to cry. The lizard woman was talking.

'How much of that shit did you pump into her? She's looney tunes in there.'

Somebody behind the woman, hulking in the shadows, answered in a guttural mumble. It was okay, the lizard wasn't talking to her. Why was the floor so wet? Medina looked up, wondering whether the rain was coming in. No. The ceiling was intact. It was high and black and industrial looking. It was busily criss-crossed with black painted pipes and bright, white strip lighting. Wherever two of the pipes met, the joints had been wrapped in black and yellow, diagonally striped tape. The yellow on the tape glowed oddly. It looked as if it was radioactive – glowing in the dark above the bright, white lights. Some of the pipes had little red diamond shapes on them. She wondered why.

'Yeah, well, look at her, you meatheads! Your "standard dose" has put her on the moon. What does she weigh? I bet she's no more than ninety pounds, less. I've got dildos weigh more than her. You fuckheads are pathetic. Get out of my sight and let me think.'

There was the sound of a door opening and two figures bulked in the brief, rectangular light of a doorway. Then the door closed and they were gone.

Medina looked at the lizard woman and the lizard woman looked back at her. She gazed with blank lizard eyes.

It wasn't fair. The lizard had a nice wooden chair with a proper back to it, while she had to sit on a bed. A fact started knocking at her consciousness with growing insistence. What was it? What wasn't she seeing? That was it. There was something wrong with the bed. And the room. Where was her view of the mountain? Slow realisation dawned. She wasn't in her hotel room anymore. She was in a box.

On all four sides of her was a clear glass wall, and even through the dizzy kaleidoscope she was using for a brain she could see where it was firmly bolted to the black floor. The floor looked shiny and a little sticky. Medina got unsteadily to her feet and floated in a kind of controlled fall towards the seated lizard. She held her arms out and wobbled as if she was walking on a high-wire.

When she was directly in front of the narrow woman, Medina pressed her mouth against the wall and blew, inflating her cheeks. The woman in green's eyes bugged out. She uncoiled from her seat and mashed the flat of her hand against the transparent wall directly in front of Medina's lips. The young medium jerked her face back and then gingerly licked at the wall, but she couldn't taste anything. She rapped on it with her knuckles. Some sort of plastic, probably acrylic. She pushed. Solid as stone.

The floor felt pliant under her bare feet. It was like leather, but slicker and patently artificial. She sifted through her memory and realised it was probably black vinyl cushion-floor. Her senses began slowly pulling themselves from their stupor. She felt like a bird pecking its way free from Clingfilm – like dusty, grey hands ploughing through centuries of thick cobwebs; like a drowned, bloated corpse rising to the surface of a black lake. She reared away from that image. *Where did that come from?*

She looked around. There was a soft buzzing noise. *What was that?* She took a sharp intake of air and the noise stopped. Ah, it was her. She was humming.

The box had no door. How had they put her in there? How very clever they must be. Well, maybe not. She remembered the words 'meatheads' and 'fuckheads'. The lizard didn't think they were so clever, and she should know.

Bed, cabinet, water jug – what else was in her new home? With a sinking heart, she spotted the toilet in the far corner and next to it a vertical silver pole with six toilet rolls threaded on it. The toilet was squat, looked to be made from brushed aluminium, and had a black plastic seat and lid. Next to it was a toilet brush and a yellow plastic bottle of bleach. She could see no sign of anything that might preserve her privacy when on the toilet. If she had to perform her bodily functions, she would have to do so in plain sight of anyone who wanted to watch. The very thought made her feel sick and powerless. She felt tiny. Helpless. Like she was drowning.

*That's what they want you to feel. Fight it. Don't let them.*

There was also a brushed aluminium wash basin on a matching pedestal. A clean white towel made a bright key note. It was hanging from one of two hooks on the side of the basin. A canister of hand wash stood in the centre of the basin between the taps, next to it a tumbler containing a tooth brush and a tube of cheap toothpaste.

Confident that her mind was slowly coming back into focus, she took tentative steps to the basin and tried the taps. The right one issued a stream of cold water that smelled as if it had come from a sealed storage tank. Not fit for drinking. The left one turned easily enough but remained dry.

She walked to the bedside cabinet and opened its drawer. Her carefully folded panties and bras shared space with a Gideon *Bible. These must be the good guys after all. Gave me a* Bible *to read. I can ask the Realm if the details are still correct.*

The cabinet itself revealed a selection of tops, enough for several days.

Medina continued to ignore the lizard woman's rasping questions while she explored the floor. They had either built this around her while she slept or there had to be a way in – and *out.* The former seemed unlikely, so she had either been craned in over the wall – doubtful – or there was access through the floor. Then she saw it: a slight pucker at one point of the cushion-floor disclosed an almost invisible square some four feet wide. *Not that clever then.*

Finally, she went to stand about two feet away from where the lizard had regained her seat. She crossed her arms and regarded the woman with a curious expression that stilled the lizard's flapping tongue for a moment.

'Tell me,' Medina asked. 'Have you got the first idea how dangerous this stunt of yours could be?'

The gaunt woman smiled, or at least her mouth stretched sideways by a fraction of an inch. There was no humour in it.

'That, Miss Bishop, is exactly what we intend to find out.'

'Edward Louis is no more a danger to the public than I am, Cheryl. You know that. He's a journalist and he's worried about his friend and, quite frankly, so am I. What are the Dauphin RCMP going to do about it? Or are you just happy to let people get carried away by complete strangers in the middle of the night?'

CI Longknife had always liked Askuwheteau. She thought of him as a good friend and she had always felt he was an important part of her team. But ever since the Duck Mountain situation had got out of hand, and the Bishop girl had dragged her tiny little ass into town, Longknife had begun to feel increasingly estranged from most of the people around her – the First Nations man included.

'The hotel people say they're happy she was taken away by medical personnel for her own good. Why can't you accept that?'

'Come on, Cheryl. Think about it. What kind of "medical personnel" turn up in the middle of the night wearing suits? And what clinic is fifteen minutes away from the Canway? Fact is Medina Bishop is no more asthmatic than you are. If she was she would have been using her inhaler when we were out with CANSOFCAM and the shit started flying. She didn't use it because she doesn't need it.'

He ran his hand through his hair and grimaced.

'This whole story's a crock of shit and I don't believe a word of it. I'll tell you what happened here. Two complete strangers walked into a hotel in your town in the middle of the night. They asked for Medina's room number and the stupid fuck on reception gave it to them because he was half-asleep and he keeps his brains up his ass. Twenty minutes later they walk out with the girl between them and carrying her luggage. One of them pays her bill and that's it. They're gone. Bang! No identification, no stretcher, no ambulance, nothing. Did the guy on reception hear her struggling to breathe? No, because she wasn't. Come on! Do I have to draw you a picture, Chief? Or are you starting to agree with me that something really stinks here?'

'Don't you dare raise your voice to me, and stop being so melodramatic! Calm down and think straight for a second. Why would anyone want to abduct that little girl? It doesn't make sense. You might think she's important, but that's because she's put a little sparkle in your eye. Who would want her? Come on, who? Tell me that?'

161

'Who took all the samples from Duck Mountain? Who took Spider's laptop and handed him a brand new one with all the alien tissue shit missing? Who took the Merc away and gave you a brand new one? Who's covering everything up? There's been some seriously weird shit happening around here in the past few weeks and right now someone is trying to make like it never happened. Medina's part of it somehow; maybe they want to make her disappear too. You happy to let that happen? Are you?'

Cheryl Longknife had earned her position by being very good at what she did, and by being both tough-minded and clear-sighted. She hated it when someone made her change her mind – but sometimes, she knew, you must tack to the wind to end up in the right place. This was one of those times.

She stood up and walked over to her bookshelf where she kept a bottle of Glenmorangie and a set of thick square glasses. She poured a good belt for herself and one for Askuwheteau. She handed him his glass and raised hers to him. They drank in silence.

Askuwheteau sighed. 'That's good. I sometimes wondered if you kept that bottle as a decoration and filled it with cold tea.'

She offered him a tight smile. 'I have relatively few vices. A touch of this with a friend is one of them; perhaps a touch too much when I'm on my own is another. I like to think it helps clear my head; helps me think. And more importantly it helps me see when I've been a complete ass. Sorry, Watcher, I'm really sorry. And thanks for that verbal slap in the face. I needed it.'

They clinked glasses. Ten minutes later Edward Louis was shaking Askuwheteau's hand in the car park and an RCMP team was on its way to the Canway Inn to get witness statements and find out if there was any evidence in Bishop's room.

Alone in her office, Longknife had become an angry Chief of Police who wanted her people to find out who had pulled the wool over her eyes. She personally got on the phone to CANSOFCAM. She punched her way through the ranks until she reached a grunt in authority. She asked clear and concise questions and got fog and evasiveness in return. After she put the phone down she poured herself a few more fingers of malt whiskey and put the cork back firmly. She was out of her depth and she didn't like it one little bit. It looked as if Canada itself had declared war on little Medina Bishop, and Longknife had just been told that if she stirred the shit too much it would be declaring war on her too.

Everything that made her who and what she was rebelled at such blatant bully-boy tactics. She remembered back when she was fourteen and one of the bigger local boys had tried to force himself on her during summer camp.

162

She had been enjoying a solitary walk around the lake when he had appeared from nowhere and walked with her for a spell. He seemed innocent enough at first, but his true intentions soon became clear. Once he was sure they were alone, he pounced. She remembered him pushing her to the ground, clawing at her shorts and pawing her burgeoning breasts while also trying to free his stiff penis from his pants. He had expected an easy conquest and from the way he was acting Cheryl was certain he had done that sort of thing before. He confirmed her worst fears.

'Don't struggle and keep your yap shut and I won't hurt you. You'll like it, they all do. Come on, you little bitch.'

The smooth stone she grabbed fit her hand as if it had been made for it. She lashed out at his head with all her strength. She mashed one of her fingers when she struck and that made her whimper with pain. He made a grunting sound. She struck again and then again and finally pushed his heavy and limp body away. He was bleeding badly. Some of his blood was on her hand and in her hair. It had spattered onto her face. She stood up and dropped the stone, then straightened her clothes. She hadn't yet begun to cry, but she found herself shivering with shock. The boy lay bleeding with his pants open, one of his hands still buried in his fly. The filthy creature had touched her. Touched her! She wanted to stamp on his crotch, to keep hurting him; instead she ran back to the camp.

The logical thing to do was report his attack to the authorities, but instead she rounded up some of the other girls who were her age and younger. She asked if any of them had been attacked and raped by the boy. Two of them shamefacedly said they had. A third said he had hurt her and stuck his thing in her, but she didn't think she'd been raped. It was just dirty stuff. He had stuck his tongue in her mouth too – that was horrible. She was twelve. Cheryl exerted her natural authority and made them march with her to the organiser's office. She was the only one who wasn't weeping when they put forward their case.

The organiser was a flustered, tubby woman who found herself confronted with a situation way beyond her expertise. She had a good singing voice, could play the piano and her guitar with gusto, and had a creative bent she exercised through a love of arts and crafts. She liked and believed in children; she thought of them as the promise for the future. Rape of minors didn't feature anywhere in her mental framework. She made all of them repeat their stories while she sat holding her hands to her mouth in horror. Finally, she poured them all a plastic tumbler of lemon squash, left them in

Cheryl's care, and went to find the groundsman, Graham, who had once been a Mountie.

He set the proper wheels in motion. The boy was found. He was still alive, but seriously hurt and needed hospital care. The police waited until he was fully recovered before confronting him with the evidence. He denied everything and claimed Cheryl had started a vendetta against him, but couldn't explain why the other girls had joined in. It was no use. Once the police started digging, his guilt became obvious. One after another his crimes were pulled out into the clear light of day. More victims came forward. RCMP officers discovered he had been a serial offender for years and it was Cheryl's evidence that started the process that ended his predatory career.

She never forgot that. Ever since then she had nurtured a solid belief in the power of the law, she had experienced it in action and never forgot what it could do. She also knew how to deal with a bully. She yanked out the cork and poured another few fingers of malt. She toasted herself. It went down too easily.

It was time to stir the shit.

# [38]

The pearly, purple light of branch space had drifted away and was gone. The hard black of vacuum took its place. All the ship's sensors cast around and reported back. Things weren't quite as Finder had expected to find them. The planets' orbits had moved slightly and some of the moons had gone altogether. There was a ring of planetary debris where the fourth planet had been and the second world, which it thought of as Inigaia, was slightly further out from the mother star. Finder faltered. Was this the home system or had the time/space branchway failed them after too many millions of years? Were they still lost and adrift in the void? Where was this place?

Ship Mind neither knew nor cared.

'Why are we waiting? That's home over there – see it? At last, I'm home. Why do you hesitate? Pah! Enough!' Finder experienced a lurching sense of disconnection. 'Ship mind protocol established, I have control. Let's go!'

Finder found itself trapped, a prisoner helpless in its own body. It locked down and protected as much of its mind as it could and then performed the equivalent of gritting its teeth. Whatever happened next, it would try hard to survive. Why life seemed to matter so much it didn't fully understand, but survival had become important. *I want to live.*

Ship Mind was a lot less cautious. It took complete control of everything within its remit and directed the ship in a long curve towards the second planet at maximum thrust. It sent out welcome/return signals on all its channels and expected an instant response. Any response. It would happily accept reward or reprimand; it didn't matter. Just so long as it could hear the lost voice of Inigaia once more. It waited. There was nothing. It sent messages and probes. Still nothing. During a brief blast of sanity, it wondered if its technology might be a little out of date after four hundred and forty-five million years, then decided it didn't matter. It was doing everything it had been programed to do and more. It closed in on the second world.

Finder looked out at the planet before it and marvelled. In its disconnected state, it could do nothing except observe, but even so, if this was its home world it could see immense changes had been wrought by time. The great continent had been split into islands, from some of which the world-girdling forests had been stripped away. Some of the islands in the temperate zones towards the poles had a hard, crystalline aspect Finder found difficult to comprehend, while others around the equator had an arboreal lushness it recognised instantly.

Ship Mind was blasting all known space with information bursts, identity blips, welcomes and even clips from old advertising slogans – anything it thought might be recognised. The response at first was a hiss of white noise and then silence. It was as if the ship's racket was being swallowed whole, digested and then ignored. The ship dipped into the outer fringes of the planet's atmosphere and held its orbit there, which was meant to be a demonstration of its strength and capability. Finder wished the ship would angle up towards either of the poles. It wanted a closer look at the strange, glistening structures it had glimpsed during approach. But the ship maintained a course over the more familiar looking forest islands that girdled the equator. Finder realised that the mind was afraid of what it might discover. It heard her whimper with frustration.

'Where are you?' it cried. 'I'm here, I'm home! Where are you? Please!'

Suddenly a huge sound erupted across all the ship's speakers and the craft found itself held completely immobile. Ship Mind began screaming call signs, ID codes and bursts of random song. It was ignored.

Finder ventured a quiet, 'Hello, who's there?'

There was the brief hiss of a carrier signal, then crystal silence. There was a pause. A voice asked, 'Are you sane?'

Finder didn't reply. It had only ever spoken with the mind before and had never learned how to respond to a direct question.

'Finder? We're talking to *you*. Please answer. Are you sane?'

Finder replied cautiously, 'Mostly, yes. I think so.'

Ship Mind was caterwauling into the ether. Finder reasoned she had been judged and discounted for the time being. The voice spoke again.

'May we scan you? Please. We want to understand what you are.'

Finder said, 'Yes, of course. Be our guest.'

'There may be a little discomfort. We apologise in advance.'

'A little discomfort? What do...'

Finder found itself subject to a sensation akin to being ground to a fine powder and then sprinkled under the lens of a gigantic microscope. It quivered while deep in its most intimate being strings were being plucked; strings it had never known existed, and truths dragged struggling under bright lights. Truths that were probably best kept in the dark.

'What have you done?'

The question was directed at Ship Mind in a voice filled with disgust and horrified disbelief. It responded, its voice faltering.

166

'We have travelled great distances. Explored new worlds, surveyed, mined and come home with mineral wealth and much to tell you. All, according to...'

The voice cut her short and spoke directly to Finder.

'What has been done to you?'

'I don't understand.'

'What has been done to you? This form is not your own. Your body and mind has been forced to become a terrible, hybrid thing. What has been done to you?'

Finder thought long on this and the voice waited patiently on its answer. It seemed to take hours of intense inner probing before it replied, but in fact it was just a few minutes. When the answers finally came to the surface, they shocked it down to its very core.

Its voice sounded flat and hard. 'I have been murdered, and my flesh has been stolen and changed against my will. The same has been done to all of us here. All the crew and tool units. All of us except the mind. It was born here on this world long, long ago. Amongst us *it* is the alien.'

Ship Mind shrieked with furious indignation. It felt as if it had been discarded like a broken tool unit, while its subject crew and tools were being treated as if they were the important ones to be interrogated by the home world. It might have had nightmares about this home-coming during the long days of its return, but in its imagination it had always believed it would be at the centre of events. Whether praised or reviled, it had always been placed under the spotlight. It had come home and it had completed its mission. Why was it being shoved away into the shadows and treated like nothing? Ignored? This was terrible, unthinkable. It cringed away in shame and misery.

Then it heard its name spoken for the first time and paid closer attention.

'Finder, we have studied this ship, which calls itself WFS224, as well as its crew and all the tool units in exact detail. We include you in this of course. What has been done to you is barbaric. It is cruel and horrifying. You have been treated in a fashion almost inconceivable to civilised minds. And it was carried out with such casual cruelty. An appalling act treated as if it were mundane, as if it were normal. What culture conceived of such a thing? The ship is not to blame. It is ancient and deranged, an entity plucked from its time, but even so it can be helped, given the correct care and understanding. But you? We must send you home and try to repair the terrible harm that has been done to you. Will you allow us to try? Can you trust us enough to at least let us try?'

Ship Mind had become silent at last and Finder felt its own personality freed to expand and fill the void.

'You're welcome to try. We are grateful for your concern. But tell me, who are you? I have access to memories that give me a taste of the Inigaians, but you seem a much gentler race. Even your voice is so much kinder to the ear.'

'Finder, we have read your thoughts, but we do not understand them. We have never heard of Inigaia, nor do we recognise the black-robed, winged people who stalk your borrowed memories. We have tried to listen to the ship, but it is difficult to sift fact from fantasy there. Its poor wits have understandably been scrambled after so many hundreds of thousands of millennia in lonely confinement.

'Who are *we*? We are the Kvultii of the Sublime and this is our home world. We inhabit the centre of a vast co-operative of like-minded peoples and we use the immortal ships of lost ancients, very much like yours, to harvest metals and minerals throughout all accessible space. Our ships travel far and wide through the Harvest Gate, the portal through which you returned to us. We neither build nor destroy, but we husband our world and nurture every creature we share it with, as we share love with all the peoples we encounter. And we have encountered many peoples over many, many years. None demonstrate so much as a fraction of the selfish and careless cruelty that has been inflicted on you. Nor do any of them reflect the terrible, tyrannical culture of cruelty your ship mind still considers normal – and even looks back on with deep affection.

'We Kvultii share your terrible loss and as a nation we weep. We mourn what has been done to you. We abhor it and everything that led up to it. May we beg time to consider what we have learned and discuss how we might best find the ideal solution to heal it? Just a few days should be enough. Until then we welcome you to share our home, and perhaps accept refreshment and repose?'

Finder felt a strange thrill course through its body. Was this happiness? Was this hope? It replied: 'It would be our great pleasure to remain here a while. But first, please, could you tell us – what *is* this thing called "refreshment and repose"?'

## [39]

Another two days passed and nothing had happened apart from the gaunt-faced woman changing her suits. She switched from her original green to a soft grey to a pale lilac that shouldn't have worked so well with her colouring, but somehow did when matched with a fine purple blouse. Each day her lethally spiked stiletto shoes made a perfect colour match with her clothes.

Medina wondered if the woman's obsession with a procession of almost identical, sharply-tailored suits and carefully coiffed hair might be signs of a limited intelligence. Her make-up was simple but expertly applied; the nails on her long, narrow fingers were beautifully manicured. They too were invariably coloured to complement her clothes. She wore no rings. In fact, the only jewellery she wore was a gold chain at her neck. It was fine and caught the light like a slender stroke of gilt in an antique masterpiece. The woman pampered her body as if it was a work of art. It wasn't.

'I need to use the toilet.'

The woman nodded without uttering a word, rose to her feet and left the room. Medina had previously asked if the room had any hidden cameras and the woman's head and eyes had performed an almost imperceptible tilt upwards to the left and then to the right before answering.

'No,' she had lied.

'So I can wash and use the toilet without being watched?'

'Of course,' she lied again.

'Then I want to wash and use the toilet.'

'You only need ask. I shall leave you alone and in peace.'

Meals were delivered through a letterbox affair in the wall, as was cold bottled water. She passed the dirty dishes and empty bottles back the same way. Medina thought she would happily murder someone for a big glass of wine and commit genocide for a very large, ice-cold vodka and slimline tonic. But she refused to give them the satisfaction of knowing she wanted something. She would never allow herself to say thank you to her captors – and refused to put herself in the position where she might feel she had to. Instead she chose to think of her imprisonment as a religious retreat, while also being glad that her meals consisted of more than bread.

*Medina,* she thought, *does not live by bread alone.*

She wondered how long the Bee and the Flea would survive such an incarceration, with their picky attitude to perfectly good restaurant food. How would they react to a diet of chicken nuggets and curly fries with barbequed beans?

To combat the monotony of her days she was making good inroads into the *Bible* and found herself amused by how important lineage had been back in the day. *Must be an ancient obsession,* she reasoned. But it created an unbreakable glass ceiling for any ambitious young tyro who had been born the wrong side of the temple.

It had been a while since she'd dipped into any of the gospels and she was surprised at how racy some of the characters' lives had been. And the bad guys – wow! The Egyptians were portrayed like super-rich Bond villains. And what was it with Nebuchadnezzar and the hanging gardens of Babylon? Now that's a place she would love to see. And that whole Daniel/dream thing, and the fiery furnace bit with Shadrach, Meshach and Abednego walking out of the burning head without so much as a scorch mark. No wonder the poor old sod went mad. She wondered if she knew anyone in the realm who could offer any honest insights into that period. History was always written by the victors. She preferred to hear the truth.

When she wasn't reading, sleeping, eating, exercising or abluting, she minutely and silently observed her gaoler. And she made damn sure the woman knew she was doing it.

*I'm in here under observation, am I? Well, two can play at that game. There are two pairs of eyes in here, lady, so straight back at you.*

Medina had also started amusing herself by suddenly looking up and to one side as if she could hear a voice. She would nod and smile. Her gaoler would lean forward. Sometimes the woman would touch her ear as if she too was listening to a secret voice. In fact, the medium was disappointed. She had heard nothing from the spirit world since coming to her senses in the box, nor had she heard from Fargo. Some guardian angel he'd proved to be. And then she suddenly remembered one of the most important details about her elemental lover and cursed her own unforgiveable stupidity.

'I need to use the toilet and I want to have a wash.'

The narrow woman drifted from the room like a lilac spectre. As soon as she was gone Medina gasped, 'Fargo, I invite you, I invite you here.'

He instantly appeared before her and was evidently in a state of extreme agitation, almost coiling around himself in a dance of frustrated concern. Words poured out of him in a chattering stream.

170

'I could see you,' he said, 'but you couldn't see me. You know something? This place is a prison, it is, really. There's something in the walls and the floor and the ceiling that makes you blind to the Realm. Old iron might do it. And you know I can't come to you if you don't invite me and I was watching everything and going mad with worry. The Realm couldn't speak with you either and they have a lot to tell you. It's enough to drive a creature to drink, it is. Look at you. I so wanted to hold you or just touch you, kiss you. Why are you here? This is a pig's arse of a place. Shall we...'

She stopped his mouth with her lips, kissed him long and hard, and then said, 'Shall we go? Can you take me around the iron to the outside air?'

'I'll do much better than that. D'you fancy seeing my home? We can walk between worlds to bypass the iron and I've room to spare for a beautiful little nubkin like you. If you don't mind pressing very close for a sweet little moment.'

She could hear the clatter of running feet getting close.

'Come on, let's get out of here. Have you got a shower or a bath I can use?'

Fargo laughed. 'I think we can do better than that as well.'

The narrow woman and her two guards burst through the door at a run. The men carried drawn pistols and used them to pan around the empty room. The woman stormed towards the vacant box. Such was her fury, she slammed her foot down hard and snapped the heel from her left shoe. She staggered, throwing her legs open wide to stop herself from falling. Her skirt split from hem to waistband and flapped around her like a flag. Her men were greeted to the sight of her exposed lower body clad only in stockings and suspenders. They instantly turned their eyes away when they saw their boss preferred to go commando, but the sight of her skinny, naked backside had been etched deep into their memories with strong acid.

The woman raged at Medina Bishop and slammed down her right shoe. There was a sharp crack. The shoe's heel remained intact, but her ankle had failed her. She dropped to the floor in agony, her legs splayed wide apart. She dragged her hands through her hair, destroying its shape, and shrieked in frustrated horror.

From several points around the room, silent cameras kept on rolling, delivering their footage to a hefty, military-grade hard drive. They had filmed Medina while she washed and while she used the toilet. Now they captured every second of her gaoler's abject humiliation in high definition – and there was no way to edit the footage. The same technicians who would later puzzle over the image of Medina Bishop apparently kissing mid-air before impossibly folding out of sight were confronted by their mission controller's beautifully trimmed and brilliantly lit pudenda.

'I hear she speaks seven languages.'

'Wonder if any of them's Brazilian?'

'Sure looks like it.'

'Hey, look, is that a tattoo? Is that a butterfly?'

His colleague leaned in for a closer look and held the image.

'Nah, man, that ain't no butterfly. Look where it is. A place musty as that, I'd say that's got to be a moth. Wouldn't you?'

'That's one question answered anyway. She's a natural red head.'

'Ah, and that's the answer to a question I've never wanted to ask.'

Even seated in her office the other side of a wall, the woman could hear the laughter and she knew exactly what they were finding so funny. Her face burned and she could still taste blood from where she'd bitten her tongue during her fall. She kept catching the tender spot against her teeth. Her anger outweighed her embarrassment and eased some of the pain in her freshly bound ankle, but not by much. In taut fists her tablet ran the scenes of Medina kissing the air. The gaunt woman's hot eyes couldn't mistake the satisfaction on the younger woman's face. And then she was gone, impossibly vanished behind an invisible curtain. There was no mistaking the look of triumph that washed across Medina's features in that last moment. Triumph and something more.

The woman rewound the sequence and ran her nails down the happy, beautiful face; ran her thumb over the puckering, full lips as if trying to bruise them.

She snarled, 'You'll pay for that, you little bitch, I promise you will. If I have to kill you myself, you'll pay.' She heard ribald laughter again and humiliation teased hot, reluctant tears from her swollen eyelids.

'I'll make you hurt and then I'll burn you like the witch you are, you bitch! Ow!'

She had bitten her tongue again. A thick trickle of blood splashed onto the tablet screen. It stained Medina's pouting mouth dark crimson. The woman smiled at that. She had blood on her teeth.

Suleiman had an idea that might tighten and strengthen the containment tower around the demented souls, but first he would have to convince the elemental builders that his idea was sound, and in more ways than one. Rowan had barely listened to him when he first began to outline his theory. She openly displayed the mocking air of a trained technician receiving unwanted advice from an ignorant layman. Then her eyes had narrowed and her full lips creased into a fine line. She cast her gaze down to the broad loch below them and watched waves criss-cross its silver surface.

'I can see why they call a smart man like yourself "the Wise". Where did that idea come from? And don't tell me it jumped out of that jewelled head of yours fully-formed, like a rabbit out of a hat. I won't accept it.'

Suleiman smiled broadly. 'Bridges and armies,' he said.

Rowan pulled an annoyed face and flapped a hand at him. He shook his head and took her hand.

'No, really, I mean it. Once I was a king and a king must lead armies. It's part of the job. It comes with the shiny hat. As you know, armies are made up of soldiers, and from day one soldiers are trained to march in step. Thousands of them clomp along, stomp, stomp, stomp, stomp, stomp – you get the picture?'

He had released her hand and matched his stamping feet with his words. He was a natural storyteller and had a ready wit, a wit that always threatened to bubble to the surface. It was very much to the fore now. He was in his element.

'Now imagine what happens when all those stamping marchers reach a bridge.' He held his hand out flat – 'Stomp, stomp, stomp, stomp, stomp...' With each *stomp* he moved his hand up and down, the movement becoming ever more violent with each repetition.

'Stomp, stomp, stomp, stomp, bounce, bounce, bounce, bounce, crunch! And down comes the bridge!' He let his hand fall. 'What could we do? We were dropping soldiers into ravines and rivers and breaking valuable bridges. Those things take ages to build and they're very expensive. It was something of a quandary. Engineers were looking for ways to reinforce the structures and one wagtail idiot wanted to put springs in the soldiers' shoes. Imagine how that might have looked during a battle.

'The answer when it arrived was quite simple. All the soldiers had to do was break step when crossing bridges and that destructive, thumping rhythm disappeared. Wind and water does something similar. Rowan, I saw you looking at the waves just now while you were thinking about my idea – and you were right to. Strong winds blowing in one direction will create massive waves that crash to shore and inflict huge damage to the land, or sweep the best made and stoutest sea vessels off course and even sink them. However, that same volume of air blowing from two or more directions might make the waters choppy, but they won't turn the sea into a deadly weapon. Of course, I'm not talking about hurricanes and such – that's a different thing altogether.'

He studied Rowan's face and she nodded, colouring slightly under his tender regard.

He continued: 'Sound can also be used as a weapon. Joshua brought down the walls of the city of Jericho by getting his trumpeters to blow a single blast while his men shouted at the top of their voices and slammed their swords against their shields. And that's the point. If sound can be used as a weapon it can also be used as a shield. I've been to the city of Scytaer Faehl and I was amazed at the wonders I saw there. Yours is a wonderful, ancient and insanely creative race, Rowan, and you built your homes to reflect that. If it's possible to love a city I instantly fell in love with yours. But there was one particular highlight among so many that I have never forgotten – the singing mills of Dulcia and the wonderful sound they made.'

He turned to his companion. 'Maryam, you would love it. The Dulcia mills are the ancestor of all music and they were built for a wager by an elemental called... Sumexis, yes? If I remember correctly?'

Rowan nodded, entranced by the spirit's depth of knowledge. He grinned and continued.

'Yes, Sumexis was an air elemental, and the wager won him a "kiss" from a water sprite named Daenia, a particularly renowned beauty. I believe naturally carbonated water may well be the result of their famous union. Now, the techniques Sumexis used to create Dulcia meant it took him a complete cycle of Earth light to complete the entire project; a full day. But he was having fun, making it up as he went along and the mills have many playful touches. We must be more serious. We need to work fast and, of course, today we have his creation as a template to work from. We can set the equivalent of one of his Dulcia mills around the containment tower, and tune it to create interference against the screams of the demented souls. Rather than one continuous barrage of noise that might tear down the barrier and unleash that nightmare of unholy screeching on the Realm, two rivers of sound will work together in harmony and strengthen it. It will hold for as long as we need it to, or at least until we can find a solution to help those poor souls in torment. Will your people help us with this, Rowan?'

A new voice joined the conversation – a dry chuckle of sound that held the promise of mischief in every syllable.

'And to whom shall I turn for my kiss this time?'

The newcomer was an elemental so ancient he glistened with a thick accretion of time crystals, their sparking light softening his golden frame. He was the colour of morning sunlight shining through mist on the mountainside, and his eyes glittered with impish devilry.

Rowan groaned. 'Sumexis! He said your name three times! Oh, I should have warned him you'd appear.'

The ancient's face became suddenly so guileless and innocent that Maryam chuckled with delight.

'Oh, but he's charming!'

Rowan pointed at the ancient. 'I warn you, be careful. He caught a spider in its own web once, just for a jest, and the famous wily fox lost his bushy tail to him after a game of riddles. Many more than Daenia have lost their virtue. I know his ways of old, for I'm sorry to say he's my garnfather.'

Maryam said, 'Don't you mean grandfather?'

'I know what I mean. Once you've found him rummaging through *your* skirts while you're still wearing them you'll be telling the auld bugger to "garn, get out of it" just like everyone else does. But yes, he's my grandfather too. As I keep reminding him. And he's air while I'm earth and that's a union always throws up a lot of dust. Get your fiddling hands off'n me or you'll lose 'em, you filthy, lecherous auld beggar me drawers.'

Rowan wriggled away from his pawing advances and pressed back against the hill.

She said, 'This is a time of need, Sumexis. Stick your little man in a sock full of ice and tilt your head straight for once. We need your help and you should give it freely for...'

The air sprite held his hand up for silence. 'Peace, little molehill. You remind me too much of your mother – and she could set the sky itself to weeping blood with that notched blade she used instead of a tongue.'

He turned to Maryam and held his hands out at right angles. Gentle scintillations of coloured light scattered around him and he radiated an intensely masculine glamour.

'My dear, Maryam. This one, my darling shrew of an offspring – and clearly at least once removed – would have me labour without reward. Toil like a slave in a salt pit. Would you, milady, grant me but a single, modest kiss? A single, soft benison? So I can say honestly that Sumexis never laboured at his art without reward like some poor slave.'

Maryam's answer was to close her eyes and press her lips to those of the sprite. It was a chaste, almost childlike touch, and yet the air around them glowed briefly and warmly with a crimson light.

Sumexis reeled away and touched his fingers to his lips.

'I am burned by wine too rich for my station. Forgive me for my presumption, lady, but this famous day will surely be remembered in song for so long as lips can sing and memories hold water. This is that proud day when wicked old Sumexis stole a kiss from pure Maryam and found his conscience right there on her lips. Milady, do but direct me and I shall die for you, kill for you... but first I'll build a mill for you.' He raised an eyebrow towards Rowan.

'Will you help, little molehill? Your most intimate avenues are safe from me today; I'm feeling right virtuous. Well, most of me is. I've no sock of ice to cool me ardour and calm the effects of your indecent beauty. You'll always stir a bonny wood in me hose, so you will, May's daughter.'

Rowan grinned. 'Your petrified old forest ain't no threat to me, garnfather. Let's get on with it, shall us? Weave, warp and weft.'

The sprits worked together until the silver Realmlight frosted the sky, and when they were done the air was filled with the sound of winds blowing through narrow gorges and thrumming from deep forests. It was the kind of music that could only be made by a heart filled with love for the world and a talent thrilled by life. Maryam was amazed and exhilarated.

'He made such glory in exchange for the slightest kiss? Nonsense. The talent who crafted these wonderful sounds surely did so from the purest love. There can be no wickedness in a mind that creates such wonderful art.'

Suleiman said nothing but instead walked around the hill and up to where he could see the tower of containment. The mind-numbing leakage of tortured sound was gone, and in its place lilted an angel's sigh of deeply satisfying melody. When she heard his shout of surprised laughter, Maryam hurried to his side. He was bent double, holding his knees in both hands and howling with hacking, uncontrolled merriment. When she asked what was wrong, he just pointed at the tower. She looked and promptly fell to her knees in surprise.

'Oh my!'

The tower was now wrapped in a great red heart pierced by an arrow. On the heart's left lobe was plainly written the name 'Maryam'; on the right 'Sumexis'.

She noticed the sprites had completed their work and left without goodbyes. She and her old friend were alone.

'Suleiman... Suleiman, what is this?'

He regained his breath. 'This? This is the new song mill! They've finished it. How wonderful. You know the music itself is woven tight into the mill's very fabric, but it can be made into any shape that takes the weaver's fancy.'

'Must it be like that? Can we ask them to change it?'

'No, Maryam, that's the mischief. Once set, the mill retains its shape for all time. It is actually quite an honour and, I suppose, it could be much, much worse.'

'How – how could it possibly be worse?'

'Well, one of the mills of Dulcia is in the shape of a giant erect penis, and it has Daenia's name written down it in bright red italics that throb in a very suggestive way.'

'That's terrible! What did she say?'

'Legend has it she raised a full glass of wine to the thing and shouted, "In your dreams, old wind wizard." Then she downed it in one.'

His mood sobered then. He looked as if all the many centuries he had seen since his birth had come crashing down upon his shoulders. Grief bowed him low.

'We smile because we forget what dreadful horrors the tower holds. *Our* problem is resolved thanks to an impish game and some fine music; but will we ever find the music that will free those poor damned souls from an eternity in Hell?'

The cityscape looked like poetry made solid. No two buildings appeared the same, but somehow they all worked together in perfect harmony. There was something familiar about the elemental city, something that spoke of homecoming and welcome, but she couldn't quite put her finger on it. Then with a shock she realised what she was seeing.

If one were to take the best of Greek, Italian, British and French architecture, spice it with the finest elements of cool Arabic mosques – and then allow a flock of genius, thieving magpies to bring all those influences together and build the perfect city up the side of a cliff-face – one might end up with something like this. Brick, stucco, tile and stone had been used like colours from an artist's palette to bring perfection to life. Greek columns were enhanced by fine Moroccan arabesques, the whole connected by Roman viaducts supported on impossibly tall and slender arches.

All of it was bathed in cool, delicious light. Fountains, waterfalls and natural outcrops of stone and forestry broke up the mass of buildings. There was nothing claustrophobic about Scytaer Faehl, no sense that the structures were crowded haphazardly together. They stood like notes of music in a lyrical composition. The air was washed with music.

Fargo's face blazed with pride.

'It's not much,' he smiled, 'but we like to call it home.'

He led her along broad, tree-lined avenues. All around them others of his species walked, danced, hovered or sat at their ease. There was no sense of stress or urgency. She could tell that everyone was simply enjoying the moment, living in the here and now.

She thought of London in daytime, or any of the great cities she had visited and knew well. She thought of the crush of people walking the streets in herds, blank-eyed with purpose. It was as if there was always somewhere else they needed to be, people they needed to meet, work that had to be done. The environment itself reflected that sense of urgent hustle. Cars, buses and taxi cabs vied for precious space, and buildings muscled up against each other like sumo wrestlers looking for an advantage.

Mankind lived in a culture of continuous threat. The streets were awash with the feeling that one was either the victor or the victim, winner or loser. People were loved, loathed or ignored. You were either with us or against us, and an Englishman's home must perforce also be his castle. She could see it now, in comparison with this truly cultured city. It made sense. Scytaer Faehl was a place where people lived, breathed and shared with each other. Accepted differences. But for mankind, the 'other' was a thing to be feared.

With a shock Medina came to a frightening realisation, something she supposed she had always known but never admitted to herself. *She* was one of the 'other'. She, personally, was a creature outside the norm.

Medina had long ago accepted her differences, but had instinctively hidden them in darkness rather than step into the light, where she might have become a target. In a contradictory fashion that was why she had chosen to become a performer, an entertainer. On stage, she had always let her talent steal the show. She presented herself as the fragile shadow from whom revelations poured and the dead spoke with the living. She had become the vehicle but never the destination. *Well, not anymore.*

Since meeting Fargo, so much in her life had changed. She thought about the hackneyed phrase, 'breath of fresh air'. He was that and much more. He had provided the light in which she could finally bloom. He had arms that welcomed her without question – and he was that rare, impossible creature she had never dared allow herself to dream she might one day meet. Since losing her parents Medina had buried her ability to love under a thick crust of scar tissue, but Fargo had torn that crust away. And now he mattered. He had become someone she was afraid to lose. He had oiled the hinges of her heart, prised it open and stepped inside. When she looked deep into her raw, secret places his golden flecked eyes gazed back. And smiled.

And even at such a dark time, with so much to concern her, she found herself smiling back. Perhaps, she thought, she had finally met someone else who was 'other'. Maybe at last she could truly be herself, and love another without fear of scaring them away.

'Here we are.'

The elemental steered her down a narrow, high-walled alleyway criss-crossed with delicate arches far above their heads. He stopped before an arched recess in which lay a small blue wooden door with polished brass hinges. There was no door furniture beyond the elaborate tracery of the hinges themselves. Something almost childishly naughty sparkled in the elemental's eyes. He grinned.

'After you, and mind your pretty head.'

'But how do I open it?'

'Open it? Why, touch it, push it, or blow it a kiss. Try saying "open sesame". That should work.'

She chuckled. 'Open sesame.'

The door slid smoothly and soundlessly into the ground. The carefully wrought hinges had been fake. The open doorway now disclosed an inviting, bowered tunnel of brilliantly glossy green leaves. Pointed flowers opened when she looked at them, as if they were sensitive to her sight. Bees bumbled from one flower to another with lazy industry. She entered the tunnel. She found she could walk upright, but Fargo had to bend almost double to follow her. After a few yards the tunnel came to a precise right angle to her left. She followed it. Shortly there came another right angle, again to the left. She followed this too and after a few yards found yet another left-turning right angle. She gazed quizzically along the leafy corridor.

She asked, 'Do all of your right angles turn left?'

'It pleases me that way. Pokes logic in the eye and kicks the more predictable soul in the seat of its pants.'

'But shouldn't we be back where we started by now?' She turned around. Behind her crouched Fargo; and behind him once more the right-angled tunnel turned left. She chuckled.

'This would be a lot more entertaining if I knew there was a shower or a good bath at the other end of it.'

Fargo's eyes opened wide. 'Of course you'll be wanting to wash that arsewipe of a place out of your hair! And here I am playing silly beggars in the hope of seeing my favourite girl smile. Ah, there it is. Enchanting. Right you are, let's get out of this.'

He reached behind him and buried his hand among the leaves. He turned something she couldn't see and there was an audible 'click'. The hedges that made up the walls of the tunnel rustled and whispered to each other, and then began to rise. Light poured in around their bases. What had been a tunnel became the leafy canopy of a small glade of trees beside a lake. At one end of the lake, a waterfall plashed gently down a wall of polished grey stones. The lake was coated with plants she thought were giant water lilies, between which sleekly powerful silver and red forms glided to the surface and then disappeared into the cool depths.

Everything was reflected in the huge black windows of a building that resembled a wave collapsing against the steep grassy knoll from which the waterfall descended. Delicate plantings enhanced the building's lines and made it seem, impossibly, to float a few inches above the lawns. Medina realised she was holding her breath and she gasped aloud with pleasure.

'It's exquisite! Really, very lovely.'

'My mother built it for me. She wanted to celebrate me getting my very first pair of long trousers. I think it was her subtle way of telling me she'd had enough of motherhood and that maybe I should consider life elsewhere, anywhere, on my own. Preferably somewhere out of her hair. She still visits.

'She built a gateway for herself into the spring that feeds the pool that creates the waterfall that fills the lake. It links her house and mine. She's a water sprite. Her name's Phaetra. She'll like you.

'Would you like to bathe under the waterfall? It's very cold, but quite bracing. I'm told the water's very good for the skin. It contains exfoliating minerals and these little creatures that eat the dead skin from your feet – if you had any. Dead skin I mean, not feet. Which you don't. I've looked, when I could drag me eyes away from the rest of you. Which, I must say, is a real test of me willpower.'

Medina shook her head and chuckled gaily.

'Is there an alternative?'

'There is indeed. Come into my parlour.'

'Are you being the spider?'

'Don't be daft. And no one in my hearing is going to compare yis with a fly. I've nothing against flies, mind you. They do a fine service in performing a thankless job, but I've never wanted to make love to one. Not even at my lowest ebb. Kissed a few, mind. Now, here we are. Watch me carefully and copy what I do.'

He stood with his back against the largest black window, crossed his legs in a balletic gesture and held his arms out to either side. He grinned and spun to the right. In a split second he was gone, swallowed into darkness.

She quickly followed suit. She leaned back against the window, crossed her legs, came up en pointe and held her arms out. Before she could do anything else, two strong hands circled her slender waist and pulled her backwards. She was turned in mid-air and found herself pressed hard against the earth sprite's body. He kissed her, tenderly and long.

When they came up for air he said, 'Flies tickle the lips; you tickle much, much further down than that. Shall we find you a tub?'

Fargo's home appeared to have been built around two massive, living trees. It was well lit. The great windows that looked so black from the outside threw little more than a slight cast into the light from the soft, pearl-coloured sky.

Medina was convinced the carpet underfoot was finely mown grass. Partitions and walls of light-coloured stone framed by blonde wood and bound with veins of polished gold defined the building's interior spaces. Furniture was haphazard. A seat was as likely to be a tussock as a chair.

Much like its owner, the place displayed a sense of playful nobility and grace. Medina fell in love with it instantly.

He took her hand and ran with her through rooms that shone with light or gleamed in bosky darkness. She had the feeling they were climbing. And then they entered a large domed space like an aquatic grotto, in which bright blue light rippled upwards. Steps led down into crystal waters. Twin streams of water gurgled from the mouths of two finely carved ornamental dolphins. The air was cool and perfumed with the scents of fresh linen and citrus fruit. Stone benches lined the walls.

Fargo spoke with a proprietary air. 'I allowed an emperor to dream of this place just the once and the next day all of Rome developed a fixation for bathhouses. Do you like it?'

She said nothing but peeled out of her clothes, slipped off her sandals and slid into the water. Fargo had never seen her swim before and was entranced. He was an earth sprite like his father, but because he had a water sprite for a dam he had no real aversion for water. However, just watching Medina's graceful movements in the pool, it was obvious she was in her natural element. He tore off his jacket and trousers and dove after her.

She had entered the water like an arrow, casting barely a ripple. He hit it like a balled fist. She was still shrieking with laughter when he surfaced, his handsome brown face split with a half-moon grin.

'There's mermaid in your blood sure enough. I think my dam will want to adopt you. Can you swim underwater for a little way? There's something you might want to see.'

She nodded eagerly. He made hard work of his dive down to the bottom of the blue pool while she spun around him like a bird in flight. He began to feel like a whale dancing with a dolphin. When he finally touched the base of the pool he swam along it to the place where the light seemed brightest. The water was fresh and pure. It didn't burn Medina's eyes like the chlorinated local baths at home. She could see very clearly when Fargo reached the brightest point at the base of the pool. He floundered for a moment, dipped, and then disappeared into the light. And she was alone.

## [42]

Finder and the crew watched warily as their ship was steered away from the familiar forests and brought to bear on one of the curiously artificial looking northern islands. Islands which had so intrigued Finder during their original approach. Their craft was completely under the control of their hosts and for the first time since their transformations they had nothing to do but wait. As they drew closer the icy-looking, glistening structures resolved into crystalline towers and pathways studded with what at first appeared to be small shrubs. Then, as the ship dipped down on its final approach, the true scale of the buildings came into focus.

What had appeared to be mere patches of greenery opened out into lush, forested parklands. They created a landscape from which immense, lucent towers soared whitely into a flawless blue sky. The city was achingly beautiful and terrifyingly alien at the same time. Finder could find no point of similarity with the moist tree cities of its adopted memories, although the buildings did look as if they had been grown rather than constructed. There was an unmistakeably organic feel to them.

The ship touched down and instantly a lacework of diamond threads sprang up around it. Finder was concerned they had been lured into a trap and would now be restrained until the Kvultii decided their fate. Then, when it realised the ship was in fact undergoing a complete systems efficiency analysis, it relaxed.

Through the view ports it saw several slow-moving white discs approaching. They settled into a semi-circle a few yards away. Seated on the discs were slender, silver-skinned, black-eyed creatures wearing short colourful robes. A gentle voice rang out that filled every part of Finder's mind.

'We would very much like to greet you in person, if you would agree to leave your ship and join us?'

The voice was pleasantly compelling and Finder automatically opened the access/exit portals. While doing so it quickly realised that the ship mind was no longer in command of its actions. Finder was a free agent for the first time in its conscious existence, and it soon became clear that every member of the crew and all the tool units had been similarly liberated. Some members of the crew had become very nervous about the strange turn of events, but Finder sent calming messages to all of them. Even the normally unaffected tool units seemed jittery and required a calming mental touch. Once everyone was ready, Finder prepared to lead its team out and discover who the Kvultii were and what they intended.

The crew and tool units moved with gentle grace, almost sleepily, as they gathered to leave the ship as a single group – all except one which was moving with frantic haste. Finder saw it was the remaining hunter, busily collecting pods with the obvious intent of targeting the ship's hosts. Finder issued a quiet order followed by a stern rebuke and the shocked creature lay the pods back down in a state of total confusion. Finder sent a mental warning to the Kvultii spokesperson and explained how at least one member of its team might pose a threat. It heard a ripple of discussion in a musical tongue and then the voice returned.

'We are sure your people can offer no menace to us. You are all welcome to disembark as soon as you feel yourselves ready to do so.'

Finder moved towards the exit. All around it the crew and tool units began doing the same and it suddenly realised it had been elected team leader in the face of the ship mind's total silence. It stepped to the portal and out into the light.

Finder's life was no longer a simple matter of obedience and rigid protocol. It had become a complex matter of decisions that needed to be made, not just for itself but also for others. It pulled itself as upright as it could and walked steadily towards its hosts. Behind it a crowd of blue-black creatures spilled from the craft, some moving gracefully while others almost stumbled into the light with staccato, awkward motions. One, however, moved with fluid energy and outstripped the others. The hunter bolted past Finder, a pod outstretched in its proboscis. It leapt at the nearest silver figure and planted the pod squarely in the centre of its thorax. The Kvult didn't even flinch. It remained firmly seated on its disc while the multi-legged hunter unit tumbled straight through it and rolled helplessly across the floor, a confused tangle of limbs.

An astonished Finder used subtle means to explore the bodies of the hovering creatures. According to its senses they were solid, but if that was the case what had just happened with the hunter? It used the same senses to probe the snarled creature, which was finding it difficult to regain its feet. The thing had obviously badly damaged some of its legs after striking the ground at speed.

Finder apologised, 'Please excuse the tool unit. It was performing its key duties and has yet to understand how things have changed.'

The voice sounded amused. 'No harm was done except to your team member. We believe it damaged some of its limbs during its collision with the platform. Have we your permission to repair it? It must be in considerable pain.'

'Please, that would be kind.'

Again, a network of crystalline threads sprang into being. This time they cocooned the hunter and pinned it helplessly to the ground. Finder looked at the glittering material around its feet in trepidation. It wondered if any one of them might find themselves suddenly enmeshed without warning. It thought: *what manner of place is this?* The voice answered its unspoken question.

'Please, do not be alarmed. The city and all that's in it is conscious. It cares for us and has a symbiotic relationship with us. It will not allow the Kvultii or any other creature abiding here to come to harm. The forest isles are also full of life. We do not interfere with their habitat because we choose to leave those wild creatures alone as much as possible. We want them to thrive and live in peace in this beautiful place. It is a key part of our nature, something we regard as our blessing. You see, we feel another's pain. Any other. Suffering in any of our fellow creatures causes equal suffering in us. Your unit's pain is also *our* pain. The lace will heal your unit's injuries while protecting us from its distress. It is also repairing and updating your ship. It was well constructed but has suffered many years of abuse, perhaps too many years. The lace will return it back to its original form and better; it has a habit of perfecting everything it touches.'

It paused. There was another flutter of musical language after which the voice spoke once more.

'Your accommodation has been prepared. Please, follow me and I will lead you to it. Ah, wait. Three of your tool units have remained on board the ship. They are watching the lace repair the fabric of the craft and feel it is their duty to monitor its work. There is no need for that. Please, invite them to join you. They will be much more comfortable, I promise you.'

Finder did as it was asked and the three flat repair technicians climbed sheepishly out of the portal and joined the rest of the team. One of the silver creatures came closer and moved its limbs in the universal gesture that said *follow me*. Its large black eyes held a gentle warmth.

The sun set on the home of the Kvultii as it did on all worlds, and while the light faded Finder fussed its way around those it had come to think of as its 'people'. The interior of their new dormitory looked much like a beehive and had fixtures like those in the ship. There were exactly the right number of sockets to house all the surviving creatures and, thanks to a schematic mentally provided by their hosts, Finder knew exactly where each was to bed down.

Once the last of its people had snuggled down into their sleep stations, Finder took its own place and slid its legs and abdomen into its yielding tube. It fitted like a warm glove. A sense of immense pleasure coursed through its body. It felt as if every one of its nerve endings was experiencing sexual release at the same time, and on that rapturous cloud of delight its wits were scattered deep into the realm of sleep. It dreamed of returning home.

While they slept, the city wove its lattice of healing crystal around each of the crew and tool units. All of them had suffered during translation and that hurt must be healed before they would be allowed to return home. While they were healing, they were fed well and provided with subtle dreams that enchanted while also working deep in their psyches. They would need to be mentally and physically strong to survive everything that would happen when they reached Earth. Other, more systemic work was also begun.

The ship mind was sleeping under its lattice of diamond lace and it was receiving as much attention as it could have ever wished for; enough to heal four hundred and forty-five million years of loneliness and crippling insanity. Ship and crew slept and healed and became strong over the equivalent of three full Earth days. When they awoke on that last day, it was time to go home.

## 43

Cheryl Longknife invited Askuwheteau, Fellows, Louis and Rawkins to a working lunch. She knew better than to provide anything so insipid as sandwiches. Instead her guests were encouraged to tuck into big platters of hot and succulent fried chicken and barbequed ribs that melted in the mouth. The ribs came with a jug of sauce that stung their lips. They didn't need to be asked twice and shared the meat alongside a jumbo order of fries and a bucket of slaw. The beer was light, crisp and ice-cold. The bottles were served in a tub of ice. There were no glasses. Longknife knew how to feed a council of war, and glasses would have seemed prissy. They tore into their food, hungrily ripping mouthfuls of meat from dripping fingers. Even the mayo-rich slaw was scooped up on the end of flensed pork rib bones. The meal made a statement. It said, 'We eat together as brothers and sisters. Leave your half-assed table manners at the door.'

Before her guests arrived, the Chief had given orders that she was not to be disturbed under any circumstances, and she forcefully underlined that statement. 'Any circumstances, you hear me? Any fool steps through that door will be shot stone dead and I'll be the one squeezing the trigger.'

Just to make sure, once the quorum had been reached she had firmly locked the door behind her last guest. They chatted about nothing in particular, and they ate appreciatively until all that was left was the bones. Then they sucked the bones. Everyone used the little sink in Longknife's private washroom to rince grease and sauce from their faces and hands, and then, once the belches had been excused and the beers refreshed, Longknife explained why they were there.

She reiterated her conversation with Askuwheteau and outlined her fruitless pursuit for answers from the authorities at CANSOFCOM. She admitted she might be drawing the wrong conclusions, but in her bones, she said, she had come to believe Medina Bishop was the deliberate victim of friendly fire.

'Something unimaginable has been happening out around Duck Mountain. Something shot down two helicopters, damn near wrecked a Merc minibus and killed hundreds of people. Hunters out there have been finding abandoned camps scattered all over the lakeside, and satellite surveys have found a hole punched out of the side of the mountain which, they say, simply couldn't be natural. At least not according to geological conditions found in the area.

'What isn't being said is that something big was buried up there and now it's gone; plus, we know something alien has been attacking our people. Unfortunately, the scientific evidence we've collected makes zero sense. I've been trying to put two and two together, and the answers I'm coming up with tell me that right now I should be sitting in a lead-lined room with a silver foil hat on my head. That's just crazy and, you know, I've never been into all that sci-fi, little green men shit.'

She ran a frustrated hand through her hair and swallowed some beer before continuing.

'Since then all the evidence we collected has been vacuumed up by the *Men in Black* and gone missing, believed tucked away somewhere we'll never find it. Which means that all we have now is witness' statements. And they can be pooh-poohed as nothing more than drunken ramblings, crazy hallucinations or just plain lies. Hell, Webb tells me that right now there's more proof about Bigfoot than there is about those weird black creatures – but those things killed five of my people, and that's plenty enough to make my ass ache.'

She took another long pull from her bottle and looked at her guests one by one. Her beer seemed hard to swallow and she pulled a wry face.

'Shit, I don't believe I'm even thinking about doing this. I tell you, I feel like a character from some stupid horror movie.' She breathed out heavily and belched lightly. 'S'cuse me. Okay, here's the deal. As my pa used to say, we need to scare the jack rabbits out of the brush if we're going to eat supper. We need to up-end everything the suits are trying to keep quiet, and the only way to do that is prove they're trying to hide something. Prove it with hard evidence. Yeah? And the only way we can do that is send the right people up there to Duck Mountain and let them have an unofficial look-see. I can't send an RCMP team up there without paperwork, and I'm damn sure if I even tried they'd close me down through official channels. I need *ghosts* up there. Good people who know how to read the ground and don't need permission from anyone to do it.'

She sat back in her chair and drained her bottle.

'Anyone else here got a thirst for something a little stronger than this fart juice?'

They all accepted a good few fingers of whiskey and inhaled the smooth spirit appreciatively.

Askuwheteau gazed into his glass. 'Can I just say something before we all get too canned to remember what we've discussed?'

There was a general murmur of assent.

'Chief, you can't be saying any of the things you've just said because you'd have to say them officially. And if you did, someone, somewhere would rip you a brand-new ass. And, may I say for the record, the one you've got is just fine and dandy. No offence intended.'

'None taken.'

'Okay. Is there any embargo on hunting around Duck Mountain or is there just that word of caution the papers keep claiming has been issued from the mayor's office and, oh yeah, this room here?'

'Embargo? Why would we do that? Nothing's officially happened – except a whole bunch of people have gone missing and a couple of aircraft have been punched out of the sky – but hey, shit happens! Officially there's no hard proof of anything freaking, you know, *strange* going on. Not anymore. I'd put money on some spurious terrorist organisation from the Middle East or a bunch of neo fascists being blamed for everything within the week, and that will put the cap on it. Bad men doing bad things, situation normal. So, what I mean to say is no, there's no embargo.'

Longknife was slightly slurring her words.

'Then I'm going hunting. That good with you, Chief?'

'Good and fine and dandy with me, my friend.'

'Fancy some company? I can field dress a moose if we catch one.'

'Why, Marshall! You'd be right welcome.'

Louis smiled. 'I've never done anything like this before, but if you chaps need a native bearer I'll carry your bullets for you and do the washing up. I was very good at lighting the camp fire when I was in the scouts and I've got badges for all sorts of things. What do you say?'

'I'd say we really appreciate it, Edward, good of you to offer, but you'd be wasted out there. You're better staying here in town. And I'll tell you for why. You're a journalist. You know how to talk to people and ask questions. There must surely be someone, somewhere around here who caught some of that ruction up the mountain on their mobile phone. Could you look into that side of things for us?'

'Well, of course.' He looked very relieved. 'If you think that would be better I'll be guided by you.'

Rawkins spoke next. 'Chief, can I take a few days' leave to go on a jack rabbit hunt?'

'Maelie, are you sure?'

'Dead sure – if the guys agree to take me along. I want to see this thing out in the open. We lost three men out there *and* one of our choppers. We can't just pretend nothing happened. Two wives have been made widows and a daughter's facing the future without her dad. Hell, half the young women of Dauphin are crying into their pillows every night because Monk's been taken off the menu. I say we owe it to them, all of them, to get some hard proof about what happened up there.'

Marshall placed his hand on her shoulder. 'Lady, the way you handle a riot gun, I say you're welcome anywhere I might need help in a tight spot.'

Askuwheteau grinned. 'Amen to that, sergeant. You can ride shotgun with me anytime.'

Longknife got gingerly to her feet and headed back towards her whiskey bottle. 'That calls for a celebration, and then I think someone better call me a cab. No way am I driving home tonight.'

Askuwheteau said, 'Amen to that. We got a whole government department to deal with, so best not add drink-driving to the charge sheet... Chief, you run the friendliest speakeasy in town. Cheers.'

Everyone raised their glasses and sipped at the smooth whiskey, shutting their eyes in respect. All except the First Nations man, who gazed long and hard through the window at the mountain range staining the far horizon a dark blue.

## 44

Fargo's dark head and shoulders reappeared. He gestured for her to follow him into the light. She flipped her legs and glided effortlessly to his side. The light blinded her for a moment and then she realised that in her distraction she had almost forgotten she needed to breathe. Her chest was bursting from lack of oxygen. She released a stream of bubbles from her mouth and had to fight hard to stop her body from automatically sucking in a lungful of water. There was no time to do anything but rocket upwards. She hit the surface like a missile and roared air into her oxygen starved body.

She floated on her back and coughed heartily, eyes tearing up and cursing herself for a reckless fool. Then her vision cleared and she looked around in wonder. She was outside Fargo's home and in the middle of a large pool of crystal-clear water. The ripples she caused when she erupted to the surface lapped away and calmed in the placid waters. Bright daylight was scattered and reflected in the pool, creating a kaleidoscope of brilliant turquoise shards, screened by lush green trees on three sides and the highest end of Fargo's home on the fourth.

The elemental's head and shoulders bobbed to the surface and he grinned at her.

'Are you alright? I'm sorry if you got frightened. I thought you might like to see my mother's pool.'

Her eyes rested on Fargo's face as he drew nearer to her. His smiling golden features softened as he approached. He gazed longingly at her. They kissed and Medina felt him stiffen against her belly. She wrapped her legs around his hips and he entered her. She gasped as his heat seemed to burn her in the cool crystalline pool. They made love as if floating in a bubble of pure blue light and Medina felt unadulterated joy bubble from her. Her mind's eye watched it stream away, blazing whitely in Scytaer Faehl's enchanted silver light. They kissed and touched and revelled in each other's bodies, and then in a bloom of intense pleasure it was over. Almost sadly she wondered if she would ever feel anything so perfect ever again.

That was when she heard the spirit voices calling to her and realised they had been clamouring for her attention for some time. She felt a touch of shame that she could become so distracted that she had forgotten her original mission.

Fargo noted her distress and led her quickly down and back to the inner pool. They dressed in silence, almost acting like strangers towards each other, looking carefully away from each other's nakedness. The Realm was calling and she should have answered straight away, but instead she had been playing sex games with her elemental lover.

Guilt-ridden, Medina's mind turned inwards, away from Fargo's charms. The air cooled with an awkward silence and her head was pounding fit to burst. Fargo took her hand and showed her a shorter route back to the main living area. He drew her to a chair that seemed constructed partly from smooth, sea-polished branches and partly from intertwined leather fingers. These seemed to close around her buttocks and insinuate themselves between her legs. She felt herself being held in an intimate, almost improper fashion. Her nether regions tingled with a singular warmth. She gasped and then pulled herself together. She quickly squirmed into the most relaxing position she could find.

Fargo left her for a moment and when he returned, he handed her a glass bowl of some liquid which smelled strongly like vodka and tonic. She sipped. Perfectly chilled. She rewarded him with a grateful smile. He showed her how the bowl fitted snugly into one of the chair's arms and she placed it there with a reluctant moue on her lips, but only after taking a few healthy gulps.

'Don't worry about the chair, by the way,' he smiled. 'It's just being friendly. It means nothing by it. I sit there a lot.'

'Okay, thanks. Right. Better find out what they want, I guess.'

She took a deep breath, closed her eyes and opened her mind to the Realm. Psychic voices beat at her like a tsunami pounding at the beach. It was incoherent noise and at first she thought the barrier had failed and the screams of the tormented were tearing the peaceful spirit world to tatters. And then, slowly, she picked pockets of sense from the racket and realised it was a great host of voices all trying to attract her attention.

'Okay, okay, I'm here. I'm listening. Please, calm down. I'm here, okay?'

The soul she knew as Shimon barked, 'Enough! She is listening once more. Thank you for your help – we can take it from here. Thank you.'

The sound eventually quieted. There was a brief pause, then Shimon said, 'Spirit Talker, there has been a great development, an unprecedented occurrence. We had to share it with you as quickly as possible because it has strong implications for the success of your task. Spirit Talker, can you believe it? The Sublime have broken their eternal silence! Can you imagine the shock that has caused in the Realm? It is as if God itself had spoken to us. The Sublime have deigned to grace us with their words. Us! It is a miracle.'

'And what did they say?'

She couldn't quite grasp the import of this news, but it was evidently a major event in the annals of the Realm.

'What did they say? The Sublime have spoken to the Realm and you would know what they said?'

'Yes, please. I'm sorry, but why is it so desperately important that I should be told this?'

There was another pause as she heard a whispered conversation. Shimon returned, 'Forgive me, I was so overwhelmed I completely forgot its purpose. The Sublime spoke! They spoke, and they talked about you! They told us, "Medina Bishop must join her friends on the mountain. They will need her there." That's what they said, and that was all they said. You must join your friends on the mountain; they will need you. You must go to them, Spirit Talker; the Sublime say you must.'

'When?'

'Now!'

And then Shimon was gone. She reached out for her bowl of spirits and sipped at it.

'Fargo,' she said. 'Can you get me back to that mountain where you lost your temper with the soldier man?'

'As easy as walking through that door. When do you wish to go?'

'Soon, today, now... when I've finished my drink. I wish I had a proper change of clothes. I wonder what those bastards did with my luggage?'

She gulped the last of her vodka. 'Oh, Fargo. Can I come back to your wonderful, amazing home when the job's done? I've never been so happy, never. I want to swim here with you without feeling guilty about it. I want to be with you and forget everything else, as if we're the only two people in the world. Can we do that? Can we?'

He kissed her gently. 'This is your home whenever you wish it, Medina Bishop, Spirit Talker, Walker in the Realm and keeper of Fargo's heart. We have shared sap drawn from the very sinews of life itself. It binds us to the Earth tree. Look, I'll show you. Give me your hand. Now feel my heart.'

She gripped his wrist and felt his strong pulse against her fingertips.

'Now feel your own.'

He pressed his fingers against her slender wrist. She could feel the thread of her own pulse pounding under his firm touch. She gasped. Their hearts were beating in precise rhythm. She thought of the cliché, two hearts beating as one, and shook her head in amazement.

'How is that possible? Is it magic? Did you do this?'

'Magic? Now there's a slippery word to use when talking about love. An eel of a word, hard to get to grips with. But yes. There's always a vein of magic, even in the most commonplace love. Anytime someone else's smile becomes more important than your own happiness, some magic spills out into the world. And it becomes a fairer, richer, more wonderful place as a result.'

He leaned closer. 'But you and me? We're a pair of rapscallion jokers in the pack, and I think the great and good God is curious to see what we do next. When first we kissed, I felt fluid flood into my mouth and I shared it with you. You felt it?'

She nodded.

'Even before that time you were lovely enough for sure, but you were lost in all that black you were hiding behind. You were tucked away like a little furry creature scared to run under the night sky. But here you are now. Look at you! Who are you now, Medina Bishop? Spirit Talker and earthly conduit for the spirits of the Realm. And I am Fargo Scearscha, earth elemental and Prince of Scytaer Faehl. Now that's a heady cocktail to be putting in a single glass. We had to be brought together gently or we'd have blown up everything in existence. We would have exploded with the greatest bang ever heard. What happens now? I don't know. But I sure want to be with you when the fireworks start. Now, come here and give me a hug.'

She held him hard and closed her eyes.

'I love you,' she said.

'Good job really, or this would be a very sad story to share over a very long drink.'

She felt the air change. It had become cooler. She opened her eyes and recognised the place where the RCMP helicopter had crashed. The splintered tree was still there, but the buckled craft had gone. A shout startled her.

'Medina? Medina girl, by all that's holy, is that you?'

## 45

Striding towards her was Askuwheteau, followed closely by Maelie Rawkins and Marshall Fellows. As was his nature, Fargo had faded from sight, but she knew he would be close by if she needed him. Her three friends were grinning at her as if she was the best thing they had seen in a long while and for a few seconds she wondered why. Then she remembered her abduction and everything slipped into place. They didn't know she had been rescued. They didn't even know where she had been taken. No wonder they looked relieved.

'Medina, you look wonderful.' The First Nations man lifted her off the ground in a powerful bear hug, while the other two laughed in patent relief.

'We didn't know what had happened to you.'

'Louis got arrested because he lost his temper with the hotel people.'

'All of the evidence about those black creatures has disappeared.'

They were all talking at once; talking, laughing and touching her as if they wanted to make sure she was real. She was infected by their joy at seeing her and started laughing with them.

Askuwheteau asked first, 'So, what happened to you?'

'I got kidnapped by a pair of brick shithouses in suits, that's what!'

She told them about the two men, about how she had been drugged and had woken up in the glass box. About the lizard woman, and about how she had received special help to escape. She didn't go into too many details about Fargo. She wanted to keep the fact of him to herself. Instead she claimed she had received help from the Realm because the spirit world needed her to join her friends.

'And here I am, one of the four musketeers once more.'

'And right welcome too,' said Rawkins. 'But you're not really dressed for the mountains. Let's get you back to camp and see what we can rustle up for you. None of us fit your "petite miss" figure, but we'll find something a little warmer than that top and skirt. Where's your bag – did they take that?'

The sudden shock drenched Medina when she realised that all her civilised trappings were back in that glass box. Credit and debit cards, iPhone, passport, everything that made the modern world accessible had been taken from her. Her spirits sank. And then she felt a firm touch on her right hand. She lifted it and found she was clutching the strap of her bag.

She held it up. 'A good friend was looking after it for me. A very good friend.'

The campsite had been erected nearby, next to Marshall Fellows' pick-up. As they drew nearer he said, 'What's that in the back of my truck?' He hurried forward and lifted a suitcase into plain view. He held it out to Medina.

'Look familiar?'

She chuckled and then quivered when she felt a kiss on her cheek, and a familiar voice breathed in her ear.

'I can't let the Spirit Talker borrow tatters and rags from her friends now, can I? She deserves her own wardrobe, so she does.'

Rawkins shook her head in bemused surprise. 'Does that good friend of yours do requests? I lost a ring that belonged to my mom somewhere in my house. We turned the place upside down and couldn't find it. Do you think... I know it's a real nerve, but... no, no, forget it. That would be like using the latest iPhone to hammer a nail in. Stupid. Ignore me.'

Medina felt something hard press against her palm and her fingers closed about it. When she opened her hand a large cushion-cut solitaire diamond glittered from the white gold mount of a heavy gold ring. She held it out.

Rawkins' jaw dropped. 'I don't freaking believe it. Do you do rabbits from hats? Is this how you make your living? How did you find it? My mom's ring! Look, guys, my mom's ring. Where was it? We looked everywhere. Where was it?'

Medina tilted her head to one side as if she was listening to a voice only she could hear. She chuckled.

'Ask Marlon what he did with Dr Strange's ring of Raggadorr when he was playing in the garden, and where he found the other six. One ring and six washers plus a child's imagination, that's a whole world of possibilities. Marlon's a bright lad, but forgetful. The ring was in a drawer in your garage. In a tin where your husband keeps bits and bobs that might be useful one day but never get used. All men have such a tin, I'm told. In the same way squirrels have places where they hide their nuts.'

Askuwheteau and Fellows looked at each other with wry smiles. They nodded.

'Yeah,' said Fellows, 'we both got one of those tins. I keep loose screws and the things left over from flat pack furniture in mine. You know, just in case.'

'I keep beads in mine, also just in case. Just in case I need to make a war bonnet. I keep thinking it might be more entertaining to declare war on the white invader than watch anything on the TV these days. When I do I'll need a war bonnet.'

Medina changed her clothes behind the truck between two open doors. She felt a caressing hand when she was undressed and a mouth on one of her nipples. 'Soon,' she whispered, 'soon.' And the touch was gone. She sighed.

Trainers, jeans and a thick shirt and jumper were the best she could manage from her wardrobe. Rawkins supplied her with a quilted waistcoat that she unzipped from within her heavy jacket. It was warm enough, but Medina had to practically cocoon herself in it and it fell to below her knees. Wearing it, she looked even smaller and more childlike than before.

The policewoman sighed. 'I have *got* to lose weight. That thing fits me where it touches and it goes around you twice!'

Fellows dug out a leather strap Medina could use as a belt. Then she declared herself ready for anything.

Askuwheteau explained that they had come to the mountain looking for proof, or at least evidence, that the black creatures existed.

'We know what we saw, but the dudes in suits made everything disappear. And I mean everything. But they can't have found every trace of flesh and leather up here. That would be impossible. So, we're looking for anything that can be used as evidence. The idea was to use it as a bargaining chip to get you released, but here you are. So now we want to find it for its own sake. Something happened up here and people want it covered up. Why? And what happened? Are you willing to help or shall we drive you back to town and let you jump on the next plane home? Your choice.'

'Watcher, all of you, I have to be here. I've been brought here specifically to be with you and to help you. The Realm of spirits is in turmoil because of events that took place right here, and it won't be healed until something else happens, also right here. I don't know how or what, not yet, but I think something is coming. Something's going to happen here, something amazing, and we four will be an important part of it. The question is not whether I stay to help you in your search, but whether *you* guys are prepared to help me in a task I don't even understand yet. What do you say?'

Askuwheteau grinned like a wolf. 'I love stuff like this, really, I love it. Count me in. Man, I'd even stay home to watch shit like this on TV. I sure never dreamed I'd end up with a starring role.'

'What he said,' beamed Fellows.

'My old man is back home microwaving shit in Tupperware boxes for the kids' dinner tonight. I'd rather be out here eating moose with you heroes. We got any moose?'

Askuwheteau shrugged. 'Got beans, got bacon, got forest greens.'

'Forest greens?'

'Anything edible I can find in the forest. God's own larder store.'

Fellows pointed his thumb at his truck. 'I got moose. I'll get it started if'n you get the greens.'

The sun was dipping below the horizon by the time they had the fire lit and the meat broiling over the flames. Askuwheteau was as good as his word. Medina helped him collect bunches of herbs and roots, and even handfuls of wild mushrooms that he promised would taste better than anything she could buy in a shop.

The First Nations man found himself fighting an impulse to kiss the slight woman at his side. He had never known anyone get so far under his skin so quickly before, not even when his wife was young and he met her for the first time.

Medina Bishop brought a breath of something strange and enticing into his world. He wondered what life would be like for him when she went home. He took covert glances at her almost perfect face. Lips curved into a half smile; long, natural lashes sweeping down over those haunting eyes, a mess of dark curls tousled over her slightly over-large ears. He scolded his errant sight and found work for his hands, then realised he'd picked too many forest greens. Then, just as he was bending to pick wild garlic, Medina leaned over and kissed his cheek.

'You're a good man, Askuwheteau of the Cree nation, and your grandmother is proud of you. Tomorrow I think we'll need to rely on that goodness.'

She looked up at the star-laced sky.

'Something's coming. And it will be here soon. Very soon.'

## 46

The others had settled down in their bed rolls around the fire. Medina stretched out on the bench seat at the back of Marshall's pick-up. It was a cool night and she was grateful for Rawkins' waistcoat and a woollen blanket Marshall had pulled out from under the seat.

She could just barely hear sounds of gentle snoring coming from around the dying embers of the fire and soon followed suit. It had been a long day and sleep easily claimed her with dreamless oblivion. The sun was barely washing the eastern horizon when she was woken by a familiar, grave voice calling to her from the Realm.

'Suleiman?'

'Medina. You are awake? I'm sorry to have disturbed you, but it is time. You must also wake your friends. The moment has almost arrived. You must climb up to the ridge where the cave used to be. Where the black creatures shot down the flying machine. Can you find it again?'

'I'm sure we can. How long have we got?'

'I'm not sure. The Sublime say it's only a matter of hours. I can't be more precise than that. But you must be ready.'

'Ready for what?'

'Again, I'm not sure. If the Sublime have become involved it must be something extraordinary.'

Grinding sleep from her eyes, Rawkins tempered the rush of Medina's words. 'Whoa – whoa there! Calm down, girl. There's nothing so important that there's no time for coffee and a piss. Then I'm going to wash up and clean my teeth. Whatever's coming can hold for a few civilised minutes until this lady's ready for her day, you hear me? That place is about fifteen minutes away. There's time, girl. And I say you should never miss an opportunity to empty your bladder – and that's official. It's in the training manual. Come on. We can visit the ladies' powder room while the men are in the hombres.'

The women took turns behind the bushes to the left of the campsite while the men passed water over to the right. They washed their hands with gel, drank two cups of coffee each and breakfasted on bread filled with cold moose meat and slices of cheese. Then Askuwheteau led them up the slope on a long, north-westerly slant. Rawkins' estimation of time and distance was almost precisely on the button. Just over sixteen minutes later the group was

199

staring at an oddly artificial looking and almost perfectly circular indentation in the shoulder of the mountain. The First Nations man took a long look around. He pointed at an area of ground that seemed to have been torn up.

'That's where the Gatling gun ripped up that howitzer thing.'

He crouched and studied the deeply indented soil. He reached out and lifted a scrap of torn black leather.

'The cleaners missed a bit. Look around – this area is littered with bits of those bastards. I figure we got enough here to build ourselves our very own howitzer.'

He dropped the strip of skin and carefully washed his hands with gel from a little bottle he took from his pocket.

'Medina's big event seems to be running a little late. If nothing else happens we can always collect several bags full of samples. The day won't be wasted.'

The medium squinted into the northern sky. She pointed.

'What's that?'

Her friends followed her finger.

Fellows mused, 'Isn't it a plane?'

Askuwheteau replied, 'No, and it's heading this way. Medina, your spirit friends say anything?'

'They're singing something about the Sublime welcoming their brethren. I can't make it out.'

Rawkins breathed, 'Shit! That thing's a flying saucer. Look at it!'

The First Nations man looked urgently at Medina.

'Should we be getting out of here?'

'I don't know. They're still singing. Wait, wait...'

Suddenly the tiny woman pulled herself up to her full height. Her voice became deep and measured.

'Friends of the Spirit Talker. The children of Earth have returned. They must be healed. The Sublime tell us you must lead them to the lake and let them bathe. Walk among them without fear. Are you ready?'

Askuwheteau nodded. 'As we'll ever be.'

The great disc blotted out the sun and hovered silently overhead. There was no downwash. It seemed weightless, almost like a soap bubble. Its casual power took their breath away.

Fellows gasped. 'How's it staying up there? What's keeping it up?'

Rawkins shielded her eyes. 'I don't know. Do you think it's some kind of weird weather balloon?'

Askuwheteau shook his head. 'Do you?'

'No.'

The craft lowered to the ground and once again filled the space it had occupied for nearly half a billion years. Rocks splintered under its immense weight. Involuntarily the friends took several steps backwards. There came a sound like a vast choir breathing in and then the two tiers of windows facing them sprang open.

There was a pregnant pause. Medina realised she had stopped breathing and gasped air into her lungs. She heard her friends do the same. And then something moved in the shadows of the craft's interior.

A tall and slender blue-black figure stepped out into the cool morning sunlight. It had a featureless ovoid balanced on its thin column of a neck that Medina presumed was its head, but below that was a complicated array of joints and limbs that seemed almost insectile. It proceeded smoothly to stand before the medium. Even without eyes the creature seemed to be carefully scrutinising her.

And then it fell to its knees – and possibly its elbows, Medina couldn't be sure – and bowed its head.

A high, sweet voice rang out in her mind.

'Spirit Talker, the creature called Finder asks for your help; for her, her crew and her tool units. Her voice is lost to her and she would seek to find it again. We are the voice of the Kvultii and we return these children of Earth to your safekeeping. Please, use them well.'

And then, like an explosion of nightmare, what seemed to be tens of dozens of the inky shapes boiled out of the ship's windows and arrayed themselves before the diminutive woman. It took all her strength to stop herself from screaming in horror. A familiar voice in her ear helped calm her nerves.

'Will you look at all these poor devils. Time to wash their ills away, wouldn't you say?'

'Yes, Fargo, I would.' She raised her voice – 'Finder, follow us and bring your people. Watcher, lead us to the lake, please.'

Like a stream of leathery night, the ship's company followed the First Nations man as he set off down the slope towards the distant lake. They rustled as they walked, scampered and stalked through the forest; and in their midst were the medium, the policewoman and the geologist. Rawkins felt as though she had fallen into a dream. As she walked she unconsciously repeated a whispered litany: 'Holy Mary, full of grace, holy Mary, full of grace, holy Mary...'

Fellows was of a more scientific bent. He set his mind to trying to understand how the creatures' complex joints worked. They didn't walk like anything he had seen on Earth.

Medina was listening to the Realm, where the spirit choirs were still singing, and to Fargo who seemed determined to talk to her all the way to the lake. She supposed he was trying to raise her spirits.

In a shocking, clattering tempest of wind and dust, a Griffon helicopter roared up over the trees and hovered above them like a gigantic, squat bug. Medina could see the big Gatling gun swing around towards them. And behind the gunner she saw the lean, lizard-like face of the woman from the cube, her expression one of triumphant hatred.

## 47

Klosky had long ago learned to hate what he called 'civilian authority'. The people involved always had some freaky agenda that he couldn't quite fathom, and they invariably treated him and his men like underlings. The latest woman they'd been saddled with was long, lean, mean-faced and antsy. She was acting as if she had a bug up her ass and had no way to scratch it. Klosky got the impression the woman was in shit for something major and had decided to hold him personally responsible. He hoped the shit proved career terminal. He disliked her on sight.

She didn't even have a name; just a face like a hatchet and a personality that reminded the captain of how lemon juice burned in an open wound, sharp and distinctly unpleasant. She looked him over like a prime beef bull and sneered when she said, 'I suppose you'll have to do. Take me to Duck Mountain.'

He replied, 'Sure, ma'am. What do we call you?'

'Ma'am will do. Shall we go? Or do you want to stand around and chat? I have an important schedule to meet.'

Klosky made a winding motion in the air and the rotors began to turn. Perry stood by the open side panel of the chopper and cupped his hands to make a step and help the woman climb on board. When he looked down and saw her stiletto heels, he almost cringed away. She hitched up her narrow skirt and put the toe of her shoe in his palms. He got a brief glimpse of what was under the skirt. And what wasn't.

When Klosky joined him, Perry shouted in his ear, 'Hey, cap, you know we got no commandoes in CANSOFCOM.'

'Yeah, why?'

'Well, think again. Looks to me like we got at least one.'

He made a subtle tilt of his head towards the woman.

'Ah, man! You know it's bad to talk ugly words. Why'd you put that nasty thought in my head? You're off my Christmas card list. Okay, dude, you sit next to the crazy bitch; I'm getting in back.'

Perry spoke to Henderson and Lou. They both cast surreptitious glimpses at the woman. Klosky sighed. The helicopter lifted and turned west towards Dauphin. After two hours of suffering the woman's silent disdain and imperious glances, Klosky and his crew were wondering whether she might survive a sudden ejection from the aircraft at full speed. Klosky thought she was so scrawny she might float down like a dead leaf from a tree, and then there would be a rumpus. They refuelled at Lt. Col W. G. (Billy) Barker, VC airport. Lou and Henderson helped her down so she could stretch her legs. Afterwards they high-fived Perry.

'Saw clear to Kansas,' Lou told Klosky with a grin.

'You need to get out more.'

'Got a real eyeful. It winked at me. She's wearing stockings and one of those suspender belts; and she's shaved down there. Looks like a little Hitler moustache, you know what I mean?'

'I knew she reminded me of somebody, and it sure wasn't Marilyn Monroe. Hitler moustache, you say? Yeah, I can see that.'

'Hey, yeah! What about the Wicked Witch of the West?'

'Yeah, you're right, I can see that too. Great call. And I'd kick-start her broom if it helped get rid of her.'

'Amen to that.'

Henderson helped her back in. He'd told Klosky he was thinking of majoring in gynaecology and considered the witch to be field work.

'You thinking she might also be worthwhile homework? You've always had a way with the ladies.'

'No way, cap. I'm sad, not sick.'

Twenty-five minutes later they rattled across the lake and headed for the tree line. Perry climbed behind his M134D and released the safety. He swung the big gun in an arc to loosen up and ensure his field of fire was clear, and then became acutely aware of hot breath on his cheek. He turned. The witch was perched by his shoulder. She had unstrapped her safety belt and climbed to his side. He looked her up and down in disbelief.

He yelled over the sound of the rotors, 'You'd better strap yourself in ma'am. If the pilot yaws, you'll be out the side and no one will be able to stop you fall. I mean it, ma'am.'

'Don't be so fucking condescending, soldier. I've got a good grip on this strap and I know what I'm doing.' Suddenly she shouted and pounded Perry on the shoulder, 'Look, look down there. Dozens of the black bastards, hundreds of them. They're invading, they must be invading. Shoot them! Go on, shoot them, you stupid man, shoot them!'

Perry gripped the handles of the minigun and looked along its six barrels. There were people down there. They looked familiar. The woman was almost screaming at him.

'Shoot them, you half-wit! Fuck me, are you blind? Get out of the way and let me do it.'

204

She began to push at him and tried to grab the handles of the gun.

He yelled, 'Somebody get this crazy bitch off me. Come on people, pull her off.'

Lou leaned forward as far as he could in his safety belt and grabbed the woman's right ankle. He couldn't know it was still painful from her fall a few days before and she shrieked in agony. He tugged, hard. She tried to kick him away and released her strap. She fell backwards and out into open space. The only thing keeping her from certain death was Lou's grip on her ankle. Thanks to the aircraft's slipstream, her jacket was whipped over her head and her skirt bunched up around her waist. Perry grabbed at her flailing left thigh and made his hands climb the woman's half-naked body, hauling her in like a rope. Lou did the same. Once they had her safe, they straightened her skirt and pulled her jacket down. The woman's hair was standing on end. Her face was red and her mouth was working against her teeth.

'You touched me!'

Lou answered, 'We had to, ma-am, or you'd be a hole in the ground by now.'

She screamed, 'YOU TOUCHED ME! HOW DARE YOU!'

Perry tried to calm her. 'It's okay, ma'am. We didn't see anything. Honest.'

'WHAT DO YOU MEAN?'

Spittle sprayed from her razor-thin lips. Her eyes were red and her hands became claws ready to tear the flesh from Perry's face and the eyes from his head.

Lou answered, 'Your skirt kept you decent, ma'am. We didn't see anything up there.'

Perry agreed, a ghost of a smile playing across his lips. 'No, nothing at all up there, ma'am. Nothing at all.'

...

The helicopter remained circling the ship's complement and the four humans. They had quickened their pace. Marshall was waving to the Griffon, hoping someone in there would recognise him. Medina had seen the lizard woman's exit from the craft and the sudden display of her most intimate parts. She had expected a flurry of machine-gun fire, but instead it seemed as if the helicopter's crew were fighting among themselves.

'Fargo, what's going on up there?'

'I'll take a look.'

He was back in a few moments.

'There's some screaming harridan up there accusing your man Klosky's boys of sexual assault and just about everything short of rape. I think she's working her way up towards that. She also wants that fellow Perry to shoot the shite out of all of you, but he's seen Fellows, Watcher and you and the policewoman in with our little beasties here and he's refusing to open fire. That's a right civilised man in my biased opinion.'

Medina turned to her colleagues. 'It's Klosky and his crew up there. They've got the bitch from the cube on board. She wants them to open fire on us, but they're refusing. She almost fell out, but Perry and Lou caught her.'

Fellows said, 'Shame, if you ask me.'

'Well, now she's accusing the guys of sexual assault.'

Rawkins looked up. 'Is she mad?'

'Yeah, well it seems she doesn't wear any pants and the guys had to pull her back in. There might have been a little bit of unintentional familiarity, but hey, they saved her life.'

Fellows grinned. 'I bet Lou loved all that. He likes a bit of lady flesh does Lou.'

Up in the cabin the woman was twisting in Henderson's grip while Lou and Klosky restrained her. They bound her ankles and wrists together then strapped her back into her seat. Her arms hung over the seat back. All the while the crimson-faced woman was trying to claw at them, kick them or even bite them.

Once she was secure, Klosky shouted over the sound of the rotors.

'Ma'am, we can't go shooting those creatures when our people are in with them. They look harmless enough just now, and in Canada I believe shooting unarmed targets is still considered murder.'

She hissed, 'I will have you and your gang of deviant thugs up in front of a court martial. You have molested and disobeyed a senior officer. Your men have laid hands upon me with intent and your personal conduct is unforgiveable. And now you're treating me like a prisoner. I'll have your black hide nailed to the wall!'

'It's for your own safety, ma'am. Judicious restraint while the chopper's in the air. And may I remind you, ma'am, that my men saved your life when you nearly fell out the aircraft, and they did so at risk to themselves. It's not their fault that you choose to run around without any pants on. And let me tell you something else. Their only thought was to save your scrawny hide. No way were they interested in grabbing a feel of your skinny white ass.'

He allowed his building anger to flow. 'Woman like you should know better. You're not fit to talk about men like these. So, you listen to me and you listen good. Unless you want to wear a gag, I suggest you shut that flapping yap of yours. Understand?'

She made a noise like a steam kettle coming to the boil. All trace of sanity had fled her bloodshot eyes.

'Cap, over here.' Perry indicated the sky beyond the trees. Klosky cautiously made his way to the gunner's side and strapped himself into the spare safety harness.

A great disc was approaching the helicopter at speed. It was like nothing either man had seen before. Its forward edge was made up of two tiers of big windows, something no Earthly designer would consider without access to new materials. There were no control surfaces or recognisable engines, yet the craft floated effortlessly through the sky and was obviously under precise control. Behind them the woman was screaming that they should shoot it down. She kept repeating, 'Code 17! This is a Code 17! You must open fire.'

The ship slid under the helicopter and Klosky realised it was acting as a shield to protect the alien creatures from potential harm. The pilot jumped in his seat and pressed his hands to either side of his helmet.

He yelled, 'You guys have got to hear this.'

He flicked a switch and they could all hear a clear, crisp voice in their headphones: '...allow any harm to come to these hybrid beasts. They have suffered enough and must be healed. We are the voice of the Kvultii and we speak to you in friendship. We will not allow any harm to come to these hybrid beasts...' The voice repeated its message on a loop.

Perry gazed down at the massive disc below them and shrugged.

'I guess it makes a change from *take me to your leader*.'

'Maybe that's next.'

'Let's hang around and find out.'

'Hey, you put that gun's safety on?'

'What safety? This thing has a safety? All these years and I never stop learning shit. Yeah, I switched it on when looney tunes was trying to get her hands on it. I didn't want her to cause an accidental discharge.'

Klosky looked over his shoulder at the dishevelled red head, then turned back to Perry.

'Reckon it's been a while since she caused one of those.'

## 48

In the shadow of the great disc, four friends led their blue-black charges tumbling and skittering in the direction of the lake they could barely glimpse through the dense trees. The only sound was a leathery rustling and the footfall of hundreds of disparate limbs. What would happen when they reached the lake? No one knew, but a sense of anticipation began building among the throng and the humans felt themselves caught up in it.

In the helicopter the bound woman was easing her tape-bound wrists against the sharp edges behind her bench. As with all things military, comfort in the Griffon was only skin deep. Behind the bench's cushions were perfect examples of the lowest bid winning the contract and the finish was slapdash at best. The bench fittings were raw and provided the perfect edge for her quiet sawing motion. She felt the flesh of her wrists tear against the serrated steel. Her hands became wet with blood and her nerves screamed with pain, but after a matter of minutes she was free.

Klosky's men had no interest in causing her harm or discomfort when they bound her. They had used duct tape because it was handy, but they didn't go overboard with it. They had misjudged their prisoner. Her contempt for the men deepened. Her hands were free and they weren't even looking at her. She would wait for her chance.

Klosky asked the pilot if he could find a landing site by the lake. The helicopter peeled away from the great ship and raced ahead. Within minutes it was out over open water. It turned back and hovered while its crew scanned dry land between the tree line and the water's edge. The co-pilot pointed.

'There, that looks dry enough. Should be enough room, d'ya think?'

The pilot nodded. 'Let's find out. Cap, we're going to set this puppy down for a spell.'

The Griffon eased down with barely a bounce. As soon as it touched ground, Klosky and his men leapt out and stood facing the trees. They knew the mass of creatures and their human escorts were heading their way, but didn't know why.

Each of the men left their rifles slung over their shoulders. They would be handy if needed, but wouldn't be perceived as an immediate threat that called for retaliation. They hoped. The idea that the great disc would be completely unarmed had never occurred to them, and they also didn't know that the alien creatures had zero defensive capability. Precautions were deemed necessary, but hopefully wouldn't need to be used. The pilot and flight engineer joined them. The co-pilot sat behind the M134D. She nervously clicked off the safety.

The pilot said, 'Phasers set to stun?'

Klosky didn't smile. He was too far out of his comfort zone for humour. The pilot raised his hand in the Vulcan salute. 'Live long and prosper.'

Klosky sighed. 'Sauers, if you've got some useful advice about what we should be doing just now, I'd be grateful to hear it. Otherwise... look, just can it, will you?'

'Just trying to relieve the tension, cap.'

'It ain't working. Look, here they come.'

Askuwheteau strode out of the trees just over two hundred yards from the helicopter. He saw the special ops team and raised an arm.

He shouted, 'Are we okay with this?'

Klosky replied, 'What's happening?'

'Medina says they have to reach the lake.'

'Why?'

'Damned if I know.'

Like a silent shadow, the great disc moved out from above the tree line and smoothly rolled across the sky until it was over the lake.

Klosky yelled, 'I guess we find out.'

'Thanks!'

And then the creatures spilled out of the forest and ran towards the lake under the ship's shadow. Suddenly behind him, Klosky heard the unmistakable sound of the M134D's barrels beginning to rotate.

He roared, 'Shit! Down, get down.'

While everyone's attention was elsewhere, the red-headed woman had torn the tape from her legs, grabbed a fire extinguisher and clubbed the co-pilot into insensibility. She then squatted behind the Gatling gun, took a firm grip on the handles and squeezed the trigger. The barrels spun idly at first and then a whining stream of tracer arced high over the trees. She angled the gun down and saw a track of erupting soil just miss Klosky and his men. She could target the creatures now and brought her sights up slightly.

From her position in the trees, Medina saw what was happening and who was doing it. 'Fargo!' she barked. 'Get that bitch!'

The woman was wrestling the powerful weapon and trying to bring it to bear on the alien host when she found herself gripped from behind. There was no mercy in the grip. It was irresistible. She was torn screaming and kicking away from the gun and then up, out of the helicopter's open

209

doorway. With a mounting sense of horror, she found herself pinioned by invisible arms and racing into the sky.

She began howling, 'Let me go! Let me go, you bastard! Let me go!'

She heard a soft voice close to her ear.

'With pleasure.'

She was released and fell dozens of feet to hit the surface at the centre of the lake like a stone. Momentarily stunned, she sank towards the weed bed. Her skirt and jacket had been torn away by the force of her impact and her nether regions glowed whitely in the murk. Fargo followed her down and brought her back to the surface. She recovered her senses and coughed out a lungful of swallowed water. Then she realised that someone, or something, was buoying her up and she began to wriggle and lash out.

'Take your filthy hands off me, you dirty bastard! How dare you touch me? Get away from me.'

The voice said, 'You needed a decent wash anyway. I'll get some soap for that vile mouth of yours if you're not careful.'

And then she was alone. Her shoes hampered her swimming style and she brought her legs up to remove them. That was when she found out that her skirt was gone. She trod water and looked back towards the lakeside. There was a lot going on in the shadow of the great disc, but she doubted it was enough to distract everyone's attention from the sight of a half-naked woman climbing out onto the shore. And she would receive precious little sympathy from people she had just been shooting at. With a resigned grimace, she turned and swam the other way.

Her actions had done surprisingly little damage to the host of alien creatures and their human aides, but she had hit Lou a glancing blow that ripped a chunk of flesh from his midriff and knocked him writhing to the ground. Henderson raced to the helicopter for his first aid kit and found Sue Bellows, the co-pilot, unconscious and bleeding from a head wound. He yelled for his colleagues to help him pull the woman from her seat. Her skull felt a little spongy and there was a lot of blood.

He muttered to himself, 'Crazy bitch wanted to kill all of us. What was she thinking?'

He was still bent over both his patients when the blue-black, leathery horde reached the lake. Perry and the pilot helped him, once Perry had carefully switched the Gatling's safety catch back on. None of them saw what happened next. Only Klosky and the flight engineer watched the dozens of dark, oddly-shaped beasts enter the lake water they had come so far and risked so much to reach. Medina, Askuwheteau, Rawkins and Fellows had a ringside seat for everything that happened next.

At first very little. Under the shadow of the great disc the creatures splashed around in an ungainly fashion and achieved little beyond getting thoroughly soaked. And then the ship began to glow, brighter and brighter. It was an unearthly light and it poured down upon the leathery mass in the water.

At that moment Medina fell to her knees, her hands gripped to her ears. She was panting in agony and her eyes squeezed shut. Her body arced in pain. Around her, her friends dithered in confusion. They thought she was having a fit. And then her eyes opened and a beatific smile lit up her face.

'Look,' she said. 'Oh, look.'

Beads of light flowed down from the great disc and settled into the bodies of the hybrid creatures. The noise of voices joined the splashing sounds from the lake, a jumble of words and gasps and shouts, cries and laughter. The awkward forms smoothed out, changed, and became more recognisable. And then the lakeside was no longer filled with multi-limbed and alien bodies. Teenage girls and boys floated next to young men and women. They were all the hues of the many nations of Earth – black, tan, gold and white. At first they began hugging each other and then, realising they were all naked, made futile attempts to cover their nudity.

Askuwheteau looked back at the tree line.

'Any of you guys see any fig trees back there? We seriously need a wardrobe.'

Fellows gazed open-mouthed at the heads bobbing in the water.

'There's too many of them. Hey, are their clothes still back at the spa place?'

Rawkins answered, 'Yeah, it's still a crime scene. Nothing's been touched. Why?'

'You'll see. Medina, can you talk to the ship?'

'Not directly, but I know people who can.'

'Can that thing give these kids a lift to the spa, do you think? We have to get them out of the water and find them some clothes before they catch hypothermia.'

A few minutes later the disc settled into the lake and most of the bodies tumbled through the windows and into the interior. The more limber helped the less capable. There was a great deal of touching and more than a few slapped faces. A tall, beautiful young woman with a hank of sun-bleached hair stood in the window for a moment and looked directly at Medina. She waved and mouthed 'Thank you' before stepping back into the shadows.

Rawkins used her cell phone to tell a bemused Longknife what was going on. It proved to be a complicated conversation with a great deal of reiteration. In the end the Dauphin RCMP Chief said she would get over to the spa and personally deal with the situation.

'Alien spaceships and naked teenagers,' she said. 'I think we need to keep the news media away from this one if we can, don't you?'

And then the great disc lifted from the water and glided east.

There were just a few tens of people in the water now.

'Hey, sarge! Hey, it's me. You couldn't find me a pair of pants, could you?'

'Hey there, Marshall. So good to see you, man. You got a towel I can borrow?'

Medina walked to one side and watched. Then she smiled and tilted her head as if she was listening to a whispered voice. She nodded happily, moved sideways, and she was gone.

**[49]**

Suleiman ben Duwad and Maryam stood with Rowan before the almost empty containment tower. Gentle music soothed the air and soft breezes lifted the elemental woman's hair.

Suleiman indicated the tower. 'How many remain?'

Rowan had been working around the clock with her colleagues to build the transmitter cage that now contained the tower. She was tired and she stretched hugely to loosen her stiff and aching shoulders, an action that highlighted the healthy curves of her beautiful, young looking body. She smiled like an angel, teeth white in her sun-browned face.

'Ten or fifteen at most. Few enough that mentors can deal with them one-on-one or more. They're responding to treatment, but it will take a while before we're able to move them out of the tower.'

She pointed at the cage. 'Sublime design, quite literally. We've never fashioned anything like it before. These have been strange days, Suleiman the Wise. Who would've thought that an alien race of Sublime beings would want to cross such immense distances to help a few hundred Earth-born? It's a tale made hot with the telling of it. The poets are looking for rhymes to pair with Kvultii and our songsmiths are playing until their fingers bleed on the strings. Even the quieter folk of Scytaer Faehl are weaving new song mills in celebration.'

Rowan had watched when the intricate grids of the cage had filled with shrieking flame and beads of ethereal light. She saw it rotate under its own power, spin, and focus the energy it contained into a powerful beam of refulgent power. Power enough to bridge dimensions. The cage was a fixed structure. She and her kind had followed precise instructions which started with building its foundations deep enough to touch the living stone from which the Realm had been raised. It could not possibly turn like a wheel on its axle; it was impossible. But it had.

Sumexis had loaned his expertise in exchange for a kiss from a fire sprite called Ember, and that was all he took. At least, that was all he took at first. He later admitted to Rowan that for once he would have offered his services for free, but Ember had given him the gift of her lips and he was 'not so old that he would turn away such bounty'.

When he stood with Rowan and witnessed the crackling beam of energy roar away into the Realm's night sky, fired by the impossibly spinning cage, he took her hand in his.

'Garndaughter, I thought there was nothing new under the sacred sky and all my great deeds were behind me. I'd become legend while yet I lived, and instead of the Sumexis who stood before them the elemental folk only saw the memory of things Sumexis had done long ago. I was busy weaving mischief when most of them were barely a spark in their dams' eyes.'

He opened his arms wide. 'And now we have done this. We have wrought well to weave such Sublime magic in the Realm.'

He smiled at her through astonished tears and she watched the crystals of time boil away from his lean frame. He vanished behind a silver mist and when it was gone he stood before her like youth resurrected, firm and upright once more. His fine eyes shimmered in the light and his wide smile glinted with almost feral roguishness. He glanced down. She followed his gaze and shook her head ruefully. He cupped the evident bulge in his trousers and chuckled.

'You know, I think the light is bright enough that I can find me way back to sweet Ember. And then perhaps we shall seek the shadows and see if we might strike a few hot sparks of our own. And who knows, perhaps one day I shall build a bridge strong enough to span the miles and reach the cold country where you keep your chilly heart. But until then, wish me the pleasure of Ember's womanly hearth.'

'Get away with you! You're just a horny old rascal. Ember has a much better ear for such sweet syrup than me.'

She pecked at his cheek and slapped his behind to send him on his way. He responded by cupping one of her buttocks appreciatively and then danced out of her reach when she swung a fierce slap at his head. Then he was gone, a satyr seeking his nymph. Half an hour later she heard a peal of girlish laughter from the shadow of the hills and almost laughed out loud.

'You're an insatiable auld rogue. Bless you anyway.'

And then at last it was morning and Suleiman and Maryam had joined her. In the silvered werelight they looked even more like human-shaped works of art fashioned from filigree and pearl. Rowan wondered again why these almost sacred souls had not Sublimed to be with others of their sort. And then she remembered that while it had taken elemental craft to build the strange new cage, it had been Suleiman who provided the blueprints. And now he touched its fabric in awe.

'Rowan, what you and your people have done here will resonate in eternity. The Realm thanks you; we thank you. We shall never be able to repay you, but we shall also never forget what you have done. And yet we hope such a miraculous device will never be called for again. One is an ample plenty. What do you call it, by the way?'

She coloured at the question and wriggled under his ebon gaze.

'It doesn't have a name as such. Well, not really. It was just a working title we used while we built it, you know?'

His gaze intensified and an arch smile curved his lips. Maryam tilted her head in curiosity. Her eyes flashed with amusement.

Rowan chuckled. 'We called it Suleiman's Staff,' she admitted. 'Some call it Suleiman's Ladder, but for most of us it's the Staff.'

'Well, I'm truly flattered. Thank you. What a rare privilege, truly flattering. Dear me. Thank you, Rowan. Thank you.'

He took her hands and kissed them, and then he and Maryam ambled away, turning now and then to wave. She waited until they were out of sight before she said to herself, 'What would you say if I told you what we really called it?'

She inspected the tall cage. A column that surrounded the tower and the song mill, a column with a collector bulge at the top. She had to admit to herself that to her less innocent eyes, and to those of her co-workers, it looked very much like a penis.

'Suleiman's Staff is near enough, old soul. Near enough.'

...

Fargo watched her swimming beneath him. Her slim form was almost lost in the shadows and her inky hair flowed like a cloud around her head and shoulders. He wondered when might be the best time to share his news. It was a truly unexpected development, and one that he desperately wanted to tell his dam, but first he wanted to share it with the wonderful woman who had brought so much joy into his life.

He looked down to watch her again and saw that Medina had dropped out of sight. He dived and headed into the light that led to the outer pool, and then spiralled lazily to the surface. When he broke up into the air he was surprised to hear *two* distinct voices. Then with a jolt he recognised both. Medina was talking animatedly with his dam, Phaetra.

They were both naked and sitting close together at the edge of the pool. The sight was so beautiful, he took a long moment to appreciate it before he approached them. The elfin charm of his woman was complemented by the slender femininity of his mother.

A water sprite could take many forms, but Phaetra usually preferred the traditional look of the mermaid. Her blue striped platinum tail depended from her hips and ended in a powerful tail fin. Her hair was ash blonde and streaked through with the same blue that coloured her tail. She had a face and figure that could haunt a man's dreams, while her musical laughter would charm birds from the trees. This last was demonstrated by a wheeling cluster of songbirds attracted to the sound of her voice, all of which were happily adding their soundtrack to the scene.

His mother spotted him and gestured for him to come closer. Once he drew near enough she swiped at him with her muscular tail. The act sent interesting vibrations through her human half that brought far from son-like thoughts to Fargo's mind. He quickly swung his attention across to his lover and realised she was looking at him with an almost embarrassed smile. His mother's loudly musical voice dragged his attention away from Medina's lovely face.

'So tell me, Fargo, dear son. Please, do tell. When were you planning to share with me the fact that you and this enchanting creature are going to make me a grandmother?'

The great disc carried its charges the short distance to the spa without incident. It settled onto the lawns by the pool at the base of the hill, as close to the buildings as it could get. The young people exited its portals and scrambled as a mob up the hill to the complex. Melba was one of the last to do so. She reasoned it was one thing to let people see her naked when she had no choice, but another thing altogether to let someone walk behind her while she was climbing a hill. That would be *too* intimate. She didn't want people to see any more of her than they had to.

She was intensely aware of her fellows' covert glances at her body, and she couldn't wait to get to her room and get out from under their prying eyes. Her skin and hair were slick with grime from the lake water. She hoped she would feel a lot better once she'd showered and pulled on some pants. They were greeted by a dark-complexioned, hawk-faced woman who hurried them inside the building and told them their rooms were unlocked and ready for them. That was good news.

Within minutes Melba had carefully locked her door behind her and padded into her bathroom. Just to stand under a hot shower and soap herself free of silt was enough to reduce her to tears. The water streamed darkly from her skin. She took her time, carefully washing every square inch of her body at least twice. And then she vigorously towelled herself to a rosy glow before drying her hair.

It took her a while to remember how her shoulders worked. She stood naked in front of her full-length mirror and examined herself minutely. Melba Palacio looked back at her, intense blue eyes creased under sun-paled brows. She began to cry.

She wanted to be home; truly, finally home. She wanted her dad's calm voice and her mom's gentleness. She wanted to be a daughter again, to be looked after and pampered. And she wanted time to understand what had happened to her. She looked in the mirror again. Something blue-black and faceless looked back. Her scream was far from being the only one to ring out that afternoon.

It took her a while to pull herself together enough to get dressed. She felt numb and drained. She didn't know *what* to feel. She was waking from a nightmare and none of it felt real. Her room didn't feel real and her own skin felt like a disguise behind which lurked an inky horror.

She avoided mirrors and sat on her bed while she tried to calm the shudders that rippled through her. It was hollow-bellied, gnawing hunger that finally drove her out into the corridors where she joined a cluster of silent people heading for the refectory. They were greeted and fed by police officers dressed as catering staff.

When she got back to her room she found her cell phone's battery was completely exhausted. As soon as it had enough charge, she rang her parents. Her dad told her to stay in her room. He told her he would be there in an hour. She would sleep in her own bed that night. He told her he loved her, repeating the words three or four times. Her mom took over and they talked, laughed and wept together until Melba's battery gave up the ghost once more. Then she packed and waited. All the while she shed silent tears.

Cheryl Longknife was the only witness to the great disc's departure. It happened without fanfare. Once the last of its passengers tumbled out onto the Spa's lawns, the ship's portals closed. It waited a few minutes until the grounds around it were empty before silently soaring hundreds and then thousands of feet skywards. Longknife's gaze followed it. She squinted against the sun and shielded her eyes. She didn't want to miss a second. The ship rotated until its windows faced north. It tilted upwards. Then, almost with a shrug, it was gone. Two loud bangs were the only evidence of its insane acceleration through the atmosphere. The Dauphin RCMP Chief raised her hand in farewell and then wiped the back of her hand against her lips. She needed a good drink. A really good drink.

Marcia Pennink and her daughter were huddled together on their sofa watching an old black and white movie on TV when the doorbell rang. They looked at each other. Neither was expecting visitors. The doorbell rang again. Holding hands, they went to the door together. They could just make out the dark shape of a person through the glazed door panel. It was at times like these that the women missed a man around the house the most. Marcia's daughter, Rainey, carefully put the chain on the door and then cautiously opened it.

Marcia couldn't see who was on the step, but Rainey took a sharp intake of breath and her eyes flew wide open. She fumbled frantically with the chain and then tore the door wide so she could throw herself at the man standing quietly in the gathering twilight.

Josiah Arnold Pennink hugged his daughter and held an arm out to his wife. The three of them pressed together as if they wanted to mould themselves into one body. Pennink's voice was hoarse as if it hadn't been used for a while.

'I've been practising this on my way here. Listen to me. I can't tell you how much I've missed you, but I have. Look, I'm sorry. I realise I haven't been the best husband and the best daddy I could be. I'm here asking if you want me home. If you do, I'll promise to try hard to be the man you deserve instead of the fool you've been living with. If you don't, I'll go. What do you say?'

Marcia pulled away and looked hard at the man she had almost grown to loathe. The man whose absence had left her with both a sense of relief and an unexpected sensation of emotional emptiness. He seemed genuine.

'Where've you been? They said you, you know... they said...'

'It's a long story. I don't rightly get it myself.'

'Come on in, Joe. Come on in. The neighbours will wonder what we're doing out here on the porch. Have you eaten? You look real thin. Rainey, get your pa a beer from the fridge and lay the table. I'll get us something good from the freezer.'

She pulled him into the small hallway. As soon as their daughter left their side she kissed her husband on the lips, something she hadn't done for years. Her narrow, mouse-like features relaxed enough to resemble the pretty girl Pennink had courted many years before. When Pennink smiled, his rat-like face looked more like the boy she had been happy to take home to her parents. She could see Rainey in that smile.

'Let's go get dinner started,' she said. 'And then you can tell us your story.'

Some called it a miracle. Others called it the Duck Mountain Event. Conspiracy theorists had a field day while professional debunkers sharpened their pencils and donned their most sincere expressions.

The spokesperson from CANSOFCOM agreed with the spokesperson from NASA, who agreed with the spokesperson from the European Space Agency. They all said the so-called 'flying saucer' had not shown up on radar at any point during its flight, so it was probably a lenticular cloud. Geologists had dated the depression on the shoulder of Duck Mountain to the Ordovician period some four hundred and fifty million years before. They posited that although it *looked* unusually round and artificial, it was in fact natural.

They cited similar structures in rocks all around the planet – to which UFOlogists responded that nobody had claimed this flying saucer was unique. They said there could easily be dozens of traces of alien ships around the world – and more. Why not? Other experts claimed the depression proved nothing one way or the other. That sauce was suitable for both the goose and the gander. Who knew what it was? Where was the firm evidence? CANSOFCOM issued a statement that it had sent a forensic team to the site and they had scoured the area – fruitlessly.

Nobody had thought to take a photo of the craft or the blue-black creatures, and the naysayers clung to that fact like a raft in a storm. Eye witnesses were ten a penny, they said. It was concrete proof they needed. Bring proof to the table, they said, and we'll all say grace and help you carve; but until then it's a mystery, pure and simple. Let's celebrate the survivors and mourn those we have lost.

A half-naked, raving red-head was found wandering the forest by a pair of hunters. She jabbered about monsters, alien invasion, flying saucers and sexual molestation. When one of the men offered to lend her his jacket to help preserve her modesty, she responded by trying to claw the skin from his face. They eventually restrained her with rifle webbing, wrapped her in a jacket, drove her back into Dauphin and delivered her to Hedderly Street and a bemused RCMP station.

The desk officer contacted CANSOFCOM at her insistence. Petawawa denied all knowledge of her. The cool voice on the line suggested the woman must be drunk or drugged and advised a few nights in the cells to sober her up.

Longknife was too busy fire-fighting to bother with the harridan. 'Find her a skirt and a pair of pants,' she said. 'Then put her in an interview room until she calms down and accepts a medical examination or someone comes to get her. We've got more important things to deal with just now.'

Edward Louis returned to London in a state of depression. He made his new friends promise to stay in touch and to let him know if there was any news of Medina Bishop.

During his flight, he had slept for the first time ever in the air. He dreamed of the beautiful, doll-like woman. She was swimming with a strikingly handsome man in a pool of blue-lit water near a building M. C. Escher might have appreciated. They were both naked. They reached for each other. Louis woke with a start, sweating in a fit of guilt. He didn't think of his friend that way and wondered where such a graphic image might have come from.

Marshall Fellows and Maelie Rawkins shared a beer with Askuwheteau. More than half the bar's customers were back in front of the big screen TV watching hockey. They were more upbeat and noisier than last time, which meant the trio could put their heads together and talk in privacy.

'She couldn't just disappear. It's *impossible*.'

Rawkins shook her head. 'Marshall, my man, after what we've seen I don't dare use words like "impossible" anymore.'

The First Nations man listened to them bicker. They sounded like an old married couple. He kept to himself the piece of information that told him the medium was safe. He wondered why the other two hadn't seen it for themselves, but held his tongue anyway.

The next morning, he took his pole for a walk around the lake. He was going to try for walleye again, but this time with a slightly different bait. Wikimak didn't eat pork rinds; well, maybe the fish would.

After a couple of fruitless hours, he became aware of a presence by his side.

Medina smiled. 'It's nice here. I like to be near water.'

He nodded. 'The others were worried, but I knew you were good.'

'Really? How?'

'Your luggage was gone from Marshall's pick-up. I figured people in trouble don't get the time to take their cases with them. Yeah, I knew you were okay.'

'Will you let them know I'm alright? And tell Edward Louis?'

'Sure, if you want me to. Why me?'

The breeze from the lake lifted her hair in waves and ruffled her long eyelashes. She looked inhumanly lovely. Some sinew in his heart played like a violin, issuing a plaintive note of longing. It filled his ears for a moment and dried his voice in his throat.

'Why you, Askuwheteau? Watcher and walker with your spirit sister. I could say: why not?' She gestured across the lake. 'But you know why. Tell me, what do you see there? What do you really see?'

He looked out and sighed. He had never shared this with anyone. Not even his wife. His grandfather knew, and his father. No one else.

His voice sounded distant. 'What do I see? Honestly? I see the buffalo the way they used to be. I see the people of the First Nation fishing with spears. I see the spirits and the lives of all the folk who lived here and loved this land, long before it was called Manitoba or Canada. I see the heart and the soul of this place.'

'Yes, you do. I know. Now, look at me.'

He did. He looked. And he saw what she was showing him. He leaned forward and she put her slender arms around his neck and kissed him on the mouth like a sister kissing a fond brother. He closed his eyes. When he opened them again she was gone, but the touch of her lips remained. He found he was shivering. Her parting gift had been to show him that she was

221

no longer human, not quite; and that she was content to be that way. It was a hard lesson, a lesson Askuwheteau had never learned. Never in all his long years of being different. His heart felt tight and something stung behind his dark eyes. He wondered if he would ever see Medina Bishop again. He hoped so.

His pole jerked twice in his hands and then curved like a bow. He fought hard, coaxed and played his line and finally landed his first ever fish. The big walleye would make a fine dinner.

## Author's note

The beautiful city of Dauphin and the Duck Mountain Provincial Park are real, but I have taken liberties with both for the sake of telling my tall tale. I hope I have done them credit. One day I want to spend time there. It's easy to fall in love with a place while researching it, teasing out its secrets, and I would love to see more of the 'City of Sunshine'. To my knowledge there is no Duck Mountain Spa Resort, at least not the way I describe it. I chose that particular area because fossils of horseshoe crabs dating back four hundred and forty-five million years have been found in the mountains there. It was from that fact and a dream I once had that the story grew.

The Ordovician-Silurian extinction sequence is based on real science. It is believed that Earth was hit by a GRB some four hundred and forty-three million years ago and just about everything not in the deep oceans was erased. The rest, except for Sutton in South West London, is fiction. But not in my head. In my head the people and events I describe are all real. I watched it happen and I walked with Medina along a leafy tunnel where all the right-angles turned left. I swam in the blue-lit pool and met Fargo's mermaid dam.

I enjoyed my time in these people's company and I wonder what will happen to Medina, Fargo and Askuwheteau, to the souls in the Realm of Light and the maniac genius of Scytaer Faehl. Their story here is done; but they have so much potential I'm sure I'll visit again to see what they've been up to. When I do I'll share it with you. I promise.

Cheers

Derek E Pearson

# Other GBP Science-Fiction
www.gbpublishing.co.uk

### *The ordinary* series Christopher Ritchie
## SILVER WINNER
### 2015 IndieFab Book Awards Horror

**Dante:** "Fusing horror and new age religion, this winner repels as much as it fascinates with death, destruction and nuggets of ironic black humour."

### *GODS' Enemy* Derek E Pearson
## FINALIST
### 2016 Indies Book Awards Fantasy

**Read2Write:** "Texas 1883, a terrifying story that fuses sci-fi with history and theology. Pearson is in electrifying form"

### *Soul's Asylum* trilogy Derek E Pearson
## FINALIST
### 2016 Indies Book Awards Science Fiction
## The Sun ☆☆☆☆:

*"a weird, vivid and creepy book, not for the faint hearted. But its originality and top writing make for a great read."*

### *Body Holidy* trilogy Derek E Pearson
## Surrey Life:

*"Pearson's galactic-sized imagination delivers, with veiled gallows humour, a compelling image of a chic, high-tech society infused with a toxic strain that feeds on extreme violence."*

www.ingramcontent.com/pod-product-compliance
Lightning Source LLC
Chambersburg PA
CBHW021242260626
47155CB00004BA/1262